Lucilla Andrews was born in Suez, the second daughter of an English father and Spanish mother. Her late father was then a manager in the Eastern Telegraph Company. At three she began her education in an English private girls' boarding school in Sussex and when she was eleven she wrote her first novel—an epic of love, lust and banditry in China. Unfortunately the manuscript was discovered and ended in the school incinerator.

During World War II, Lucilla Andrews entered the Nightingale Training School at St Thomas's Hospital in London and five years later left with an S.R.N. and S.C.M. Part One. She married a doctor, had one child, and when her husband's illness necessitated that she become the family breadwinner she returned to nursing.

Her first book, THE PRINT PETTICOAT, was written while she was working as an assistant Night Sister in a small Sussex hospital. Since that time it has never been out of print.

Over the years Lucilla Andrews has established herself as one of Britain's leading popular novelists. She created what was virtually a new genre—the hospital romance—written against an authentic and detailed medical background drawn from her own experience.

Readers who would like to know more about Lucilla Andrews are recommended to read her autobiography, NO TIME FOR ROMANCE, an account of her life and training as a nurse in wartime London.

Lucilla Andrews lives in Edinburgh.

Also by Lucilla Andrews

A HOSPITAL SUMMER
HOSPITAL CIRCLES
AFTER A FAMOUS VICTORY
IN AN EDINBURGH DRAWING ROOM
A WEEKEND IN THE GARDEN
and published by Corgi Books

Lucilla Andrews

My Friend the Professor

CORGI BOOKS

FOR
VERONICA LUCILLA

MY FRIEND THE PROFESSOR
A CORGI BOOK 0 552 08719 X

Originally published in Great Britain by
George G. Harrap & Co. Ltd.

PRINTING HISTORY
Harrap edition published 1960
Harrap edition reprinted 1961
Corgi edition published 1962
Corgi edition reprinted 1966 (twice)
Corgi edition reprinted 1967
Corgi edition reissued 1971
Corgi edition reissued 1980
Corgi edition reissued 1986

This book is set in Plantin

Corgi Books are published by Transworld Publishers
Ltd., 61–63 Uxbridge Road, Ealing, London W5 5SA, in
Australia by Transworld Publishers (Aust.) Pty. Ltd.,
26 Harley Crescent, Condell Park, NSW 2200, and in New
Zealand by Transworld Publishers (N.Z.) Ltd., Cnr. Moselle
and Waipareira Avenues, Henderson, Auckland.

Printed and bound in Great Britain by
Cox & Wyman Ltd., Reading, Berks.

CONTENTS

1

THREE YOUNG LADIES FOR ST MARTHA'S

THE country annexe of St Martha's Hospital, London, was ninety miles from my father's turkey farm.

"It's as off the map as we are, Frances." My father gave me my railway ticket. "So don't forget you've got to change three times. Here comes the first." He kissed me briskly. "Good luck, darling. Don't forget to write to your mother. Nervous?"

I swallowed. "Very."

He said he didn't blame me, and slammed the carriage door. The small local train lurched forward, he waved, and I was alone.

No one seemed to be travelling that day. I had a carriage to myself in all three trains. They ambled through miles of hop gardens, apple- and cherry-orchards, as if they had all eternity in which to carry me to my destination, while I practised calling myself "Nurse" aloud. By the time I was in the third train "Nurse Dorland" sounded quite unexceptional.

There was a corridor on that train. The ticket-collector came in as I was chatting to myself. "Did you say something, miss?"

I pretended I had asked if he knew anything of St Martha's annexe. "Is it near Pine Halt?"

He pushed back his cap with the stub of a pencil. "It'll be around seven miles to the hospital, I reckon. You'll have been working in the London branch, I take it? I know you young ladies all change over now and then. Make a nice break to get a bit of country air, eh?"

"Very nice, thank you." I tried to sound nonchalant and experienced. I felt very pleased with myself as he offered to get down my cases from the rack. He said he always liked lending nurses a hand, because he had been in hospital and he knew. He did not explain this knowledge as he obviously took me for an old hand, and I could not question him without spoiling my act. I wondered what he meant when I was alone again; then the elderly train rattled and groaned to another stop. Pine Halt was written in large letters on a sign just by my carriage window. My nonchalance dropped like an old coat from my shoulders. I thought, Oh, no! I'm there.

I clutched at my cases for support, and left the train reluctantly wondering what had ever made me think I wanted to be a nurse. Surely I should be far wiser to jump straight back into the carriage and meander with the train round the branch-line stations of southern England?

The train moved on, deciding my future for me. I put down my cases and looked around, uncertainly. There were two other young women waiting on the platform. They looked at me with equal uncertainty.

The girl nearest to me was fair, attractive, very well-groomed, and wearing a suit that could only have been cut in Paris. Her pale, pointed shoes had stiletto heels; her hat looked as expensive as her suit. I was on the verge of smiling hopefully, when I took in her appearance. Her clothes made me dismiss her from the possibility of being an embryo student nurse. She was obviously just a passing traveller. I turned towards the second girl. Her clothes could have come out of my wardrobe; her handbag had come from the same chain-store as the one I was carrying. I risked a smile.

She rushed up to me. "Would you by any chance be bound for the Preliminary Training School of St Martha's?"

"Yes. You? Oh, good. I'm Frances Dorland."

She beamed. "I'm Hannah More. I'm so glad I've met some one. I was feeling lost. How about"—she jerked her head at the fair girl who was studying a timetable by the booking office—"her? Do you suppose she's one of us? She doesn't look like it."

The station-master came out of his office and answered her. "Would you three young ladies be for St Martha's?"

The fair girl looked round. "I am, please."

We joined her. "So are we."

The station-master said he was glad we were all present and correct. "You'll just have to wait six minutes, ladies. The Sister from the hospital said there'd be two more nurses coming on the up train. The hospital's sending a conveyance to collect the five of you." He walked round the booking-office, and looked over the low fence that separated the minute station from the road. "That's one of the hospital cars coming along now. The porter'll look after you."

The hospital porter was a fatherly young man. He checked our names and luggage, then sat us in the back of his station-wagon while he met the up train. When the two other girls joined us in the wagon he told us to keep an eye out for the view as he drove, and to send home immediately for our bicycles, if we possessed them. "The P.T.S. and the hospital are a tidy step from the bus route, Nurses. No buses run up our hill, see, it being private, like. So if you've got bikes you get your mums to pack 'em off sharpish."

The fair girl had not spoken a word since Hannah More and I joined her. "Would I be allowed to have my car?" she asked quietly.

Hannah More had very dark hair and eyebrows. Her brows shot up. The porter glanced round momentarily. "I can't say as I know the answer to that, Nurse, seeing as you're the first nurse I've known to ask it. You'd better have a word with the Sister about that."

One of the new girls had sandy hair and thin lips. Her companion was a rather pretty brunette with a lovely complexion. They stared with open hostility at the fair girl. She looked at her hands, and relapsed into her former silence.

"Obviously," I said, "a car or bike is a must if buses are out." Hannah agreed, introduced herself and me. "What are your names, girls?"

Sandy hair was Fay Kinsley. Her friend, Agatha Carter. I looked expectantly at the fair girl. I had not heard what she said when she gave the porter her name. "I'm Estelle Dexter." She smiled, a polite and strangely anxious little smile. I smiled back, wondering if she was really anxious or only shy. Then I noticed Hannah's eyebrows were on the move again, and Fay was visibly nudging Agatha Carter. The atmosphere in the back of the station-wagon had not been particularly amicable, but at that moment it was positively and—to me—unaccountably electric with disapproval.

I had never been able to tolerate atmospheres. I had to say something. "Any of you girls done any nursing?"

"Have you, Frances?" queried Hannah.

"No. The only time I've been inside a hospital was when I went up to Martha's for my interview with Matron. The prospect before us scares the daylights out of me."

Estelle glanced at me in silence. Agatha Carter and Fay Kinsley exchanged smug smiles.

Fay said, "I suppose it must be rather frightening for you. Personally, all I feel is that starting again is going to be the most awful bore. Agatha and I were discussing it on the way down to-day. We've come together. We worked in the same hospital in our home town."

"You've done another training?" I asked. "Children? T.B.? Fevers? Mental?"

She gave us the impression that, although they had no specific qualifications, there were few branches of the nursing profession in which they were not highly experienced. "Of course, it's going to make all the difference to us at Martha's. Frankly, I simply can't wait to get back into a ward."

Agatha nodded. "It'll be like old times."

"Honest to God," murmured Hannah, "is that so? It must be nice to be an old hand."

"You'll feel like that a year from now," Fay promised.

Hannah caught my eye. "Maybe. Mind you, it took me more than a year to feel at home when I was doing my children's."

"Children?" demanded Fay. "Have you done that training? Where?"

Hannah named the most famous hospital for sick children in the British Isles.

Fay was speechless. I asked, "Why do a general training on top of that? And if you're qualified for kids why do you have to come to the P.T.S.? Can't you start off as a second-year?"

"In most hospitals. Not Martha's. If I want a Martha's certificate as well as an S.R.N., which I do, I've got to go through the whole works again—only I don't take Prelim. State twice, naturally. I want a Martha's certificate because—frankly—it's a key to any hospital anywhere in the world. Even in places where an English S.R.N. doesn't carry much weight a Martha's certificate can tip the balance. It's well worth an extra year to get that." She looked at Estelle Dexter. "I don't suppose you've done much nursing?" she asked not unkindly, but as if she knew what she was talking about.

Estelle shook her head. "No."

"I'm glad some one else is green," I said, as the station-wagon began to climb an apparently endless and very steep hill. "I've been wondering how I'd make out among all you experienced characters."

Hannah said Estelle and I would probably get on far better for being green. "No two hospitals agree even on bed-making. I expect I'll have to forget a lot of what I've learnt and keep quiet about the things I can't forget." She glanced at Fay. "It doesn't pay to know anything in a P.T.S."

The porter joined in. "You've got something there, Nurse. That Sister P.T.S. is a one for learning the nurses in her way and not no other. Got a proper name for that, she has." He jerked a thumb to the left. "Take a look between them pines, Nurses. There's the hospital."

The trees beyond the fringe alongside the road had been cleared; the long, low, white-painted buildings were sprawled all over the clearing, and connected by a long covered ramp. We passed quite close to one of these buildings. Two nurses were pushing a patient in bed out of one of the open french windows of the ward. They were laughing as we drove by. Their laughter surprised me. I thought the most hospital nurses were permitted was a gentle smile.

Hannah asked about the land. "Does it belong to the hospital?"

"That's right, Nurse. It did belong to one of our gentlemen. He used to live in the P.T.S. house when he was a lad—see? He give the lot to the hospital when it was bombed bad in the War. That was afore me time, but me dad told me about it. Me dad was Head Porter in London for twenty-three years." He swung the wagon round a hair-pin bend and then into a wide drive.

"Here you are, Nurses. Your house. I'll give you a hand with them bags, then I'll have to get off." He turned, grinned at us, and raised a thumb. "Best of luck, all."

Sister Preliminary Training School was waiting with her Staff Nurse, in the open front doorway. Sister P.T.S. was tall, youngish, with straight hair parted in the centre and draped severely over her ears, then drawn back into a Jane Eyre bun. Her eyes were small and keen; her back was like a ramrod.

Her appearance momentarily made us into a band of sisters. "Heavens, what a battleaxe!" muttered Fay. "Thank goodness that Staff Nurse looks human. She's got a sweet smile. I'm sure she'll be a dear."

Hannah recovered first. She took another good look at the pair in the doorway, called "Good afternoon, Sister," politely, as she jumped out and helped the porter unstow our luggage.

Fay and Agatha went in first. In the shelter of the wagon back doors, Hannah murmured, "Don't be too shaken, girls. Looking a battleaxe is part of the stock in trade of any Sister P.T.S. Take my tip and reserve judgment and—be as meek as two little lambs. The old girl may be human underneath."

I found it hard to believe her then. I did, later. Sister's formidable exterior hid an acute sense of humour and a very kind nature. Staff Nurse Naylor's sweet smile and gentle voice were soothing at first meeting, but her smile meant only that she was showing her very good teeth. She smiled all the time; she often laughed at us; she never laughed with us.

We were the last arrivals in our set. Sister shook our hands, and told us tea was ready. "You will be shown your rooms after tea, Nurses. Go and wash in the downstairs cloakroom."

Tea was perfectly dreadful. Sister and her Staff Nurse sat at each end of the long table; polite conversation was made only at the ends of that table; no one else said a word. I sat between Estelle and Fay, and thought how lucky Miss Nightingale had been. P.T.S.'s had not been invented until long after she returned from the Crimea. If she had had to go through this, even she might have had second thoughts.

After tea Sister gave us an introductory lecture on ethics, then showed us how to make up an ordinary bed in the approved Martha's manner. When she finished she handed us over to Nurse Naylor. "Nurse will show you how to make up your caps and wear your uniform correctly. Then you may go to your rooms, unpack, and get into uniform. I shall expect you to have finished your unpacking and have your empty suitcases ready for removal when the first supper gong sounds."

Naylor surveyed us as if we were so many angel-children, and in the softest voice tore our attempts at cap-making to shreds. "That is supposed to be a cap, Nurse Dorland. Not a pancake!

I don't know what you think you are doing, Nurse Kinsley. You are certainly not making up a St Martha's cap."

She sounded really saddened by Estelle. "We'll have to do better than that, won't we, Nurse?" She ripped out the cap-wire Estelle had painstakingly inserted. "And something must be done about your aprons. They're nearly two inches longer than your dresses. Surely you could have had them attended to?"

I wondered why she stressed the 'you,' and why Hannah, Fay, and Agatha looked so knowing. I felt very sorry for Estelle, who was staring fixedly at the floor. This was all so reminiscent of my first day in boarding-school that it had stopped bothering me, but possibly she had been to a day school, and was unaware of the unwritten institutional law that insists all newcomers must be made to feel as stupid as possible.

Eventually Naylor dismissed us to our rooms. We dispersed in obedient silence. In the middle of my unpacking I found one suitcase was missing. I went out on the landing and saw it sitting outside a room two doors away. Estelle's room was next to mine, as we had the same surname initial. Her door was open. She was standing surrounded by unopened suitcases, gazing blankly at them. I looked at her as I went by the first time. On my return I stopped. I had wanted to talk to her since we arrived in the house. She seemed so lost. But every attempt I had made at conversation had met with either a monosyllablic reply or a polite smile. I watched her unnoticed for a moment, and was reasonably sure I recognized what was wrong. I had three sisters. My second sister Pauline was often petrified by shyness. People thought that she was a problem-child or a square, depending on their age group, when she was only dumb with nervousness.

I tapped on her open door. "Can you manage? Anything I can do?"

She looked up slowly. "No, thank you."

She did not move. Nor did I. She was reminding me too much of Pauline. "Nearly finished?" It was an absurd question, as she had obviously not started.

"No. Not yet."

"Shouldn't you get on? Supper's at eight. It's nearly half-past seven." I went into her room. "Sure I can't help? Maybe you don't like unpacking? Lots of people don't. My mum says the sight of a filled suitcase unnerves her."

For some reason this made her blush. "I—don't—know. I've never done any unpacking."

"First time away from home? That's tough. I know. I felt like you do now, when I first went to boarding-school. How I loathed it!"

She did not answer for a few seconds. From her expression she was making up her mind about something. She must have reached a decision. "I know this'll sound crazy," she said quietly,

12

"but although I've often been away from home, I've never done much for myself." She folded one hand in the other. She had beautiful hands. "Snag is, I don't quite know where to start. I suppose that's inevitable, as some one's always packed and unpacked for me."

"I suppose so." I tried not to sound surprised. "Don't give it another thought." I shut her door, left my case on her mat, lifted one of hers on to the bed. "Behold an expert. I'm the oldest of four girls, and as our mum's allergic to suitcases, I've had to learn the form. Got the keys?"

She gave them to me without more argument. "What can I do?"

"Pull open all those drawers and your wardrobe door."

She did this in silence. She went on being silent. Pauline would have behaved like that, so I behaved as if she was Pauline, and talked about the P.T.S., the hospital, the Dorland family, and turkeys.

She thawed slowly. She told me she was an only child. "My mother loves travelling. I've lived with my grandfather. I can't remember my father. He died when I was four."

I was no longer surprised she looked lost. "Did your mother nurse?"

"No," she murmured, and froze again.

I changed the subject to Hannah. "She looks fun. Kinsley looks—well, as if she'll be taking over from Sister, very very shortly." I noticed the label on the dress in my hands. "Blow me! No wonder it looks good!"

She smiled slightly. "I like their cut."

"Like?" I held up the dress. "Isn't that the understatement of the year? It's perfect. Do you get all your clothes there?" I suddenly remembered the time. "We'll have to get on. Can I look at these later?"

"If you like." She smiled properly for the first time in our acquaintance. "Do. Any time."

We were in my room, when Hannah came to say Estelle was wanted to take a phone call in Sister's office.

She looked worried. "It'll be my grandfather. He said he'd ring. Will Sister mind?"

"Shouldn't think so. Better hurry."

She looked from Hannah to me. "What do I do? Walk in?"

Her ignorance of the most elementary facts of normal living surprised me yet again. "Knock first, then go in."

"Thanks."

Hannah looked after her. "She bringing out your maternal instinct, Frances?"

I had liked Hannah at sight. "She needs some one to take her over," I said openly. "The poor girl doesn't seem to know what time it is. I can't make her out."

13

"Why should she bother to know what time it is, when she doesn't have to? All I can't make out is, what is she doing here?"

"Why shouldn't she be here? If she wants to train?"

"Honest to God! You mean you don't know who she is?"

"Should I?"

She shrugged. "Don't you read newspapers on your turkey farm? Listen to the wireless? Watch TV?"

"Very often. Why?"

"Then have you never read, heard, or seen anything about Sir Hamilton Dexter, the aeroplane king? Girl, he's one of the richest men in the country! The multi-multi-type—although how he manages that with the income tax he must pay, God only knows. But he's got the lolly, all right. And one heir. His granddaughter. Name of Estelle. She was deb. of the year—they had 'em still when she came out—and she had the lot. The Sunday papers were marrying her off weekly. Who wouldn't want to marry her. And here she is with us. Just a lowly P.T.S. pro."

"Wow!" I sat down on my bed. "That explains those Dior labels—also her car and her helplessness. Poor girl."

"To inherit the odd million?" she asked drily.

A fraction would be fine. The lot—no. It would be crippling—and look what it's done to her. She must want to nurse pretty seriously to be here—she's in for a hell of a time. She doesn't know how to unpack, how to mix, has obviously never made a bed in her life. She's probably had a wildly expensive education, but it clearly has not taught her one thing about the life of a working girl."

"Fay Kinsley was holding forth about her bed-making in the sitting-room just now. Maybe it's as well you've decided to hold her hand, Frances. The Fay Kinsleys in Martha's will go to town on her mistakes. You, my child, have got yourself a full-time job."

Hannah was right and wrong. Estelle needed a great deal of help during our first days in the P.T.S., since everything we did was new to her. I knew nothing about nursing, but I had made beds, used dusters, swept floors, before. She genuinely did not know one end of a broom from another. As we were both 'D's,' generally we worked as a pair, which suited us both. I got into the habit of keeping one eye on my own work, the other on hers, and whenever she ran into trouble she rushed to me. "Frances, what does Sister mean about my bath having a rim? How can I take it off? Isn't it the edge of the bath?" "How do I high-dust? Do I stand on tip-toe?" "What does Naylor mean by my corners being ragged?"

I translated or helped, and when in doubt, asked Hannah. Between us we managed to carry Estelle through those early days. And then, slowly but very definitely, she realized what she had to do and how to do it. Once she grasped any fact, she never forgot it; she was quick on the uptake, and in her movements.

14

Hannah and I were delighted. Fay Kinsley was infuriated. "Of course this is just a passing phase for Dexter! She won't last out at her present pace. She'll be bored and leave long before half-term."

The term settled in and Estelle showed no sign of being bored by the regular routine of early cleaning, the lectures from nine until one, afternoons off-duty, and the evening practical nursing classes. We rolled countless bandages, bandaged each other and the life-sized dolls on whom we practised all forms of nursing; we washed each others' heads in bed; chanted the names of the muscles and bones over meals, discussed the central nervous system, the lymphatic system, drainage systems, and how to manage when there were no drains at all; gave innumerable injections of water into the sawdust pillow in the classroom until its weight trebled and it had to be put out in the sun to dry.

There were twenty-five girls in our set. After a while, although most of us got on well together, the set split into little groups. Estelle, Hannah, and I became a fixed threesome. With the exception of Fay and Agatha, the girls accepted as shyness Estelle's habitual reserve with every one but Hannah and myself. Fay and Agatha insisted she was being upstage. The sight or mere mention of her irritated them, and they never lost an opportunity to rub in the poor-little-rich-girl-slumming angle. Estelle ignored them outwardly, which inevitably irritated them still further.

One evening I found her in floods of tears in her room. For once we had attended different classes. I had been at Sister's practical nursing demonstration; she had been summoned to Naylor's extra sewing class. She had not been able to sew at all, when she first arrived. Hannah and I had turned up her aprons for her when she explained that she did not know how to hem. She could now hem fairly well.

"Hey—what goes on?" I closed the door behind me. "What's wrong, honey?"

She mopped her eyes with an unfinished many-tailed bandage. "I'm just being a little woman."

I removed the bandage and gave her a handkerchief. "My dear, you mustn't weep on that, whatever you're being. It's your test piece."

"I know." She sniffed. "That's what's so maddening. I can't do it right. I'll fail the exam. because of it—and my mother and every one'll say, I told you so. I shouldn't have come—I'll never get through."

She wept on my shoulder for a few minutes. I did not say anything. She had told me a great deal about her mother. The more I heard, the less I liked the sound of Mrs Dexter.

Eventually she calmed down. "It's all that damned bandage's fault. Naylor said herring-bone. I didn't know what she was talking about and asked Kinsley. She was sitting next to me. She

15

said I could use my eyes and watch her, but she wasn't going to do any for me, as these are our test-pieces."

"Didn't Naylor show you?"

"I didn't ask her. She'd only have made some crack if I had. I pretended I knew what I was doing. Look at it! It's a complete wreck."

"No, it isn't." I pulled out my scissors and unpicked her sewing. "Where's a needle and more thread? Oh, thanks. Now, watch . . ." I sat by her. "Herring-boning's dead easy once you know how. You go over here—over there. See? Sort of criss-cross. Now you do it."

She dried her eyes. "It looks easy. But should you be sewing my test-piece?"

"Forget that rubbish. Try it."

She tried and, as always, after a couple of false starts succeeded very well. "This bandage is filthy. Will that matter?"

"No. We'll just wash and iron it."

Afterwards I told Hannah what had happened. "That miserable Kinsley and snake-in-the-grass Naylor! They really got her down. They only had to show her."

"Frances, don't be dumb. Kinsley loathes Estelle's guts. She wouldn't help out. And Naylor, we all know, is a two-faced so-and-so who wants to be known as the dear, sweet staff nurse who is not impressed by all that lovely lolly."

"She's so hellish impressed, she never lets the poor girl forget it for one moment. She's foul to Estelle. Thank goodness Sister's got more sense."

"Problem there," said Hannah thoughtfully, "is that Naylor has Sister's ear. And Naylor's a trouble-maker. Her type in hospital is the type to avoid. Beware the curves, smiles, soft voices, Frances. Beware the girls who can hardly bear to put down their lamps to eat. Beware any one who makes such a song and dance about being dedicated to their profession. People who really are dedicated—like Sister—never make any fuss about it. It's just as natural to them as breathing. There's not one thing about Naylor that's natural. And she resents Estelle quite as much as Kinsley. Naylor would like to see her chucked out."

"But that's up to Sister."

She hesitated. "Don't forget Naylor makes a report on us too. She's caught on to how much you do for Estelle. I actually heard her telling Sister that Nurse Dexter should be grateful for Nurse Dorland's guiding hand. Sister didn't look peeved, but no one can tell what Sister thinks. You watch out. Because I don't trust Naylor. Honest to God, I don't."

"I gathered that." I smiled faintly. "I'll be careful. Thank goodness it's cooking to-morrow. No one can say I guide any one at cooking. I'm a lousy cook."

The next day was Wednesday, our half-day. The cookery

class occupied most of the morning. In the afternoon Hannah wanted to visit a hair-dresser. Sister had given Estelle permission to keep her car in our drive, so she suggested driving us to the nearest town, fifteen miles away. "Hannah can get her hair done; we can all have tea somewhere and go to a movie."

We accepted willingly. "After cooking," I added, "I'll be ready for a little escapism."

I was ready to escape when 1 P.M. came, but not free. My egg-custard had curdled into an unattractive lump; my bone jellies refused to jell; my creamed chicken, according to Naylor, would have given acute dyspepsia to any patient unfortunate enough to eat it. "An eight-year-old child could do better, Nurse Dorland! I refuse to pass such work. Come back this afternoon and really work on your cooking."

"Will some one please tell me," I demanded at lunch, "how I really work on a custard, jelly, or creamed chicken? And anyway, who would want to eat such nauseating food?"

The girls tried to explain, and said they would wait until I was finished. "You shouldn't be more than an hour."

"Two'll be more like it. I know me in a kitchen. You girls go without me. I'll have my escapism next week. Naylor's determined to have her pound of flesh from me. Let's not give her the satisfaction of having yours as well!"

They were reluctant to leave me behind, but as the last thing any of us wanted to do was to give Naylor any satisfaction, they did as I suggested. I went back to the kitchen when they had gone, feeling like Cinderella, with no Buttons or Fairy God-mother to cheer me. Naylor's quite natural displeasure at having to cut short her own half-day did not make the atmosphere any more cheerful.

"I cannot conceive why you do not take more pains over your cooking, Nurse," she remarked later as she gingerly tasted my creamed chicken. "You seem quite content to take endless pains over matters of interest to you."

I was too concerned by the gritty texture of the cream, and the fact that my new custard had also curdled, to pay much attention to what she was saying. "Yes, Nurse. I'm sorry, Nurse. Shall I make another custard?"

"Indeed you must. In your own time, and at your own expense. You have wasted quite enough of my afternoon and the hospital stores. Perhaps," she smiled sweetly, "Nurse Dexter may care to repay a little of your very willing assistance to her and help you out?"

There was a possibility she was only referring to Estelle's natural ability to cook. Knowing her and realizing now what lay behind her previous remark, I did not think it a probability. I did not want to show how annoyed I was, so I assumed my best Idiot Pro expression. "Yes, Nurse. Thank you, Nurse."

"Then you may clear up and get off to what remains of your half-day." She sighed. "I'm afraid Sister is not going to be pleased about this waste of food. I'll have to report it."

"Yes, Nurse. I'm sorry."

"So am I, Nurse," she murmured sadly, and walked off shaking her head. She came back when I had finished washing-up. "Sister would like to see you now, please, Nurse."

I dried my hands gloomily. I wanted to be a nurse, not a cook, yet it seemed my nursing career might end before it had really begun, because I could not bake a custard. It was my curdled custard that had really infuriated Naylor. I did not blame her for that; it had infuriated me. If she had not made that crack about Estelle, I should have been genuinely sorry to have spoilt her half-day.

Sister P.T.S. was at the desk in her office. My anatomy notebook was open in front of her. She was comparing my book with another open in her hand. I recognized Estelle's handwriting upside down, and wondered what else Naylor had reported.

"Nurse Dorland, did you do both these illustrations?"

"Yes, Sister."

She lowered Estelle's book. "Do you consider that fair, Nurse? How am I to judge Nurse Dexter's capabilities, if you do her work for her?"

I had an answer. I was afraid she would not like it much, but could see no alternative to giving it.

"I did both drawings, Sister, but—well, Nurse Dexter wrote the basis of the notes we both used."

Her lips tightened. "A combined operation?"

"Yes, Sister. Does it matter as it was not a test?"

She considered me reflectively. "It would not matter if this was an isolated occasion. I like my nurses to help each other. I am pleased to know that some of this work has been done by Nurse Dexter. I would feel happier if it was all her own work. I can appreciate your concern for a new friend," she went on slowly, "but I think you would be well-advised to be a little less solicitous over her. I will say no more about these illustrations now, but in future I do not want to be able to trace your guiding hand in any work of Nurse Dexter's. You may go, Nurse."

I went up to my room feeling worried and disgusted. I could hardly wait to get Hannah to myself and tell her how right she had been to warn me. Sister even used Naylor's wording. 'Guiding hand.' Bah.

Looking at it bluntly, I thought as I changed out of uniform, What good could Estelle's cash do me? I had no brothers with whom I could persuade her to elope. Our homes were at opposite ends of England, so I could scarcely entertain hopes of her introducing me to her wealthy friends, if she had any. There would be no point in my borrowing large sums of money from her, even if she were foolish enough to lend them to me, since we had no time or opportunity to spend money in the P.T.S. and, according to Naylor, would have still less time once we worked in the wards. Naylor adored chilling our spines with tales of the footsore years ahead.

I decided I was growing introspective and bitter, and must get out of the house, if only for a walk. I wandered aimlessly out of the front gate, crossed the lane, and climbed the hill beyond, forgetting that on an early summer afternoon in England, it is seldom wise to go out of doors without first having a look at the weather. I had climbed some distance before I realized the sun had gone in.

I looked at the sky. It was heavy with purple-black thunder clouds. I had on a sweater and skirt. I stopped on the hill, wondering whether to go back. I did not mind getting wet, but I did mind the prospect of being caught in a thunderstorm. Thunder terrified me when I was small, and it still did. I turned, then turned again. To go back would mean an afternoon spent avoiding Naylor and Sister. I had another look at the sky. The clouds were fairly high. They might move over. It was worth taking a chance.

There was a small plateau above tree-level on top of that hill. A squat, three-sided, roofed stone shelter had been built on that plateau as a memorial to some one who died in 1853. The name had worn off, but the date was still clear. I had often been up to the top and regarded the shelter as my private property, since I had not been able to persuade any of my set to make that climb, or seen any one up there during the various half-hours I had spent sitting on the crumbling wooden seat against the back wall, looking out over the miles of open country below. The lane did not go over the hill. It ran round about half a mile from the plateau. The crest above tree-level was covered with bracken; the gradient so steep that even in fine weather it was often necessary to use both hands as well as feet to keep balanced. I was scrambling quickly about two hundred yards from the top, when the rain began in slow, heavy drops. It was followed immediately by a sharp crack of thunder. The sky split with lightning. A second and louder crack shook the hill.

I tried to ignore the noise. I told myself it was just harmless noise. There was nothing to worry about. It was raining. Some one had told me thunderstorms were perfectly safe, so long as it kept on raining.

The rain stopped like a tap being turned off. I hurled myself over the edge of the plateau as the full violence of a dry thunderstorm broke directly overhead. Panic gave me wings. I had done those last two hundred yards at the double. I literally leapt across the plateau and into the shelter, intending to drop safely on to the wooden seat and wait while the storm rolled on. Instead of dropping on to the seat, I missed my footing after that final leap, stumbled, and went down backwards. It was mainly surprise that made me stumble. The shelter had always been empty. It belonged to me.

It was not empty that afternoon. A man in a grey suit had got there before me. It was as well he had. The shelter floor was made of stone. He caught me as I went over and saved me from a nasty crack on the back of the head.

"I think," he said calmly, "you had better sit down." He pushed me not ungently on to the seat, put his hands in his pockets, and looked at me thoughtfully. "Forgive my being trite, but next time you go mountaineering in a thunderstorm it might be an idea to look before you leap. You might have knocked yourself out just now. If you had been alone the consequences could have been quite serious."

2

A STORM AND A STRANGER

THE thunder paused, and the rain returned. It hammered like machine-gun fire on the flat roof, turned the plateau into a shallow lake, then spilled over the hillside, sweeping away twigs, stones, and bracken.

My companion had fair hair. He stood in the opening watching the curtain of water. "This plateau gets larger every time it rains. If it were not for those pines the whole hill would erode. It's certainly coming down now. You got here just in time." He turned. "Getting your breath back? Here"—he handed me a clean handkerchief—"use this as a face towel. It's larger than yours."

"Thank you very much." I mopped my face and hair. "And thank you for breaking my fall. I'm afraid I must have given you a shock, leaping in as I did. I didn't expect any one to be here. I've always had this shelter to myself before."

"So have I. It's fortunate that this afternoon has proved the exception to our rule." His smile was only polite. "You're pretty wet." He took off his jacket. "As we've no means of drying you, you had better put this on."

"Oh, no, thank you. I don't need that. It's very kind of you, but I'm not at all cold."

"You will be, when you cool down." He held the jacket by the shoulders. "You put it on."

I accepted reluctantly. "Thank you. But what about you? Won't you be cold?"

"I doubt it, thanks." He sat at the other end of the long seat. "Tell me, are you in training for a four-minute-mile-up-hill? You should make it, if you can keep up the speed you produced over the last fifty-odd yards."

"How could you see me? I came up from that side." I nodded at the wall on his left. "I couldn't see you."

"I was watching you through glasses." He produced a small pair of binoculars from the corner of the seat. "And through this crack in the wall. Here. I was actually watching a pair of falcons. They've taken over an old crow's nest in one of those trees down there. Your scarlet jersey came in my line of vision, and I followed you."

"Falcons? Up here? Hobbys? Aren't they rare here?"

He had treated me with polite detachment. He looked really interested in the habits of the hobby. "Yes. Very. That's why I came up here this afternoon. I saw them yesterday, tried to get some photos, but the light wasn't good enough. Are you keen on birds?"

"Fairly. My father's a passionate amateur ornithologist. I've been out with him a lot, and picked up all I know about them from him. He's got masses of photos, but his main interest is more bird-song than birds. I don't think there's a dyke on the Romney Marsh in which he and I have not sat with a tape-recorder."

He smiled. "He must have a good collection."

I nodded. The thunder had come back, and the shelter vibrated after a tremendous crack. I winced involuntarily.

"Worried?" he asked kindly.

If he had been a young man of my own age, nothing would have made me admit my complex about thunder. I could not guess his age exactly, but although there was no visible grey in his thick fair hair, the lines of his thin, intelligent face, and his generally assured air made me place him automatically in my parents' generation.

"Yes. I know it's absurd, but it scares me."

"I shouldn't worry about feeling absurd." His long, slender hands played with the straps of his glasses. "Every one's scared of something. Not every one has the courage to admit it." He bent forward to look up at the ominous sky. "This is too violent to last." He had to wait until the next peal faded before going on. "Violence in any form is generally short-lived."

I said I was sure he was right and wished I could believe he was. The lightning was brilliant, forked, and constant. It seemed to me to be aiming for our shelter.

He glanced at me. "I shouldn't watch it. Do you smoke?"

I dragged my eyes from the sky. "No, thank you."

"Mind if I do? Then would you feel in that right pocket for my pipe, pouch, and—I hope—matches. Thanks." He filled his pipe, and watched me over the flame of his match. "Where do you work in the hospital?"

"How did you guess that?" Then I smiled. "I suppose it's a fair guess to make about any one on this hill. We all work here."

He smiled back. "I don't." He did not enlarge on that, and as I did not care to question him I told him about the P.T.S. "It's in the large house"—the lightning made me blink—"just higher up the hill than the hospital."

"How are you getting on? Like nursing?"

"We haven't done any real nursing yet. We practise on dolls. I like all we do—apart from cooking."

He looked amused. "You can't cook?"

"No. I'm the world's worst cook. I know what I should do in

22

theory, but it never works out right. Either I produce charcoal or my food comes out of the oven raw. Our Staff Nurse says an eight-year-old child could do better." I told him about my afternoon. "I've only to look at an egg custard to make it curdle."

"What happens?"—he raised his voice slightly to be heard over the uproar around us—"to all the food you cook in your classes?"

"We eat the successes. The failures go in the pig-bucket. Some one, somewhere, is raising some fine little piglets on my cooking." I knew none of this could interest him, and he was only keeping me talking to keep my mind off the storm. It seemed only fair to meet him half-way and keep on talking. "There's no doubt, good cooks are born, not made. Estelle—one of the girls—had never cracked an egg before our term started, but all her things turn out well. Imagine—she never even curdled her first custard."

"Just imagine," he echoed soberly, and we both laughed.

"Possibly," he said a minute or so later, "you use too much heat. Do you use gas or electricity?"

"Gas."

"Then I should say you want something that resembles a candle flame. And perhaps you try and work too quickly?"

I guessed he had picked up these tips from his wife. "It might be that. Our Staff Nurse is always fussing about my being in too much of a rush. Can you cook?"

He smiled. "No." His next words confirmed my guess. "I've only acquired this knowledge second-hand. Try it out in your next class."

"I will. Thanks." I thought it over. "Hannah told me I should go slow." And I explained whom she was, and why she was training.

He knocked out his pipe, looked at the sky, refilled it slowly. "And what are your plans when you finish training?"

This time I had to wait to be heard. "Haven't any, yet. Four years is a long time to go."

"You'll probably be surprised how quickly it does go. Time speeds up as one gets older. Or haven't you noticed that, yet?"

I discovered I had. "Through my youngest sister, Judy. She's ten. A week is an eternity to her."

The walls of the shelter were positively rattling with the noise. "Have you a large family?"

"Three sisters." I looked at the lightning and then away. "I'm the oldest."

"Where do you live?" he demanded civilly.

I had to give him my attention or seem rude. "In Kent. My father's a farmer."

"What does he farm?"

"He grows turkeys."

23

"Many?"

"Six thousand—roughly." If violence was short-lived, it was time this particular spell of violence died.

"Does he breed them?"

"No. He says that's too tricky. He gets them as chicks. Day-old, generally."

"Tricky? In what way?"

I did not intend talking about turkeys, but he seemed so genuinely interested that soon I was telling him not only all the problems of turkey-growing, but all about my family and the farm.

"It's actually on the Romney Marsh? No wonder your father knows about birds."

I nodded. "In all weathers and seasons it's a bird-watcher's paradise. Good shooting, too, if you like shooting."

"You don't?"

"Afraid not. I prefer people who go after birds with a camera instead of a gun."

He did not comment on this. "The Romney Marsh is pretty big. Is your home very isolated?"

"Not really. Only three miles from our village." I told him the name. "It's a small village, but when Daddy was a boy it was quite famous for a while, because some one found the ruins of a Mithraic temple just beyond our church."

"I think I remember that." He watched the rain through half-closed eyes. "Let's hope this is the finale."

"I hope so. I've never known such a long storm."

"It'll pass. Tell me, do you miss your home much? Or are you too busy in your new life?"

"I miss the family a bit—but we are very busy."

"Are your fellow nurses pleasant?"

"Very"—I remembered Fay and Agatha—"on the whole."

"Only on the whole? Where's the rub? Your Staff Nurse?"

I smiled slightly. "She's a rub to us all. We've a problem pair in our set."

"Why's that?"

I had no more intention of telling him about Fay and Agatha, than I had had of talking turkeys. I not only told him about our problem pair, I threw in Estelle, Naylor, and Sister P.T.S. "Have you ever heard anything so stupid? What if she has lots of lolly? It's no good to me or any one else in our set. I just like her. But I don't like the idea of Sister having these dark thoughts about me."

"Apart from Sister—do you mind about the others?" he asked curiously.

"Not really. Their opinions aren't worth anything. They can think what they like."

"I don't imagine your Sister really does entertain dark thoughts on this matter. She must have a great deal of experience in dealing with young women to hold her particular job. With experience you learn to recognize certain qualities when you meet them. I should say all she meant this afternoon, was that this girl must stand or fall on her own. Which is fair enough."

A hideous thought struck me with the violence of the storm. "Are you a psychiatrist? One of our medical staff?"

"I'm not a psychiatrist. I don't work or live down here. Didn't I tell you?"

"You did. I'm so sorry. I forgot." I was infinitely relieved I had not been pouring out my life's history to some one I might one day meet in a white coat in one of the wards. "Are you on holiday?"

"Just down for a couple of days. I live and work in London."

I would like to have asked what work he did; about his family; if they were down with him. But the obvious difference in our ages, the fact that he reminded me vaguely of my parents' friends, and the austere lines of his face in repose prevented me asking personal questions, even though none of these had prevented my talking to him as if we had been friends for years.

Our conversation drifted back to birds. It was some time later that I realized the storm was over.

He stood up. "I hadn't noticed, either. Come outside. I'll show you the tree in which those hobbys are nesting."

We strolled over the muddy plateau. The air was clean and fresh as it always is after a storm, the light stronger than it had been all afternoon. I discovered he was much taller than I had previously thought, but he did not look at all strong. His face was too thin and drawn. My mother would be horrified if my father looked as he did. I wondered why his wife did not do something about it. And again, I wondered what he was. He was reassuringly unlike any doctor I had ever seen. His grey suit was of good material and well-cut, but it was far from new. His shirt was white, his tie sober. He looked, I thought slowly, very like some one I knew. Whom?

I placed that likeness a few seconds later when I watched how he walked. He walked exactly like my mother's older brother. My Uncle Joe was a Fellow of a Cambridge college. My companion had the same academic air. He would look absolutely at home wandering round the streets of any university town with his thin shoulders slightly hunched under a long, flapping Senior Member's gown.

I returned his jacket, thanked him again for saving me a cracked head, and for helping me sit out the storm. "I'm afraid I've talked far too much. I always do. I'm so sorry."

His lips twisted in a crooked and very attractive smile. "I've enjoyed listening. Please don't apologize." He looked round suddenly. "Quick—see—there's one of them."

A small bluish-grey bird with pointed wings rose from one of the trees. "Isn't that the male? I never realized their beaks were so like a hawk's."

He nodded. "That's him. I wish I did not have to get back to town this evening. This light's quite good. I'd like to try for at least one photo."

"I don't know if this light'll last. Are those clouds over there coming, or going?"

"Coming, I'm afraid. You had better go back." He looked round nostalgically. "I must go too, more's the pity."

"Did you know this hill before it had a hospital?"

He answered my question with another. "Do you see that church down there? The tower's just visible? The man who was Vicar there up to—let's see—twenty-odd years ago was my godfather. I used to spend a lot of time with him when I was a boy. So I know most of this part of the world very well."

We said good-bye then. I looked back once as I slithered and skidded downwards. He was standing where I had left him. He noticed my pause and raised a hand. I waved back.

Hannah and Estelle were enchanted to hear about my storm. "What was his name? What does he do?"

"I dunno. Watches birds. Saves young women from cracking open their heads. Keeps up their morales in storms."

"Didn't he ask your name?" demanded Hannah.

"No. It was about the only thing he didn't ask. It was a long storm. He kept me talking."

That, they said, was not difficult. Estelle asked why I had not tried to find out anything about him.

"It would have been like cross-examining one's father or uncle. It didn't seem to matter. He was nice, polite, and sensible. I liked him."

Hannah said he sounded deadly dull. "He must be aged to have good manners. Modern young men have to be angry, and that means plain rude. Now you take my cousin Bart," she went on eagerly. "Remember, Frances? I told you Bart was a Martha's student? Estelle and I met him in the high street this afternoon, just before we went in to the movie."

"It was quite a while before we went to the movie," corrected Estelle. "We had just come out of the car park."

"Well, we met him, anyway! And he just adores being an angry young man. He's for ever flying off at a tangent about something! He is good fun, but can be impossibly rude when he wants to be. I was so pleased we met him this afternoon. I did write and tell him we were here, but thought he must still be in London as he hadn't rung me. He never writes letters."

I was not sure that I liked the sound of Bart More, but as Hannah was so clearly delighted about him, I said I thought it all very splendid.

She slapped me on the back. "You'll love Bart! He's just your cup of tea. Am I not right, Estelle?"

"Quite right, Hannah," echoed Estelle politely.

I looked at her curiously. I was coming to know her well, and somehow her words did not ring true.

Hannah's mind could go off at tangents, too. "Do you mean to say, Frances, he didn't make so much as a pass?"

"Not one. Why worry? We've agreed he's aged."

Hannah said age never stopped any man making a pass. "Maybe he's queer?"

"Not with his voice, dear." I jerked a thumb downwards. "It came up from way down there. Deep and quiet. Like—like—gentle thunder."

"You might be describing Bart's voice—eh, Estelle?"

Estelle said she was afraid she was not very good at noticing voices, and changed the subject to the mid-term test we were due to have at the end of the week. "We've an hour before lights out. Shall we do some bandaging? I cannot get my ascending spirals right. Frances, be an angel and model, then Hannah can criticize."

Hannah was our private bandaging expert. "You do me, then I'll do you. I'm very shaky on fingers," I said, "and can never remember which side you tie the sling."

"Over the injured side," chanted Hannah, "over the injured side. Let's go and borrow the wherewithal from Naylor."

With Nurse Naylor's permission we loaded ourselves with crêpe bandages, and retired to Hannah's room. As first victim I lay on the bed while Estelle bandaged me under Hannah's instructions. She dropped the bandage twice. Hannah caught it both times, handing it back imitating Naylor's agonized protest, "Ten little marks gone, Nurse Dexter."

"That's not right, Hannah," I said, after the second occasion. "Dear Naylor does it this way." I sat up, simpered, and flapped my eyelashes. "Ten teeny weeny marks gone, dear Nurse Dexter," I purred revoltingly. "You naughty little nurse, you! What will Matron say! Ouch!" I yelped normally. "Watch you, Estelle! You've cut off my circulation!"

"Sorry," muttered Estelle, dropping the bandage again.

I picked it up for her. "You are in a dither to-night."

She said she was suffering from an acute attack of pre-mid-term-test nerves. "It would be grim to be chucked out half-way, and it can happen! Remember Sister warning us about it, in our opening lecture?"

The thought sobered us all so much that for the rest of that hour we concentrated only on bandaging.

When the test day arrived, our whole set was jittering with nerves. When the written work was over, we gathered in our sitting-room to wait for lunch, and commiserate with each other's mistakes.

"Will somebody please tell me"—I searched through a surgery text-book—"how many bones there are in the foot? I could not remember and had to blur my illustration with some arty-crafty shading to hide my ignorance."

Fay Kinsley said she had found the anatomy paper quite straightforward, but had been aghast by the nursing paper. "We might have been taking State Finals! Really, Sister expects far too much—setting a paper like that!"

"I don't think Sister honestly expects us to know the answers," said Estelle. "When I met her in the hall just now she said she knew the nursing paper had been stiff, but had set it intentionally to give us some idea of the questions we might get in our Final P.T.S. exam. She actually told me not to worry too much, and I'm sure she meant that for us all."

Fay snapped immediately. "We all know you don't have to worry about anything, Estelle! You needn't shove it down our throats."

I looked up from my book. "She wasn't shoving anything down our throats. She was boosting our morales. Do stop making cracks, Fay. My nerves won't stand them. I've simply got to find out how many bones there are in the foot. Oh, no!" I suddenly found the illustration I had been looking for. "That does it! I drew a hand instead of a foot! Sister'll take off!"

The others crowded round. "Look up the knee joint, Frances. I'm sure I got the capsule wrong."

The sitting-room resounded with groans as our post-mortem continued. "Thank God, there's the lunch gong," said Hannah piously. "If it hadn't sounded we'd all have nervous break-downs."

"One thing—we can't go very wrong this afternoon." I replaced the text-book. "Sister always says practical nursing is mainly common sense."

An hour later I discovered my mistake. Sister walked over from her desk as I blanket-bathed a life-sized doll called Mrs Brown. "I presume your patient is having a full course of peni-cillin, Nurse Dorland?"

I gazed at her blankly. "I'm—er—afraid I don't know, Sister." I looked at the doll's serene face. "Should she be on penicillin?"

She removed two blankets from the neat pile I had arranged on the chair at the foot of the bed, and laid them carefully over Mrs Brown. "Indeed she should, Nurse. She will need all the help medical science can give her to counteract the acute attack of pneumonia she will inevitably suffer after your ministrations. Do you realize you are bathing a patient in front of an open window, and have only covered her with one thin blanket? Shut the window, make the bed, change your water, and start all over again. And then kindly do as you have been taught. Use your eyes, consider the temperature of the room, and always close near-by windows before washing so much as the face and hands."

I said weakly, "Yes, Sister. I am so sorry."

"And I am equally sorry for any patient unlucky enough to be nursed by you at this juncture, Nurse Dorland," replied Sister calmly, looking beyond me to something on the far side of the room. "Nurse Franks—one moment, please!" She gave me a brief nod—"Carry on, Nurse Dorland"—then sailed across to Sylvia Franks. I heard her ask Sylvia whether she had ever had the misfortune to break a bone. "No? Then allow me to inform you that fractures are painful, Nurse. Mrs Smith [Sylvia's doll] has a newly pinned fractured right femur. I saw you place your heavy hand directly over your patient's injury. You may not consider your hand heavy, Nurse? You must believe me when I say that under certain conditions even the weight of a light sheet can be an intolerable burden."

A few minutes after Sylvia joined me in the improvised sluice-room that had once been a housemaid's cupboard. "The old girl's going to town this afternoon," she whispered. "She's got me so on edge that when I got soap in Mrs Smith's eye just now I apologized aloud even though Sister was behind the screen with Fay."

I refilled my washing bowl. "She's given me such a conscience about Mrs. Brown's pneumonia that I feel you may as well call me Sarah Gamp and have done!"

"Where's the gin bottle, duckie?"

"In my bib pocket . . ." I broke off as Fay Kinsley flew past the sluice door looking very pink. Half a minute later she hurtled back, lugging a heavy oxygen cylinder behind her. "What ails you, Fay?" I asked, opening the classroom door for her.

"I dropped George in the bath," she muttered furiously, "and Sister insists I give the wretch artificial respiration and fix up an oxygen tent. It's too crazy! He might be a real baby—not just rubber!"

Sylvia looked at me as Fay rattled on. "Do you suppose the old battleaxe has a sense of humour—or just knows her stuff—or both?"

I did not dare answer as Sister was watching us. I had no doubts about Sister knowing her stuff, but was not sure about Sylvia's first point. We now knew how we all stood with Naylor, but Sister P.T.S. was still very much of an unknown quantity.

When Mrs Brown had been bathed to her satisfaction she sent me next door to Naylor who was presiding over the bandaging and poultice-making tests. A girl called Alice Linton was temporarily acting as model.

"Nurse Linton has fractured her right scapula and left os calcis, Nurse Dorland. Will you apply the requisite bandages?"

Thanks to Hannah, bandaging was one of my strong points.

Nurse Naylor gave my bandages an approving nod. "You have a little time to spare since your bandages are right first time, so will you set for, then give a hypodermic injection in the sawdust pillow."

I felt quite pleased with life, and myself, as I scrubbed-up. My spirits rose still higher when Naylor passed my setting with a sweet smile. I fitted the hypodermic syringe together, and decided we had been most unjust to Naylor. Her gentle manner and soft voice made her really pleasant to work for.

She smiled so gently as I gave the injection. "Nurse Dorland," she breathed the words, "would you be good enough to remember you are supposedly giving a patient—a human being—that injection, and are not digging up your father's garden? Please wash and do it again."

My second attempt was no more successful. She merely used different words. "Nurse, you are holding a hypodermic syringe, not brandishing a harpoon. And look what you've done to that needle! Possibly you might be able to use it as a crochet-hook—you can certainly never use it again for an injection. Put it all away now and make a linseed poultice. You have just time to get one made before the test ends."

I began my poultice hopefully. Perhaps I could make a beauty and cancel the bad marks my injections must have earned. I lost hope very soon. The linseed refused to allow itself to reach the right consistency. I stirred feverishly with the official wooden spoon, then in desperation used my scissors and fingers in my attempt to spread it correctly. Consequently, instead of a smooth brown poultice, the result was something like a miniature mountain range.

Nurse Naylor considered this with an angelic smile. "How very odd that looks! Just what is it supposed to be, Nurse Dorland?"

"A linseed poultice, Nurse."

She widened her eyes. "I would never have thought it. Does your father keep horses?"

"Er—no, Nurse."

"What a pity. Never mind. Perhaps you know some horse to whom you could present it? And meanwhile, I think you had better make me another."

I made another; then a third. When five o'clock and the official end of the test arrived, I was still struggling with soggy squares of brown paper, and covered in sticky linseed. Naylor told me to remove my mess from the classroom, and my person, and go to tea. "You had better practise your poultices on your own, Nurse. Matron may well ask you to make a linseed in your Final test, and if she should," she asked brokenly, "what will you do?"

"I know exactly what I'll do," I told the girls at tea, "if

30

Matron so much as murmurs 'Linseed'! I'll burst into loud tears and hand in my lamp."

"At least your bandaging went well, Frances," called Alice Linton from the end of our long table. "Mine was a nightmare. Naylor told me to fix a right tib. and fib. on Sylvia. I got in a state and began on the right radius and ulna. Good old Sylvia kept mumbling 'Tib. and fib., tib. and fib.,' out of the corner of her mouth—but Naylor heard."

"What happened?" we chorused.

Alice grinned. "Naylor told Sylvia to recollect she had been knocked unconscious and wouldn't be round for hours. For good measure she threw in a fractured skull. That was sheer murder as Sylvia's hair's so thick!" She waved her tea-cup at me. "My only consolation was that I hadn't got you, Frances. Your curls would have been the end!" She set down her cup with a cheerful crash, the tea slopped over, staining the clean white cloth. "Blimey! I'm still in a state! I can't even drink tea this afternoon. What will Sister say?"

I stood up and smoothed imaginary cuffs as Sister always smoothed her cuffs at the start of each lecture. "That you are sadly failing in one of the most important attributes of a nurse, Nurse Linton. Every nurse worthy of the name," I announced, in a copy of Sister's voice, "should have at her finger-tips the correct method of drinking tea. Prepare to make a note, Nurses. Ready?"

"Yes, Sister—please, Sister," they chanted obediently.

"Very good. Now. A nurse may only drink tea in the following circumstances: (a) when she has a cup, (b) a saucer, (c) a teaspoon. No St Martha's nurse may consider drinking tea without a teaspoon. And the position of the hands should be—so." I picked up my cup and saucer. "Note the elbows, Nurses. No flapping ducks on the nursing staff of St Martha's Hospital, if you please. Any questions?"

Sylvia Franks choked and had to be slapped on the back by Alice. "You've got her voice exactly, Frances!"

"She's better at Naylor," said Hannah. "Frances, let Naylor take over."

I was too cheered by the discovery that I had not been the only person to make a hash of the test to feel self-conscious. I relaxed my ramrod posture and beamed at their upturned faces. "Lecturing is Sister's province, Nurses. I'm just going to have a teeny weeny little cosy chat with you. It won't take more than four or five hours, and we'll put our heads together and really get down to working on this question of tea-drinking! It may seem only a simple point, but, a good nurse is known by her simple . . ."

"Mind?" suggested Alice gravely.

"Nurse Linton! Naughty, naughty! Not worthy of you!

31

What would Sister say if . . ." my voice faded as the room rose to its feet.

The girls facing the door—which was behind me—were staring dumbly over my shoulder. I turned very slowly. Sister and Naylor were just inside the door. Sister's face was expressionless. Naylor was looking at the floor; her cheeks were tinged with pink.

Sister cleared her throat. "We have come to tell you that you may all be excused extra duty this evening, Nurses. You may go off-duty after tea." She looked deliberately at me. "When you have finished your tea, will you please come to my study, Nurse Dorland. Thank you. That will be all, Nurses. Sit down and enjoy your tea."

No one said a word for the few seconds after Sister and Naylor left us. Fay Kinsley broke the silence as she alone obeyed Sister and went on with her tea. "I tried to catch your eye, Francis, directly I saw the door open. I'm afraid," she added primly, helping herself to a slice of currant cake, "I was not surprised to see her looking so cross."

I got up. "I've lost my appetite, so may as well get this over. Write and tell me how you all made out in the test, girls."

Estelle touched my arm. "I'm sure she won't be too annoyed. She's too intelligent not to know we were all letting off steam through you, and I'm sure she's got a terrific sense of humour."

Fay shrugged. "I don't see how she can possibly overlook being publicly ridiculed, but I suppose I'm very dense."

"Stick around and I'll tell you. If I'm not sent up to my room." I straightened my cap. "Am I tidy?" I shot out of the dining-room, across the hall, and knocked gingerly on the closed door of Sister's office.

She was sitting at a small table in the bay window sharing a tea-tray with Naylor, who was pouring out tea.

"There you are, Nurse Dorland. Good!" Sister smiled pleasantly, stood up, and flicked back the neatly folded corners of her apron. "Now, where did I put it? Yes—here." She handed me a smallish registered envelope. "This arrived by the afternoon's post. Mrs Mallinson signed for it, as you were occupied in the test. Just add your name under hers in my book, to show you have collected it in person." She pushed a red-ruled exercise book towards me. "And add the date and time."

I thrust the envelope in my apron bib, signed mechanically, then waited with my hands behind me for the real reason for her summons.

She sat down, helped herself to a cucumber sandwich and smiled again. "That's all, Nurse. You may go."

I looked at her uncertainly, wondering if she expected me to apologize before she said anything. Perhaps her smile was only for Naylor. "Excuse me, Sister, I—er—think—I mean—know—I ought to apologize. . . ."

"For wasting a quantity of excellent linseed?" she queried smoothly without giving me time to finish. "I'm sure it was not really wasted. You have no doubt learnt from your failures. Go back to your friends, and have a pleasant evening relaxing after the strain of to-day. Unless," her eyes danced, "you plan to continue your most instructive course of lectures?"

I felt my face turn scarlet. "Yes, Sister—that is, no, Sister. Thank you very much," I mumbled and fled back to the dining-room.

"What did she say? Is she going to send you to Matron?" demanded the girls directly I opened the door.

I closed it, leant back, and smiled widely. "Relax! Panic over! What do you know, girls! She's actually human!" And I repeated Sister's words. "Isn't she a honey?"

Estelle came up to me. "My God, Frances—I've just aged ten years. I thought she'd be all right, but I only had instinct to go on."

Hannah said her nerves could not stand any more of anything. "Let's change and go out, before I go into a decline." She led the way to our rooms, and, as usual, we went into hers as it was on the floor beneath Estelle's and mine. "Did she just send for you to set your mind at rest?"

"Actually, no." In my relief I had forgotten the registered letter. I pulled it from my bib. "She wanted me to sign for this. It must be something special from the family," I said glancing casually at the postmark. The postmark was London. I turned it over now curiously. "It's not from the family. It's from a J. S. Slane. Slane? Whoever? I don't know any Slanes."

"Perhaps it isn't for you at all?" Hannah peered over my shoulder. "Yes—Miss Frances Dorland. Do open up, Frances. This is fascinating."

I slit the envelope with one blade of my scissors, and shook the contents into one hand. "Streuth! Photos."

Hannah seized them. "Am I seeing things? Birds."

I took them from her. "Let me see. Why, they're the hobby babies in that old crow's nest—and look—there's Mum coming in on the wing. They are good. They must have been taken with a cine."

"Most peculiar little objects I've ever seen." Hannah gazed entranced. "How do you know that's Mum? And what's a hobby when it's at home?"

"A small falcon. I know it's Mum because it looks like a hobby Mum. It's got the right markings. It must have taken him ages to get them. How cute of him to send them." I looked at the envelope again. "So he's J. S. Slane."

"Your bird-watching man?" asked Estelle.

"Must be." I was extraordinarily pleased, and took the photographs from Estelle. "Let me see them again."

Hannah removed the envelope from me. "Isn't there a letter? There's nothing on the backs of these snaps. Yes, here you are, jammed inside." She drew it out, and handed it to me. "What's he say?"

I smiled, "Not much. Listen:

"DEAR MISS DORLAND,

I thought the enclosed might be of interest to you and your father. I hope you are having a good term, and that the egg custards no longer curdle.

Yours sincerely
J. S. SLANE."

3

MY FRIEND THE PROFESSOR

"I've met a good many opening gambits," said Hannah, "but this is a new one on me."

"I suppose it is an opening gambit?" Estelle looked at me. "Why else should he send them?"

"I don't think it is." I re-read the letter. "This is civil, but hardly forthcoming."

Hannah asked me to be my age. "Men don't go round sending strange young women pretty pictures of birds for no good reason."

"Amateur ornithologists do. Daddy corresponds and exchanges bird snaps with total strangers all over the world. Male and female. This'll probably start an interminable correspondence on falcons large and small between him and this man Slane. I'll send them on home, which is obviously what he wants me to do." I replaced the photographs and letter in their envelope. "I'm glad I know his name. I detest not knowing people's names. Wonder what the J. S. stands for?"

"How did he know yours?" asked Hannah. "I thought you didn't tell him?"

"I didn't. I had forgotten that detail. How peculiar. How do you imagine he found it out?"

Hannah smiled. "A strategically dropped handkerchief with your name tape on it? Or maybe your scissors?"

"There was the father and mother of all storms going on. I wasn't in uniform—didn't have a handbag. My skirt had no pockets, my handkerchiefs are only marked with initials, and I certainly did not drop one that day, as I only had one with me and used it when I got back to get the mud off my shoes before coming into the house. Nor did it occur to me that there would be any point in giving him my name, discreetly or otherwise. Honestly. He just wasn't the type."

"He couldn't have conjured your name out of thin air," she protested reasonably, "so he must have got it from some one. Whom?"

Estelle said thoughtfully, "Are you positive he wasn't one of our men, Frances?"

"For Pete's sake, don't suggest that! Not after Mrs Brown's pneumonia, my linseed, and then tea to-day! If I seriously thought I had unburdened to a senior member of Martha's I'd walk out here and now! And he'd have to be a senior member to be on our staff at his age."

"What was he wearing?"

I relaxed. "Estelle, thank heavens you've got brains. Of course, there's our answer. He couldn't be a pundit because Naylor says they all wear black jackets and pin-striped trousers. He was just in ordinary grey."

"Sure it wasn't just a dirty white coat?" suggested Hannah.

"It was a suit he had on, neither a long nor a short white coat."

"Which rules out Senior Residents, registrars, and housemen," agreed Estelle.

"Unless he was off-duty?" put in Hannah.

Estelle remembered Naylor's lecture on form far better than Hannah and I. "He would still have been in a white coat. Naylor told us it's a Martha's private rule that all residents must wear their white coats in the hospital grounds, even when off-duty. That hill belongs to the hospital, so is part of the annexe grounds."

Hannah was determined to be difficult. "Maybe he was a student?"

"He was far too old—and not wearing tweeds or corduroys."

Estelle looked amused. "We're whittling him down. What's left? Naval, military, law, divinity—medicine's out—City, art?"

I thought this over. "He couldn't work in the open—he was the wrong colour. And he certainly couldn't work with his hands. He might be a lawyer——" I told them about Uncle Joe. "But I got the impression he was something academic. He had that kind of scholarly—pardon me while I just turn Einstein's theory of relativity over in my mind—air, some dons have."

Hannah said she was sure I had something there. Estelle was doubtful. "Why wasn't he up? The term's on at present. And he told you he worked in London."

"What about London University?" demanded Hannah. "We're close enough for him to get down in a couple of hours to look at his falcons. Perhaps he's a Professor there? His own boss? Then he could nip off and bird-watch at will. What do you guess he's a Professor of, Frances?"

I laughed. "I don't even know he's one. He was old—but not that old. He did not look Professor-ish—he hadn't even a beard. We've a splendid Professor of Zoology at home who has the most magnificent beard."

Hannah said beards were not at all essential. "There were two Professors at my children's hospital. One did have a tiny goatee, which was purely an affectation, we all thought. The other might have been a retired sailor. He was fat, tanned, clean shaven, and didn't walk the wards—he rolled round them."

"Did your Professor show any signs of a roll?" asked Estelle cheerfully.

"No. Nor was he fat or tanned."

Hannah flopped on her bed, and removed her shoes. "He's probably got a gastric ulcer. But we still don't know how he got your name, even if we think we've got him taped. Ask him when you write to acknowledge these."

I sat down, and took off my own shoes. "I suppose I must do that. I don't see how I can ask how he traced me." I half closed my eyes and reflected on the face in my mind. "No. I haven't the nerve. Anyway—can I write back? Where's that envelope? Pull out the letter, Estelle, and read the address. I didn't look at it properly."

She did as I asked, while Hannah peered forward. "Is that how you pronounce that name?"

I looked up. "What is it? A house?"

"A club," explained Estelle, "rather like the Athenaeum. Grandpa stays there when he's in town."

"Your Professor must have a good job to move in the same circles as Estelle's grandpapa," said Hannah bluntly. "Is the subscription very heavy, Estelle?"

Her expression tightened as it always did when her money was mentioned directly or indirectly, but as Hannah and I had previously agreed privately that the kindest way to deal with Estelle would be to treat her wealth as a normal subject of conversation, we ignored her expression. "Is it?" I asked.

"Fairly. It's—well, rather more exclusive. My great-grandfather was a member, then Grandpapa—and so on."

I said, "It's very handy having you here to educate us, Estelle. I like knowing things like this. One thing—my Professor knows how to bake custards. Maybe he is in the cookery line, if they have such things? I haven't curdled one since I took his advice on slow motion."

"Tell him that when you write—and ask if he has any hints on linseed," insisted Hannah. "Who knows? He may have the answer to all a pro's little problems. We can use him, if he has."

"I'll do that," I agreed lightly, intending to do nothing of the sort.

Later that evening I wrote my weekly letter home, and enclosed the bird photographs in their own envelope to prevent their being crushd. I explained how I had come by them, and added, "I've really no idea who he is, but Hannah's name seems to have stuck."

My words were more true than I guessed. From that afternoon J. S. Slane was 'the Professor' to Hannah, Estelle and me; and before the term ended our whole set called him "Frances' Professor."

When I had sealed my parents' envelope, I re-read the Professor's short note. I decided to answer it at once, in case I forgot later, which was only too probable, as I was for ever forgetting to write letters. I modelled my answer on his brevity. But where he seemed to me to have succeeded in being brief without being curt, my own effort seemed abrupt to the point of rudeness. I tried again; tore that page too. I wrote the third attempt without any fixed plan. The result covered a page and a half. I read it through doubtfully, wondering how to shorten it, and why I had allowed my pen to meander from thanking him to Mrs Brown and the linseed.

Sister P.T.S.'s head appeared round my door and prevented me writing a fourth letter. "Ten minutes after lights out, Nurse Dorland. You should have finished your letters by now." She waited while I tidied away my writing things. "If you care to give me those, I will see the postman takes them early in the morning."

I hesitated momentarily, then feeling Sister's impatience was growing, slipped the Professor's letter into the envelope I had already stamped and addressed to encourage myself, and gave it and my parents' letter to her. "Thank you, Sister. Good night."

"Good night, Nurse. And in future please see your lights are out on time."

Next day we heard the results of our test. To every one's astonishment Estelle came easily first in the written work.

Fay Kinsley took this as a personal insult. "You never told us you had brains, Estelle!"

For the first time Estelle hit back. "You never asked me, Fay."

Hannah and I were jubilant for Estelle. Hannah had done very well in the practical test, was fourth from the top in the written. My name came in the middle of both sets of marks.

"I'm only too thankful I wasn't lower down," I said as we surveyed the results on the hall notice-board for the twentieth time that night. "I wrote reams on everything, but most of what I wrote was wrong."

Sister was behind us. "I'm happy you realize your weakness, Nurse Dorland," she said not unkindly. "You must not let your pen or tongue run away with you, in future. You merely have to conquer your habit of answering all round a question and go straight for the main point. You wrote essays yesterday, where you need only have tabulated facts."

"Copy your Professor," murmured Estelle after Sister walked on, "he seems a model of brevity."

I slapped my forehead. "Don't mention him. I tried it last night—and from what I remember ended by writing him an essay on linseed."

They laughed, and Hannah told me not to worry. "He can't be horse-y as well as bird-y. The two things don't go together.

Probably he's never heard of linseed. Only horses and P.T.S. pros have any use for the stuff."

Apparently the Professor did know about horses. A few days later I had another letter covering barely half a page. "I believe an old groom told me when I was a boy that the technique with linseed is to warm all the utensils first to prevent the seeds coagulating."

I shared this information with Hannah and Estelle. At the next poultice practice we produced three fine linseed poultices. Naylor was reluctantly pleased. "You are coming along at last, Nurse Dorland."

"I feel an awful fraud," I told the others, "but I could hardly say, 'Don't congratulate me; congratulate my Professor.'"

A couple of days later we had a very complicated lecture on the formation of the blood. Sister P.T.S. was a good teacher, and normally I was able to follow her very well, but a faint thunderstorm was going on during her lecture. It did not frighten me, being too far off, it merely reminded me vividly of the last storm on that hill. My mind kept drifting from reticulo-cytes and normoblasts, to fair men in grey suits, and, above all, to the still unsolved problem of how my specific fair man in grey had discovered my name. When the lecture ended I was in a complete but oddly contented daze. I remembered every detail about the Professor, but not one word Sister had spoken. I had to write up the lecture and illustrate it with reasonable accuracy, so I borrowed one of Estelle's many medical text-books and spent my next free 'two-to-five' pouring over the highly technical words.

Estelle looked into my room from time to time to see how I was getting on. "All straight?"

"Uh-huh. I'm way out of my depth. What's a lymphocyte? Or a basophil? I didn't get either down." I showed her my rough notes. "Only those four."

"She did mention them. See here—it's like this——" and she tried to explain. It was no good. Her brain worked far too quickly for mine, and although she was very patient, she could not teach.

Hannah came in to help; so did two-thirds of our set. "It's really quite simple," they all said kindly. The trouble was, I did not find it simple. In desperation I learnt by heart a chunk from Estelle's book, wrote an essay on what I had learnt; illustrated my essay with what I considered a most impressive chart.

The chart earned me a visit to Sister's office. "What exactly does this represent, Nurse Dorland?"

I took a deep breath. "It is a diagram to illustrate the formation of the blood, Sister."

"It does nothing of the kind, Nurse. As you would know," added Sister sternly, "had you paid any attention to the drawing

39

I made on the board in my lecture. I noticed your mind was wandering, which is why I am not going to repeat my lecture to you now. If you cannot take the trouble to attend in class you must find this out for yourself. Let me have it back as soon as you have got it right."

I returned to the girls, sunk in gloom. "How am I going to get this right?"

"Why not send your Professor an SOS?" suggested Estelle thoughtfully.

"He couldn't know the answer to a thing like this. Besides, I can't keep on badgering him. I'll just have to find out for myself, as Sister said." I borrowed all her text-books. "I'm going to bed with the lot. Maybe my subconscious'll dream up the answer in my sleep."

My subconscious seemed otherwise occupied. I dreamt about my Professor all night. In the morning I felt very cheered by my dreams, but very worried about the formation of the blood. Fay Kinsley and I were paired as bed-makers in the practical nursing class that day. Sister told us to put Mrs Brown in a rheumatic bed; Mrs Smith into an orthopaedic bed; and then to make up the empty bed in the class-room to receive a patient returning from the theatre after an amputation. "Collect all necessary equipment before you start, Nurses. When you are ready wait by your beds until I return to inspect your work."

We loaded ourselves with fracture-boards, bed-cradles, extra mackintoshes, extra personal blankets, mackintosh pillow-cases, and bed-blocks.

I closed the store-room door with my shoulder as my hands were full. "I'm sure we've forgotten something—apart from the kitchen sink."

Fay looked down her nose. "I don't know why you think you always have to joke, Frances. Nursing is not a joke."

I let that pass. "There's something else we'll need. What?" I stopped Estelle as she hurried by to Naylor's First-Aid class. "We're doing rheumatic, orthopaedic, and amputation beds. Do we need anything else."

Fay's lips tightened, but she said nothing knowing, as we now all did, Estelle's memory for detail was the best in the set.

Estelle glanced swiftly over our collection. "Tourniquet to tie at the foot of the amputation bed. Lower rail. Maybe a transfusion stand, just to be on the safe side. Sorry, girls—I must fly. Naylor's waiting."

"Fly, dear. Heaven'll reward you even if I don't." I put down my load and took a rubber tourniquet from one of the shelves. "We'll have to come back for the transfusion stand. Bless that girl! She's the brightest person I've ever met."

Fay smiled unpleasantly. "She's certainly brighter than you

were. Now she's got the hang of things, she's not lending out her brains, even if you did cosset her when she was so green."

"What are you talking about? Hasn't she just done that?" I heaved my load higher. "Let's get on with those beds."

"I wasn't talking about just now," she said as we stripped the empty bed. "I was talking about the rocket Sister gave you on that chart. If Estelle had any decency, she could have saved you that rocket. She's got the facts all right, but is keeping them to herself. I suppose she inherited that tendency along with everything else from her precious grandpapa. I suppose you have to be grasping to get rich and stay rich. Personally, I think it's a pretty rotten way to act."

"Personally, so do I—about the way you're acting. She hasn't inherited from her grandfather yet, he's still alive. I've never heard such nonsense in my life."

I had to stop speaking then as Sister had come back to watch us, even though I was bursting to tell her just how much Estelle had tried to help me over that wretched chart. Later, when we were alone again, I changed my mind. It was useless trying to persuade Fay about anything concerning Estelle, but unless I got my facts right about that last lecture, she would probably spread her nasty little ideas round the whole set. That night, in desperation, I wrote a really short, urgent letter to the Professor.

He answered by return of post. This time his letter actually covered the whole of one side of a page. Accompanying it was a spare typewritten sheet of paper on which was given a very simple account of the formation of the blood; on the reverse was a clear diagram illustrating the account.

"I called in the assistance of one of my fellow-members here," he wrote. "A pathologist. He recommends the enclosed as being successful with his students. I hope it may be of some use. If not, drop me a line and I'll tackle him again."

I was enchanted by his helpfulness; doubly enchanted to be able to understand his enclosures.

The following Friday evening Sister summoned me once more. "Explain this diagram to me in detail, please, Nurse Dorland."

When my somewhat nervous explanation ended, she nodded approvingly. "I see you have taken pains with this, Nurse. Good. Did you manage it alone?"

"No, Sister. I consulted—one of my friends."

She smiled. "I thought as much. Well, Nurse, you may tell Nurse Dexter that I consider she has the makings of an excellent teacher."

This time it was Estelle who felt a fraud. "I can't take the credit, Frances!"

"Nonsense! You must. The Professor wouldn't mind, and

41

Sister would have a stroke if she thought I was writing to him about it."

My set never knew the Professor had helped me over that particular problem, but his existence was now common knowledge. When any one had a problem, I was besieged immediately. "Frances, is it your turn to write or the Professor's? Then will you ask him—this—that—or the other? Thanks."

I mentioned this to him in one of my letters, without telling him of his nickname.

In his reply he seemed amused:

I find myself enjoying this novel situation. I have never been an oracle before. I only hope I will be able to come up with the right answers. I must admit your questions lack neither variety nor entertainment value, and are infinitely preferable to crossword puzzles.

I always enjoyed getting his letters; I loved getting that one. I wondered, as I did constantly, about his background; if his wife was attractive; if he had any daughters. His tolerant attitude reminded me a great deal of my father, so I suspected he had at least two growing daughters. Perhaps he had more than two; perhaps a vast family? Estelle said Professors were reasonably well-paid, but a family can eat money, as I knew from my parents' food bills. I got quite upset at the thought of the Professor having to over-work, and do without to support his many children, and wondered if I ought to bother such a busy man with my letters. I also wondered whether his wife minded his writing, if she knew. I could not decide if I preferred her to know or not; he was older than me, but—well—not all that much older. If I were his wife, I thought finally, I would not like it at all. Yet that was sheer folly, because as he had admitted, my letters took the place of crossword puzzles and meant no more to him than that. I was a little disturbed to discover how much they were beginning to mean to me.

The second half of the term was now well under way. Our Final Test was no longer a vague date, but merely a matter of days ahead. Hannah lost interest in her hairdressing appointments; Estelle's shining car stood silent in the drive; my bicycle developed two flats, but there was no time to mend either. Every spare moment we had off-duty we devoted to working through test-papers, nursing each other in bed, chanting the muscles and bones, and finishing our many-tailed bandages.

One afternoon Estelle and Hannah were in my room for a change. We had had a very busy morning of practical nursing, and our legs were weary. I massaged my calves then drifted round the room barefoot and on tip-toe as Naylor had advised. "I can't say this makes much difference. What's this chap here?"

42

I slapped my leg. "Some name like a Rider Haggard character. Gastroc—something?"

Estelle was reading the anaemias. "Gastroc nemis—I think. And not from Haggard—it's pure Martian."

"I'm not all that up in space fiction." I leant out of my window and watched a bright blue dot appear on the winding white lane running up the hill. As it came closer the dot turned into a motor-scooter ridden by a man in a white crash helmet. "Talking of Martians—come here, girls! There's a very muscular Martian getting off a blue scooter at our front gate."

Estelle looked up quickly, but showed no other sign of interest as Hannah bounded to the window.

"It's Bart! Good! I thought he had forgotten his promise to call." Hannah scrambled for her shoes. "Come and meet him, Frances. You too, Estelle. You remember Bart? We met him in the town."

"Bart?" murmured Estelle vaguely. "Did we? Oh, yes, I remember. He was charming." She hesitated, then added politely, "Will you mind if I don't come down? I'm whacked, and must get these anaemias taped. But you go, Frances. You'll like Hannah's cousin." Her eyes met mine for a fraction of a minute.

The expression in her eyes silenced the protest I had been about to make over her absurd statement that she needed to get the anaemias taped. She had reeled them off to us only a few minutes ago, and once she learnt anything, she never forgot it. I glanced at her curiously, put on my own shoes, and said I would love to meet Hannah's cousin.

Hannah looked hurt as we went downstairs. "I'm afraid Estelle didn't like Bart. She was fearfully standoffish when I introduced him."

"She was probably only stricken dumb with shyness. Remember how she first was with us? I'll bet that's why she's staying upstairs."

She brightened. "I expect you're right. You really know her even better than I do."

I agreed heartily, but inwardly was not so sanguine. I knew Estelle well enough now to know something was wrong. I did not understand what that something could be, and when I met Bartholomew More, I understood even less.

Hannah's description of him had been quite wrong. He was no Angry Young Man; he was exceedingly gay, had pleasant manners and exceptional good looks. He had Hannah's dark hair and eyes, but his features were far more regular, the lilt in his voice far more noticeable—I suspected intentionally so.

Sister gave Hannah the choice of entertaining in the sitting-room or garden. Hannah chose the garden. It was a lovely afternoon and we sat on the lawn by the summer-house, while the

43

bees hummed over the lupins and columbines in the flowerbeds, and Hannah scolded her cousin for not visiting us sooner.

"Darling Hannah," he said plaintively, "do you appreciate the risk Luigi and I have just run? The chaps below told me I'd need a signed pass from Matron to get beyond your front gate. This place is out of bounds to one and all. And I risked it," he laid a hand on his heart, "for you, and you, Frances!"

I said, "I'm deeply touched. Is Luigi your scooter?"

"And who else would he be?" He looked round the lawn. "Where's the third member of the trio? You did say you were a trio, Hannah? That afternoon we met? Wasn't that blonde the third? Esther Something or Other?"

Hannah looked worried. "Estelle. Yes. She's—working."

I said, "Up yon." I waved at the house. "With her head in a medical book. You mightn't guess it from her fair and fragile appearance, but Estelle is the brains of our set. She's not just plain clever, she's staggeringly bright."

"Is that so?" he asked eagerly. "Maybe, now I come to think of it, there was something unusual about her." He suddenly noticed I was watching him and promptly altered his manner. "Unlike Junior," he drawled. "No brains—not even keen—just the slack type."

Hannah laughed. "Your years in Martha's haven't changed you, Bart. You always were daft."

"She mocks me," he said sadly, "mocks me. Let's ignore her, Frances. You, I know, will understand me. We must get together. When do you girls join the old firm in town?"

I smiled. I did understand him—as much as any young woman can ever understand any young man, or vice versa. I had met too many other young men of his type not to recognize it at sight. Our village at home was a very social place, oddly lacking in young women. I had never been more than mildly in love with any of them, but had been on dancing and going to Point-to-Point and Hunt Ball terms with several Bart Mores since I left school. "We don't mention the old firm yet. We still have to get over our Finals. All is dark beyond that date."

He said he knew just how it was. "Is your fair friend jittery, too?" He glanced at the house. "Is that really why she's flogging the books? It seems too bad to have to stay in in this weather. Who knows? To-day may be the summer."

Hannah said Estelle would not let a little thing like sunshine deter her once she had made up her mind to stay in.

"Strong-minded as well as bright?" asked her cousin.

"Inevitably. Or she wouldn't be here at all."

"And why wouldn't she?"

"Bart. You surely realize she's Estelle Dexter?"

He stared at her momentarily. "That—Dexter?"

She nodded. "The only one."

He looked at the house for several seconds before making any comment. "So she's the lass with all that lovely lolly," he said at last. "Well, well, well. Useful stuff, lolly." He turned slowly to me, as if it took him a tremendous physical effort. I expected him to ask what Estelle was doing at Martha's, since that was the first question every one asked on discovering her identity. He said only, "You in the money, too, Frances?"

"Not me. My father's a farmer with four daughters. I have what I earn."

He smiled faintly. "My old man's a parson. I'm the oldest of five. And I don't even earn." He glanced back at the house. "How does she fit in?"

Hannah said, "Frances can answer that. She's Estelle's closest pal."

I said, "It was tricky at first. She seemed utterly helpless. But once that Dexter brain catches on to a fact, it really catches. She's streaking ahead of us all, and fitting in very well."

"That's just great." He stood up. "And it's been just great seeing you girls, but it's time I made tracks. Be seeing you both, in town. Take care of yourselves."

We walked with him to the gate. Hannah watched his scooter vanish down the hill. "I hoped he'd spend longer with us. Never mind. We'll see him in town." She smiled at me. "Wasn't I right about him? Isn't he exactly your cup of tea? I knew you two would click. You can't conceive how differently he behaved to Estelle. He barely opened his mouth to her."

I was on the point of remarking that despite that original reticence he had managed to say quite a few words about Estelle, when she came out of the house and joined us.

Hannah hailed her cheerfully. "Bart quite understood you wanted to work. He had a fine time with Frances. They might have known each other years."

"How very pleasant for all of you. Will he be up in town when we get there?"

"I'll bet he'll be there when Frances gets there, if I know my cousin Bart," replied Hannah, who was patently in a match-making, and highly imaginative mood.

Estelle smiled politely. "That should be fun, Frances."

"Sure. Great fun." I noticed her smile did not reach her eyes. "How did you get on with the muscles? All taped?"

"I think so. That's why I came out."

"This sun is too good to waste," I said, and went to shut the gate which had just swung open. I did not remind her that she had officially stayed in to read up on anaemia. "Let's go back on the lawn. Hannah's cousin was right. To-day may be all the summer we have."

Bartholomew More was not right. The weather remained settled and brilliant. He did not visit us again during the rest

45

of our term, which annoyed Hannah irrationally, since he had only mentioned seeing us again in town. I heard twice from the Professor during those final weeks, and then there was no time left in which to open another text-book, roll another bandage, practise another bed, or write another urgent letter.

On our last evening I persuaded the two others to climb the hill. I would have preferred to go up alone, but knew they would be hurt if I vanished in the middle of our post-examination celebrations, so I insisted the exercise was what we all needed.

They said they were glad I had insisted when we reached the top. The evening was warm and golden; the sun only half-way down the sky. We lay out on the bracken, removing prickles and burrs from our hair, wishing we had brought a rug. Below us the hospital was white in the pine-trees, and on the cement ramps the scarlet blankets covering the patients lying in beds made vivid splashes of colour against the green and white.

We talked over the term, then the future. Estelle and I were going to a ward called Josephine in London. Hannah was to work in Arthur.

"I wish we could start in the annexe," said Estelle drowsily, "it's such heaven here now." She shielded her eyes with one hand. "What's that bird, Frances?"

"Flying east? That's a hobby. One of the Professor's babies. A honey, isn't he."

Hannah sat up. "Which way?"

"Thataway. East, girl. Blue-grey with pointed wings—see?"

"Think so." She lay back. "You know, we ought all to write and thank your Professor. He's given us a packet of help. Wasn't it a good thing you messed up your cooking that morning? You'd have come out with us, if you hadn't and never met him. Of course, you would then have met Bart earlier, and we might have seen more of him, but there's masses of time ahead."

"That's true," I agreed casually, glancing at Estelle. She was still watching the fast-vanishing hobby, and apparently ignoring our conversation. She had never mentioned Bart to me, but whenever Hannah talked about him, which she did frequently, Estelle made a point of not paying attention. This was odd, because Estelle was normally very good about paying attention.

Hannah twisted her head round and surveyed the stone shelter. "So that's where you nearly cracked your head? You were mighty lucky, Frances. You'd have had a fractured base almost for sure on that floor." She relaxed again. "I wonder if you'll ever come across the Professor again? Does he ever mention a date?"

"No." I said no more, hoping she would drop the subject.

"Then why on earth does he go on writing to you? The man

46

must be nuts. No passes; no attempts to date you." She looked me over. "You did say he wasn't a queer?"

"He wasn't. Why does he have to be one to write? Maybe he just likes writing letters? Maybe he's just plain kind."

Hannah snorted. "You're no raving beauty, duckie, but you're a good-looking wench with a smashing figure and the best legs in our set." She extended her own complacently. "And we've got some pretty good legs among us. I won't say that men can't be kind, but kindness is seldom the motive that inspires any man to pursue an acquaintance with a young woman." She turned to Estelle. "Aren't I right?"

Estelle hesitated. "Grandpapa says there is no such thing as a platonic friendship between a normal man and woman. Grandpapa's generally right."

"It's hardly a friendship," I protested. "We only met in that storm. I expect it's amused him to write as he has, but he'll probably get bored with it soon."

"You can't let him get bored before you find out how he managed to get hold of your name. You don't know that yet, do you? Or, really, anything about him?"

I was very fond of her, but I could willingly have choked her. "No."

She said she thought I had been disgracefully unenterprising. "Can you even remember what he looks like?"

"Sure," I said, "sure. It's engraved on my heart. Haven't you guessed?"

She laughed. "I'll bet. Since the poor old Professor's been such a boon and a blessing to us, I only hope he doesn't feel the same."

Estelle asked quietly, "Why?"

"Quite obviously he's married—decent men of his age always are. He must be decent, not to have made any passes or dates. Maybe he's at the dangerous age. Was he?"

"He wasn't dangerous, whatever his age."

Hannah said I was very young and innocent and she was very old and cynical. "You wouldn't recognize danger if you saw it."

Estelle nodded. "It's probably just as well there's not much chance of your meeting him again. Those snaps might not have been an opening gambit, but if you hadn't made some impression on him, you'd never have got that second letter. Hannah's right. Your friend the Professor sounds charming, and has been extremely helpful, but has obviously decided to stay at the end of a letter—and just as well if there's a Mrs Professor and lots of little Professors."

I had been first embarrassed, then annoyed, now I was honestly amused. "Girls, you are a pair! Poor man! You aren't giving him a chance. And you don't know what you are talking about, for all your worldly wisdom—though you ought to!

47

You've seen his letters. They couldn't be more impersonal or discreet. You talk as if they were Sunday paper love-letters."

Hannah said she would have thought it all far more natural if they were.

"For Pete's sake! Why? He's not in love with me!"

Estelle came over to my side. "He's certainly not acting as if he is."

Hannah rolled over and looked up at me. "Maybe he isn't. All the same—watch out, Frances. I'll tell Bart to watch out for you, too. When I was doing children," she went on dreamily, "we were always getting kids in with measles. We shouldn't have had them, but they developed it once they were in. Some one on the staff always caught it. Love, my dear little Frances, is like the measles. The older in life you get it, the worse it hits you. So I hope for Mrs Professor's sake, that for once Estelle's grandpapa is wrong. You'll forgive me, I hope, Estelle?"

"Even Homer sometimes nods," agreed Estelle. "But—I've never known Grandpapa wrong."

I shivered although the sun was still there. "I'm cold. Let's move."

There was a party going on when we returned to our sitting-room. Earlier I had decided to leave the party discreetly to write a last letter telling the Professor about our results. I wanted to write to him as never before. I did not. Hannah and Estelle had forced me to face all the questions I had previously refused to face. I stayed in the party until Sister sent us to bed.

4

BART ASKS ME OUT

THE sun shone on Josephine Ward balcony that Monday morning, the river was the colour of polished pewter. A small, dirty, red tug ambled lazily past the hospital. A seaman holding a rope on the narrow deck waved at us, and the two patients in beds on the balcony waved back. The tug's funnel tilted back as it approached the bridge, a trail of black smoke floated up to us. In a few seconds, young Mrs Ellis's face, hands, and clean white bedspread were spotted with soot.

"Oh, dear." I dropped my wet string duster. "I am sorry, Mrs Ellis. Did any get in your eyes?" I took her face flannel from the back rail of her locker and removed the soot from her person. "Sure your eyes are all right?"

"I'm all right, duck." She smiled. "A bit of dirt don't hurt. Makes me feel I'm back home along of the Power House. My Mum," she gasped, in the way Sister Josephine had told us was typical in acute cardiac disease, "reckons we all thrive on a peck o' dirt. But you'd best do something about me quilt, Nurse. Staff Nurse won't half create, if she catches it in this state." She paused for a longer breath. "We did really ought to have them red covers over our quilts, duck. You nip along and fetch 'em to us afore that Nurse Garret sees us out here without 'em." She looked across the balcony to her companion, Mrs Astor. "See what that tug done to me quilt, Gran?"

"Dear, dear, dear," clucked Mrs Astor anxiously. "Poor Nurse. What a worry we are for you."

They were great friends despite the sixty years between their ages. They were so obviously fond of each other that at first Estelle and I had thought them actually related. Mrs Ellis had been longer in the ward than any of our women, but both of them had been in and out of Josephine several times before.

Sister Josephine had given us a diagnosis class on our second day in her ward. She had said Mrs Ellis was very ill. I knew she had to be right, but found that difficult to remember and believe when I was with Lily Ellis. She was two months older than I was, very attractive, gay, and good-natured. It seemed impossible to associate her with my previous notions of illness.

She had scattered those notions and adopted me as 'my Nurse Dorland' from the moment when, on our third morning in

49

Josephine, I had spilt tomato soup all over the clean turn-down of her top sheet. She not only consoled me; she even soothed our Staff Nurse. "I'll bet I look real classy with ketchup on me best bib and tucker, Nurse Garret! Talk about clumsy! I always was a shocker and no mistake! There was this poor little new nurse trying"—gasp—"to feed me real lovely, and I gives her a shove and bungs the tray clean out of her hands."

When Nurse Garret had helped me change the sheet and left me with a new bowl of soup to feed her, I had attempted to thank Mrs Ellis.

She lowered one eyelid slowly. "Shush, duck. Don't say no more. If I say it was me own fault, it was me own fault, see. The patient is always right—eh? Hasn't that Sister Tutor told you that yet? She will."

She was perfectly right. Sister Tutor gave us this maxim in her opening lecture a day or so later. By then I had discovered that Mrs Ellis was a mine of hospital information. She knew all that went on in Josephine; a great deal about nursing; and exactly how to manage Sister Josephine and Staff Nurse Garret.

I did not hesitate when she said I needed to get two red check-covers. "Do I just help myself from the linen-room?"

"Half a tick, duck! Hey—Gran! Is it all clear?"

Mrs Astor was allowed to move freely in bed. She sat forward and peered into the ward through the open balcony doors. "The Staff Nurse is just going into the lift, dear," she whispered conspiratorially. "You're safe."

Mrs Ellis agreed. "She'll be off to the dispensary. She won't be back afore eight-thirty. Get weaving, duck."

"Bless you both—I will. Thanks." I shot down the ward that even after two weeks seemed four miles long and to contain four hundred and not forty beds. The linen-room lay at the opposite end to the balcony. Sister's office, and the changing-room were on the same side of the small ward corridor outside the main ward and called 'the flat'; the kitchen and clinical-room were on the other side.

Estelle gave me a faintly harassed smile as I passed the open kitchen door. I waved back, then dropped my hand like a stone as Sister Josephine came out of her office.

"Nurse Dorland, is one of my patients haemorrhaging?"

I swallowed, knowing what was coming. "No, Sister."

"Then I can only presume that my ward is on fire?"

"Er—no, Sister."

"Then what do you mean by racing in this fashion? This is the fifth occasion upon which I have had to speak to you about running on duty, Nurse. Kindly spare my having to do so again. Carry on with your work decorously."

I collected the red-check covers, and walked with what I hoped was suitable decorum back to the balcony. The women nodded at me amicably. "Always on the go, these young nurses. Shame. But, there. Got so much to learn they have."

On the balcony Mrs Astor sat forward to help me arrange her cover. "Lil, dear, has Nurse done the end right?"

Mrs Ellis was watching carefully. "Only sort of. Look, duck, tuck down them sides—see"— she breathed deeply—"not like it was a quilt. Then get to the bottom and pull up the end from the middle, like you was making an envelope. That's it, duck. Now, bung the lot under neat. There. You catch on quick." She glanced round the balcony. "Better give that wet linen bin a shove against the wall—Nurse Garret'll create if she sees it sticking out. And don't forget your wheel-chair with your rubbish. Nurse Garret won't be shutting her eyes to nothing now you been here two weeks."

If Nurse Garret had shut her eyes to anything during our first fortnight, neither Estelle nor I had noticed it. Garret was a slim, brisk, dark-haired young woman with a fine complexion and dark-rimmed slanting spectacles. Those winged frames added to the impression she gave of being constantly on the point of taking off from the ground. She moved like silent lightning, yet never seemed to distress Sister by her speed, possibly because she was so quiet. She came into the sluice as I was drying the last washing bowl. "Nurse Dorland, did you do the feet of your trolleys this morning?"

"Yes, Nurse."

"You turned them upside down and scraped the wheels with your scissors?"

"Yes, Nurse."

"Then you must have done them most carelessly. They're all over fluff. Do them again when the sluice is finished."

"Yes, Nurse," I said meekly, feeling like a gramophone record stuck in a rut.

Nurse Player, our Senior Pro, arrived in the sluice directly Garret vanished. Monica Player was in her second year—and our guardian angel. She hovered maternally over us, helping when we were lost beneath mountains of mackintoshes needing scrubbing, plates that needed heating, linen that had to be sorted, sterilizers that had to be cleaned, bed-tables that required polishing. She seemed capable of being in three places at once, and appeared to possess six hands. She came to my rescue now.

"I'll do those trolleys for you, Dorland. You get straight in here." She paused on one foot. "Have you been very careful about your locker backs? Garret's in one of her Monday morning moods. She always gets worked up about trolley wheels, and locker backs on Mondays." She glanced out of the window towards the balcony. "Have the balcony girls got their checks on —oh, yes! Good girl. I forgot to remind you when we were pushing their beds out."

51

"Actually, Nurse, Mrs Ellis reminded me."

"Thank God for Mrs Ellis," she said sincerely. "I don't know how we'd cope without her. And the others. They're a nice bunch."

Estelle said much the same when we did the flowers together at ten to nine. "They were heaven at breakfast. Garret told me to manage second cups alone. I was terribly slow without Player and the tea got more and more stewed. Sister noticed the colour when she was doing the pulses, and asked Miss Ronson if it was too strong. Dear old Miss Ronson adores weak China tea, but she swore blind the foul stuff she was drinking was just how she liked it! I could have hugged her."

Player sailed into the clinical-room in which the flowers were stacked at night. "Come on, girls, or we'll be late. All these vases must be in before I take down the screen across the door at the first stroke of nine."

Thanks to Player we were done by nine. She removed the screen that showed whether the ward was open or closed for medical rounds, and marshalled us up to the centre table. Sister dismissed Estelle for the morning; gave Player a list of treatments; told me I was to do 'morning routine' on my own. "You've been with us long enough to be able to manage, Nurse Dorland."

Player gave me a slight nod. I took the hint and smiled weakly. "Yes, Sister; thank you, Sister."

"Don't look so rattled, Dorland," she whispered as we retired to the kitchen. "It's quite simple. Errands first, then temps., charts, drinks, treatments, set for lunch, close the ward, round; open the ward; help serve lunches."

I felt even weaker. "Yes, Nurse. Thanks."

"Don't forget you mustn't start the four-hourly temps. before ten to ten. The four-hourly book lives on Sister's desk. Ask her for it if she's sitting there, if not, help yourself. Don't forget to put it back when you've done the charting, or Sister'll go through the roof."

Maggie, the ward-maid, considered me grimly. "So I've to have another of you new nurses getting under me feet all morning, have I? Then you listen to me, Nurse Dorland. I'll have no milk spilt on me clean stove, nor drips on me floor, so don't you forget it. All right—all right," she grumbled, although neither of us had said a word, "I'll put your milk on and see to the urn. And you mind you fetch all the used crocks back to me by eleven. I'll want me kitchen to meself to get straightened up besfore I goes down for the dinners at a quarter to."

I had been nodding like a mandarin. "Yes, Maggie; no, Maggie; right, Maggie. Nurse Player, do I go to Sister for the errands?"

"Dorland, Sister takes round the S.M.O. immediately after

nine." Player spoke slowly as she would have done perhaps to a backward child. "Nothing must interrupt the S.M.O.'s round. He may not be a pundit, but he is the senior resident."

"What about the S.S.O., Nurse?"

"I've told you, physicians take precedence over surgeons. Do get that into your head. And do get off to Garret for those errands. She won't like being kept waiting."

Garret did not like it. "What have you been doing, Nurse Dorland? Why weren't you here five minutes ago? Now, take this"—she handed me a test-tube—"and keep it warm. Not in your pocket, child! It'll spill and you'll be drenched in bugs! In your hand. It must stay at blood heat. Take it to the Path. Lab., before you do anything else. It's labelled—this is the request form. These notes"—she pushed a file under my arm—"are for the in-patient Lady Almoner. Leave this bed-ticket"—my other arm was needed—"at the dispensary. Tell them the digitalis can come up in the basket as I've enough until the after-lunch round. That's all for now, but hurry. I may have more errands when you get back."

"Yes, Nurse; thank you, Nurse." I rushed off to look for Player, and met her coming out of the kitchen. "Please, Nurse, which floor was the Path. Lab. on?"

"Which Lab? We've got four." She tilted her head to read the label on the tube I was clutching. "For Sir Marcus. Top Lab.—top floor over the Admin. block. Not the Lab. I took you to—that was the Central slap opposite to Arthur. Know how to get to the Admin. block?"

"Is that where Matron's office is? I think so."

"Yes. It's quite simple. Go along to Matron's office, turn right past the Dean's office, and take the lift marked 'Private, Pathological Department Only.' That tube lets you use it. Come down the same way and make for the Almoners. You know where they live. I took you only last week."

I felt breathless already. "Beyond Casualty?"

"That's them. Ask the Almoners to direct you from there. They'll do it. They're good girls."

"That's a mercy," I murmured feelingly.

She grinned. "Don't worry. Pathologists don't bite."

"Just one thing, what do I do when I reach this Top Lab.? Do I ask for Sir Whatwashisname?"

"I wouldn't if I were you. He's the Director. He doesn't deal with any one under the rank of Ass. Mat. You won't have any snags up there. If there isn't an assistant pathologist around there'll be a label. Our Labs. are stiff with labels. It must be something to do with pathology or maybe the back-room boys are just allergic to being disturbed. Do get going, or you'll not be done in time to get your temps. taken by ten."

I walked as quickly as I dared along the main corridor that

53

connected all the hospital blocks. I knew the way to Matron's office, and did not anticipate any difficulty in finding the Dean's, until I reached the Admin. block and found I was quite lost. Matron's office was there all right, but I could see no sign of anything leading to the Dean. On my right was an opaque glass door marked "Private." I turned left. The notice on the only door in sight ran, "Medical Reading-room."

I hesitated and was promptly engulfed by a crowd of students who must have been following me down the corridor. The sea of tweeds and heads hid both doors momentarily, then swept by as if I was invisible and without substance. I gazed after them wondering if I had enough courage to call one back to ask the way, when I recognized one of the heads.

"Bart More," I called quietly, "can you help me?"

He glanced round incuriously, then smiled. "Hi, there, Frances Dorland. I didn't see you. So you made it? How about the rest of the trio?"

"Fine, thanks." I had no time to waste in civilities. "Where's the Dean's office?"

He had joined me. "Taking up medicine?"

"I've got to get this"—I held up the test-tube—"to the Top Lab., and I'm lost."

"Not now you aren't, angel. Come with uncle. Out of the way, chaps. The lady wants to rise to the upper regions." He thrust his colleagues aside, and opened the glass door marked "Private." "This way. The Dean's yon"—he jerked a thumb—"and there's your lift. I'll see you in."

"Thanks." I waited as he opened the gates. "You don't know how relieved I was to see you."

"You can do the same for me sometime. Where are you working?"

"Josephine."

He closed the gates very slowly. "Cousin Hannah?"

"Arthur. Bart, I'll have to go."

"That's right." But he had not yet closed the gates completely. "How about your other pal?"

"Estelle is in Josephine, too."

He let go then. "Just press that button, angel, and it'll take you right the way up. Take care of yourself."

I stepped out into another long white corridor. I had not been up there before, but, as Player had said, there was no question of any one visiting the Lab. being in any doubt. The door directly opposite to the lift-well was marked Pathological Research Department. Beneath that was a small notice: "Will all nurses walk in without knocking."

I obeyed rather timidly. I expected to find a room filled with intelligent-looking youngish men in long white coats absently eating dusty sandwiches. I was alone in a large tiled room lined with china shelves on which stood hundreds of empty test-tubes of various sizes. A line of white sinks with long-handled taps occupied the centre of the floor; four long zinc-covered tables were in a row by the outside wall that was almost entirely of plate-glass. The room was full of light and silence; the whole of London seemed spread before me and I wished I had the time and courage to linger and look out.

As I had neither I looked round, wondering what to do next. I felt exactly like Alice when I read an obliging label. "Will nurses please put any specimens to be kept at blood heat in the incubator under this notice."

"Thank you," I murmured automatically, opening the incubator. Directly I opened it, a bell rang. It went on ringing until a door at the far end of the long room opened. A middle-aged man in a long white coat, with rimless spectacles, and thinning grey hair, stood in the doorway. "I don't think you can have closed that properly, Nurse. Turn the handle right up. That's better." He came forward. "Where are you from?"

"Josephine." The bell had unnerved me, and I forgot to add, "Doctor."

"Good. I was expecting you. You've brought Miss Yates's specimen for culture? I may as well take it now. I want to get on with it." He removed the tube I had just left in the incubator and showed me how to close the door to cut off the bell. "Right, Nurse. We'll send the report down later."

"Thank you, Doctor." I made for the door, then wondered if I should have said 'Thank you, Sir Marcus.' I decided I should have used his title as Player did, but he did not seem to have noticed my mistake. He was shaking his head over the request form and muttering something about the last Van den Bergh showing a positive indirect reaction.

I wondered what or whom a Van den Bergh might be and if Player would be able to tell me. If not I might find it in one of Estelle's medical books.

In the P.T.S., I thought as the lift carried me down, I would have written, to ask the Professor. I had not written or heard from him since we left. Although we had only left the School a couple of weeks, that term and the Professor now seemed to belong in another lifetime to another person. I thought over the man I had just seen. He was a genuine Professor—and looked it. Mine was—I did not really know what he was. As the girls said, he was obviously married: as I had said, he had obviously grown bored with our correspondence. The girls were right. It was just as well he had faded out of my life as he had. I had spent far too much time thinking about him in those last few weeks in the P.T.S. I would have more than enough to occupy my mind and time in the next four years. I wanted to make a success of my training and the only way to make a success of anything was to have a one-track mind. I was really grateful to the girls for making me look the facts in the face. From now on, men were out, as far as I was concerned. I was absolutely determined on that point. And then a strange man with fair hair walked in. He looked nothing like the Professor, but the faint similarity in their hair-colouring made me wander into Casualty without realizing it.

A bellow from Sister Casualty brought me back to earth. "And where do you think you are going, Nurse? Yes! You! You with the untidy hair!"

I swallowed. "To the in-patient Lady Almoner, Sister."

"Then will you oblige me by using the main corridor, and not using my department as a short cut? This is Casualty. Not Oxford Circus."

I apologized, backed to the door through which I had come, and lectured myself on the obvious necessity for that one-track mind. Player had warned me never to set foot in Casualty if there was a possibility of Sister Cas. being on duty. "She may be young and pretty. She can be as tough as old Sister O.P.'s—and being younger, moves faster."

The Almoners' office was a haven of peace. They gave me one of the maps reserved for patients. "It's so easy to get lost here when you are new. The dispensary's marked on it and most other places you'll need. Every one should have either a map or a guide dog. Martha's covers over half a mile of London."

"I feel as if it covers all London." I deposited the file of notes, thanked them for the map, hurried on to the dispensary and then back to Josephine.

I had not hurried sufficiently. "You must not dawdle in this fashion, Nurse," said Garret sternly. "You don't seem to realize that you have work to do. Get on with those four-hourly temperatures."

The ward was very quiet when I took the four-hourly book off Sister's desk. A cardiologist called Dr Curtis was lecturing to a group of about thirty students at the far end of the ward. His words were inaudible to me, but his voice hummed deeply like the hum of a sleepy bee.

I looked at him curiously. Sister said he was one of the coming men of modern medicine. He was wearing professional clothes, but he looked more like a farmer than a doctor. He was large, plump, and—at a guess—forty. The Professor looked around that age. My father was forty-eight, so that put them in the same generation.

"Nurse Dorland." Garret was hissing at my elbow. "You're shaking down a thermometer, not shaking out a salad. You've been maltreating that bit of glass for the past two minutes. What are you trying to do? Dislodge the mercury for all time?"

Ten minutes later Player appeared at my other elbow. "Are

you going to sleep over those charts, Dorland? For Heaven's sake, get on! The drinks should have been in by now!"

Sister frowned hideously as the cups rattled on my tray. "Less noise, please, Nurse," she murmured as I scurried past the round.

Maggie looked closer to exploding each time I returned to the kitchen. Her flash-point arrived when, in my too violent attempt to dislodge one cube of ice, I sent the entire contents of the ice-tray on to her floor.

"You young nurses! Think I've nothing better to do than clear up after you, you do! Look at me floor—and all that ice wasted!" She ignored my immediate offer to dry the mess and wielded her floor-cloth like a weapon. "And now I suppose you'll want to borrow more from Margaret as that second tray hasn't set?"

I mopped my forehead with the back of one hand. "Maggie— can you do that? I was just wondering what to do as Mrs Jenkins will only take iced milk. I thought I'd have to ask Nurse Garret."

She rinsed and wrung the cloth, tipped the ice into the tea-bucket, washed and dried her hands. "What do you want to go running to Nurse Garret for? Isn't this me kitchen?"

"Oh, yes, Maggie."

"Then don't you go forgetting it again. I don't let nobody forget it," she added sternly, "and if anyone tried it on, I'd go to Sister and ask for me cards."

I did not then know that Maggie had threatened to ask for her cards throughout the eighteen years in which she had ruled the kitchen in Josephine. I must have looked suitably shocked, because she grew more mollified. "I'll see to that Mrs Jenkins's milk. If they ask you why it ain't in yet, you tell 'em as Maggie says her fridge ain't frozen and you can't have no ice. They won't say no more."

"Maggie, you're wonderful! Thank you so much."

When I had collected the empty cups, Garret sent me down to the dispensary with another bed-ticket. "It can come up in the basket too."

The dispenser on duty at the staff counter was a solid-looking young Scot. "Josephine again, Nurse? Aye. It would be. Let's have it."

I passed the bed-ticket over. "Nurse Garret said it could come up in the basket, so there's no hurry."

He looked meaningly at the clock. "Your basket goes up in ten minutes, Nurse. It'll take all of twenty to decipher Dr Curtis's script."

I apologized automatically. I seemed to have done little else all morning.

He smiled dourly. "I doubt it's your fault, Nurse. You

wouldn't have been born when he was here as a houseman, so you had no hand in guiding him through his first scripts. When you get to being a Staff Nurse, give a thought to it. A doctor may be too busy to write clearly, but we happen to be busy, too. We waste an awful lot of time this way—and I had best not waste any more of yours or mine. Good morning."

Directly I returned to Josephine, Sister called me to her desk. "Just run along to the Physiotherapy Department with this request, please, Nurse."

I waited to consult the Almoners' map until I was out of the ward. I stopped ten yards from Josephine and drew it from my apron bib.

"Where do you want now?" asked Bart's voice.

He was sitting on one of the broad windowsills a few feet ahead. He slid off and came up to me. "And what are you doing? A private tour of Martha's?"

"Seems like it. Next time I'm on in mid-morning, so help me, I'm bringing roller-skates. I want the Physiotherapy Department. Know the way?"

He tucked the pile of books he had left on the sill under one arm. "I ought to. I've been nigh on six years in the old firm. You go in the opposite direction this time." He jerked a thumb downwards. "Via the basement. Come—I'll show you the nearest stairs."

"Thanks." I studied the map. "I expect I can manage from there."

"Not with that, you can't. It doesn't show the basement. That's for patients. They aren't allowed to wander down there, but it's much the quickest way. Now, get this"—we had reached the basement stairs, "turn right at the bottom and carry on until you pass the Blood Bank. You can't miss that. It has a dirty great notice. Then you go left—left—past Repairs and Works. Left again and you come to the physios gym. Up the first stairs and you're there."

"Bless you again. What would I have done without you this morning, I hate to think. I've no bump of whatsit like Estelle. She seems to take the right turning by instinct."

"Too bad she wasn't sent on tour in your place."

"She couldn't be. She's off. On to-morrow morning."

"Is that so?" He glanced at his watch. "I may as well take you along to the physios myself. Time I was shifting."

I accepted gratefully. "What were you doing on that sill?" I asked as we went down.

"Damn it, girl. A man must sit somewhere. This walking the wards racket is hellishly hard on the feet."

I smiled absently, being too interested in the basement to pay much attention to him. I had not been along there before. It was a new and most—to me—unhospital-like world. The apparently

58

endless corridor was neon-lit, lined with huge tubes and pipes, and inhabited by men in boiler suits, and women in laundresses' overalls. "This is very Orwell-ish."

"A little too matey for Big Brother. I like it down here, and the fact that it's technically out-of-bounds lends it added piquancy."

"It's what?" I demanded.

"Relax, angel. Not to you, to me. So what? Authority never walks this way."

I stood still. "Home Sister does. I saw her in the laundry as we went by. I'm sure she saw us. Will she mind?"

He grimaced. "I don't suppose she'll give three loud cheers. She probably didn't recognize you. She's pretty short-sighted. If she did—well, I'm only escorting you with the most honourable of intentions. Stop dithering, angel."

"Sorry." We walked on. "It's hard not to. Our Senior Pro in Josephine gave us the most tremendous pep-talk on the folly of having anything to do with the medical staff in our present junior plus state."

He laughed. "I'm not medical staff. Just a student man. And for the record, that's less than the dust."

I thought about Home Sister. "I hope you're right."

"And why wouldn't I be? After all the years I've been here? Look—I tell you what we'll do. We'll show the old girl this isn't just a pick-up and you and I are old pals from the P.T.S."

"We will?" I looked at him curiously. "How?"

He answered my question with another. "When are you off, to-day?"

"This evening."

"Care to join me for coffee and a hamburger on a park bench this evening? We could look at the ducks. Supposing I call for you at six-thirty? Any good?"

His invitation surprised me considerably. I could not conceive why he wanted to take me out. I knew very well it was not for the pleasure of my company. I had had a great many doubts about my Professor, but none at all about Bart More. He was no more interested in me than I was in him, yet I could see he wanted me to accept his invitation. Curiosity made me do so. "Yes, thank you."

"Thank you." He smiled. "Jolly good."

He left me almost immediately after that, explaining that the physiotherapist students were nice girls who could not keep their big mouths shut. "They'll all be standing on their heads in their gym at this hour. They never stop keeping fit. Most exhausting. We'd better not tempt Big Brother too much. See you later."

It was a reasonable explanation, but it rang no more true

than his invitation. Curiouser and curiouser, I thought, and finished my errand alone.

When Estelle arrived on duty at one I told her I had seen Bart. "Not once, but twice."

She smiled her polite smile. "Hannah'll be pleased. How long is he up for?"

"I don't know." Her expression gave nothing away. "I didn't ask."

Monica Player bustled into the changing-room. "Girls, do stop nattering. Sister's ready for us to report."

Hannah was at lunch. I told her I had seen her cousin, but said nothing about my date. I wanted to tell Estelle first, and there had been no time before lunch. I did tell Hannah about the basement and Home Sister.

She twisted her head to look at the Sister's table. "She generally comes to one o'clock lunch. I'll keep an eye out when she gets in and see if she gives you any dirty looks."

Fay Kinsley joined us. "Did you say something about Home Sister, Hannah? Surely you've realized Monday is her half-day? What do you want her for?"

Hannah kicked me. "Frances has a laundry problem. How's Florence?"

Fay promptly lost interest in Home Sister, and for the remainder of our lunch half-hour gave us a lecture on just how Florence Ward should be run. Hannah was off until five; I had to return to Josephine; and as Fay left the dining-room with us, we were unable to continue our former conversation.

Bart drifted into Josephine directly the ward opened to students at 2 P.M., and spent the entire afternoon reading patients' notes at the students' table at the far end of the ward. I had no opportunity to see what effect, if any, his presence had on Estelle, as she was hidden in the bathrooms doing extra cleaning until four, then vanished behind varying sets of drawn curtains to help Nurse Garret with the heavy washings. We attended different teas and only met eventually when she reported to Sister Josephine for her evening's work-list, and I reported off-duty.

I made my third daily trip to Matron's office to look for any post before returning to the Home. There were two letters in the 'D' pigeon-hole; neither was for me. I strolled on wearily feeling irrationally disappointed, and wondering how I was going to raise the necessary energy to change and go out. My legs seemed on fire. A pain shot down each calf and round each ankle, then split into wicked little white-hot tentacles that accumulated in the balls of my feet. I thought longingly of a hot bath and supper in bed, and wished I had refused this date.

The portress leaned out of her lodge as I limped into our hall.

"Home Sister's been asking for you, Nurse Dorland. Will you please go straight to her before going to your room?"

I damned all medical students. "I thought Sister was off, Mrs Higgs?"

"She is, dear. She's going out later. She's been waiting to see you."

"Thanks," I said grimly. "I'd better hurry."

Home Sister was wearing an uncharacteristically gay blue mohair coat. Her manner was iron grey and bristling with starch. By the time she had finished with me I wondered why the Wolfenden report had overlooked hospital basements.

Mrs Higgs hailed me again when I reappeared. "I've been holding a call for you, Nurse Dorland. Go into Box three and I'll put the gentleman through."

Bart having second thoughts, I decided, shutting myself in the third of the four telephone booths at the end of the hall. He wasn't the only person. "Frances Dorland," I said, between my teeth, and waited for Bart to say he had been held up on a case in Josephine.

" 'Evening, Miss Dorland. Slane, here. How," asked the Professor, as if he had been in the habit of telephoning me for years, "is the hospital?"

Home Sister's rocket, Bart, and the pain in my legs and feet, vanished from my conscious mind. So did my power of speech.

"Are you there?" he prompted.

"Yes. Yes. I'm here." I took a deep breath. "Sorry."

"I expect you needed a couple of moments to place me." He sounded amused. "It's some time since we met. I hope you don't object to my ringing you like this, but as I was down at your home yesterday, I thought you might like first-hand news of your family. They are all very well and your young sister Judy is engaged in finding names for six thousand turkeys."

That second shock jolted me back to normal. There was no question now of my wondering if I was awake. Never in my wildest dreams could I have visualized the Professor talking turkeys with Judy. "You were at the farm? I didn't realize you knew my parents."

"I only met them yesterday. Your mother was kind enough to ask me to lunch and I'm afraid I stayed on until the evening, listening to your father's tape-recordings. Luke Anderson said they were unique when he took me round to have a before-lunch drink with your parents. He's absolutely right."

I should have guessed, I thought, smiling weakly at my reflection in the mirror behind the instrument, I should have guessed, having been brought up by a passionate ornithologist. Dr Anderson, our local G.P., was almost as enthusiastic as my father. But I could not have guessed the Professor knew Dr Anderson. "Were you spending the week-end with the Andersons?"

"Saturday night."

"I didn't realize you knew them, either."

"How could you? I didn't mention it. Luke Anderson was at Cambridge with me. We hadn't met for some years, then ran into each other a few weeks ago and he asked me to go down to Kent this past week-end. You know how it is when you meet very old friends; you pick up where you left off, and then run out of conversation. I suspect," he added good-humouredly, "he was as grateful to your parents as I was. Sunday afternoon invariably seems to me to be the great argument against week-ends with old friends, and yesterday the exception to prove my rule."

"My mother would agree with you." I wondered why he had not apparently taken his wife to the Andersons and how I could bring her into the conversation. "She says that when she has visitors from Friday to Monday, she reaches screaming point after lunch on Sunday. If the lunch has been a success, every one is in a coma, so she has to refuse offers of help with the washing-up; if it's been a failure she feels like hurling a plate at any one who dares come in the kitchen."

He laughed. "She permitted me to help yesterday. Into which category does that put me?"

"Neither. You were only there for the day. She loves people to drop in like that. Does your wife? Or does she prefer to have warning?"

"I'm afraid I'm not married. I remember my mother used to insist on having ample warning. She didn't encourage stray lunch guests."

I was no longer smiling weakly at my reflection; I was grinning like the Cheshire Cat. "It can't be very easy—unless you live on a farm. Catering, I mean."

"That's so." He paused momentarily, then asked, "I've given you all my news. How are you getting on?"

"Fairly well, thanks."

"Only fairly? Why's that? Work very hard?"

"It is, but it's not that that worries me."

"Then what does?"

His tone was so in line with the tone of his letters that I answered with the truth I had used in my letters to him. "I've put up a major black to-day. According to Home Sister—five minutes ago—I'm a disgrace to the entire nursing profession and inevitably bound for the gallows."

"Are you indeed?" he queried mildly. "Specifically, why?"

I told him. "If Home Sister had stopped to draw breath once I might have been able to explain. She didn't give me a chance."

He said he thought that was probably just as well. "Explanations seldom do much good. Friends don't need them; enemies don't believe them."

"I never thought of that." I could hardly wait to pass this on to Hannah and Estelle. So much for Mrs Professor and all the little Professors! "And I certainly never thought she'd wait in specially to take me apart. I'm going to do a little of that myself, this evening. That wretch Bart More said she was short-sighted. I've got news for him. She isn't."

"Bart More? I thought her name was Hannah. Or did you say 'him'? I couldn't quite hear you."

"Him. It's a hideous abbreviation, I agree, but Bartholomew is too much of a mouthful. He's Hannah's cousin."

"The student in question this morning?"

"Yes. He's in his last year."

"And what are you doing with him this evening? Film? Dance?" he asked casually.

"Not with my feet! We're going to drink coffee and look at ducks in some park."

"Well, don't be too hard on the poor youth. He was only indulging in wishful thinking. A not uncommon failing. I hope you have a good evening, and that I haven't delayed you too long."

"Oh, no." I thanked him for ringing, and, to keep him talking just a little longer, for all the help he had given me in the P.T.S. "That diagram was superb. Even Sister P.T.S. was impressed."

"Good." His voice sounded as if he was smiling. "I'll pass that on to the right quarter. And now I think I had better get down to doing some of the work that I should have done on Saturday morning."

I could ignore his civil hint momentarily, but not that opportunity. "What is your work, Mr Slane?"

"I'm one of the many variant types of Civil Servants. That mayn't sound interesting, but in point of fact I find it extremely interesting. However I could wish there was not quite so much paper work. I am always trying to cut it down, so far without success."

So much for his being a Professor, I thought, and said I was sure his work was most interesting.

"I like it. Good night. I'm glad I was able to find you in."

"It was very kind of you to bother to ring."

"Not at all," he said politely, and rang off.

5

RED STANDS FOR DANGER

I REMAINED in the telephone booth for a couple of minutes after I put down the receiver, wondering whether to ring my mother. I had no money with me, but she would not mind my reversing the charges. I was agog to hear what my parents thought of the Professor. So agog, that I did not make that call. I knew my mother would be able to guess what was in my mind from the sound of my voice. I had never before had any inhibitions about telling either of my parents anything. They knew all about my first meeting with him, roughly, the number of letters he had written and the general contents of those letters. We were a matey family. There was, I now realized, a limit to how matey any family could be. I loved them all, but the Professor was no longer some one I wanted to discuss with them. I would wait until the next letter from home arrived with their version of his news.

As Bart was not due to call for me for half an hour, I took off my shoes and cap and relaxed on my bed directly I reached my room. It would not take long to change. I could spare ten minutes. I beamed idiotically at the ceiling and wished I had not got a date. I should be more than happy to spend the entire evening thinking about my Professor. I thought my father exceedingly clever to be so keen on birds; Dr Anderson just as clever to go to Cambridge and not Oxford, and quite brilliant in his choice of week-end guests. There was nothing like a hobby to keep a man happy. Nothing. I thought up a series of appalling puns on a hobby and the hobby and was delighted by my wit. Dear hobbys, I thought dreamily. Dear bird-songs—tape-recorders—thunderstorms. Dear every one.

Estelle woke me three hours later. No one had called me to say I had a visitor. Bart had obviously stood me up.

I blinked at her. "Off, already? I've missed three suppers."

"I wondered where you were." She sat down and removed her shoes. "I thought you must be out."

"I was, dear. Cold. Nice evening?"

It was an automatic question we all asked each other. It only required an automatic answer. Apparently she had to give it considerable thought. "Quite. I spent most of it chaperoning. We've got a new bunch of clerks in Josephine."

64

I thought about my date. "Bart More's set?"

She studied her hands. "Must be. He's one of ours."

"You been chaperoning for him?"

"Yes. God, he's slow. He held me up for ages. I thought I'd never get my routine done."

And I thought, so that's why I've been stood up. The thought only amused me.

Hannah came in with a tea-tray. "Frances, have you had any food?"

"No. I've been snoozing. It doesn't matter. Think of the good to my waist-line."

Estelle said she was. "If it gets much smaller it'll snap in two. I've got a cake and some chocolate in my room. Just the job."

Hannah smiled as Estelle left us. "She's even beginning to talk like you. Remember how upstage she was? Doesn't seem possible any one could thaw as she has. Mind you, it's only with us. I met Bart on my way over. He was very low in spirits. He told me he had spent the evening being chaperoned by her. I gather she handed him the frozen mitt."

"Hannah dear, one can scarcely be matey in the middle of a ward."

She said there were ways and ways of chaperoning. "Bart isn't used to the frozen mitt. He generally gets knocked over in the rush if he lifts a little finger. By the way—he asked me to offer you his humble apologies. He didn't have time to explain for what, because Sister Tutor suddenly came out of her office. I suppose he meant about this morning? Did Home Sister say anything?"

"She did." I told her about it and wondered if to mention my date.

Hannah was very upset. "He is naughty! He never thinks one inch ahead!"

"Never mind. He saved my life this morning. I'd still be looking for the Top Lab. and that man Marcus would still be waiting for his little tube, but for Bart."

"That man——? Frances, what is all this?"

I explained. "You don't know the morning I had," I added. "I covered Martha's."

She waved that aside. "You mean you actually spoke to him? You've made hospital history? He never speaks to nurses. No one is allowed to disturb him."

"Sorry about that. He didn't seem to mind." I smiled. "Why? Player says pathologists don't bite."

Estelle had come back with the cake and chocolate. Hannah said she was the girl to answer my question. "Just tell her what you told me about this Marcus Everly, Estelle."

She hesitated. I recognized her expression and demanded openly, "Is he due to come into a packet too?"

She relaxed. "You've got the wrong tense there. Frances, you must have heard of him!"

"I've never heard of any one. Remember, I told you—not even you."

"So you did. But your father's a farmer. Or doesn't he need a tractor for his turkeys?"

"He's got some land as well as the turkeys. Of course he has a tractor. So what?"

"What make is it?"

"An Everly—blow me down! His?" They nodded. "Then what's he doing in our Path. Lab.? Why isn't he turning out more tractors? He ought to be. English agriculture is the most mechanized in the world. Why is he neglecting the home market for the bugs?"

"Honest to God! Will you just listen to her, Estelle!" Hannah exclaimed indignantly. "The man has his Membership, an M.D., and is the only man in Martha's to have collected a gold medal for medicine and another for pathology—and she says he ought to be turning out the tractors."

"Well, who does turn them out for him?" I asked.

"My dear," said Estelle, "it's a huge concern."

"Large as Grandpapa's?"

"Almost. Same sort of thing. A man called Bryce Macindoe runs it. I don't believe our Everly has ever had much to do with it. He gravitated straight to medicine. There are a couple of other Everlys—second cousins, I think—on the Board."

"Our man," said Hannah, "has only one passion in life. Bugs. Right, Estelle?"

"Dead right. He's allergic to all else. He's so keen on his privacy that not even Matron walks uninvited into his lab. He's got the reputation of dealing in short order with any one who strays up there to look at the view."

"The view's worth seeing. He isn't. I'm glad I didn't know all this this morning. If I had, I'd have been out of that lab. like a bat out of hell when that bell went off."

"Did he deal with you in short order?" queried Hannah.

"No. He was perfectly civil in a dreary sort of way. How old is he, Estelle? Fifty? Sixty?"

"I would have said he was younger. I'm not sure. Grandpapa knows him. I've never met him. Grandpapa was at school with his father, he was—hang on—Sir Claud."

"So he's inherited a title with all the rest?"

"It's been going some time. He's the fourth—or it could be fifth."

"All that and he spends his life on our top floor peering down a microscope. Or has he a wife and kids, somewhere?"

"We've told you," said Hannah, "he's allergic to humanity. He only loves his bugs."

66

"But why? Crossed in love? Too much cash? Or just plain bats?"

Estelle said she had never heard of his having a love-life.

"People have been trying to marry him for years. No one's even got to first base. No man with his brain could be bats."

"Must be his cash. Don't you go that way, Estelle. No good'll come of it. It's agin nature."

"God," groaned Hannah, "she's on a soap-box. Come down off, Frances, and have some more cake."

Bart came into the clinical-room early next morning. I was doing the flowers alone, having for once finished my cleaning ahead of schedule. He gave me a wary smile.

"Are we on speaking terms? I hoped Hannah had given you my message, but you cut me dead when you came out of breakfast."

"I certainly did, and will do so again whenever there's a dark blue dress around. Don't you ever speak one word to me in the hospital—or mention basements. Home Sister," I snipped stalks as I talked, "took me into little pieces last evening. But all will be forgiven and forgotten if you'll just go right away—now. I know Garret's having a day off, but Sister Josephine'll finish her pulses any minute now."

He squinted into the clinical-room microscope. "I'm officially here with her blessing. I asked last night if I could come in early to use this chap"—he fixed in a slide—"and she said yes, indeed, provided I understood that at this hour the nurses had to come in here to do the flowers." He looked at me anxiously. "I'm really sorry about Home Sister and feel a perfect heel over last night. Did you get very mad at having to wait?"

"No." I explained why. "Then, when Estelle woke me, she told me she had been chaperoning for you and I guessed what had kept you."

"You did?" He looked up again. "Didn't she think it odd I was here when I had a date with you?"

I shook my head. "She didn't know you had dated me."

"You didn't tell her? I thought you girls told each other everything."

The Professor's phone call flashed through my mind. I quoted him out of context. "There has to be an exception to prove every rule. No. I didn't tell anyone." I picked up two vases and made for the door. "So that's one more weight off your mind."

He straightened. "Just what," he demanded curtly, "are you getting at?"

"Why, Bart—that you don't have to worry about feeling a heel for standing me up because I didn't mind." I flapped my eyelashes idiotically, but he was too on edge to notice. "I'm glad you came in this morning to straighten things up. To-morrow's my day off. Estelle'll be doing the flowers alone and you'd have had to go on worrying. I wouldn't want that to happen," I added quickly, and sailed into the ward before he could answer. When I returned the clinical-room was empty.

Estelle did not tell me if Bart had used my information. I heard it from Nurse Player. "We've got the keenest bunch of students I've ever known. One of them was actually in the clinical-room by a quarter-past eight yesterday morning. Long before Dexter could get to the flowers."

Bart continued to haunt not only the clinical-room but the ward. He could do this legitimately as he was one of our clerks. Whenever the ward was open, he was a permanent fixture on one of the locker-seats, talking to his patients, writing endless notes.

Lily Ellis was one of his patients. "That young Mr More's real cool, duck! Ever so nice-looking, too. He ought to be on the telly. And the way he works! Cor! Proper keen he is! All that writing an' all!"

Bart did not only write notes in Josephine. When he had to leave the ward because it was closed to men, and the clinical-room booked by some other clerk, he either sat on one of the main corridor windowsills a few yards from the ward entrance or on the steps of the statue of Miss Nightingale that overlooked the door to our dining-room, and went on with his note-writing.

In a very short time our whole set knew that Hannah's cousin had taken root in Josephine. Hannah was very bucked by her insight. "I knew you were his type, Frances."

I heard nothing from the Professor for several days after his telephone call. When my mother's weekly letter arrived her comments on him were disappointingly brief.

We were most amused to discover Luke Anderson's friend was your Professor. We liked him. Daddy says he really knows about birds, and gathered he works for some Ministry. We agree he should have been a don. He is very like Joe. We hope he will come down again, some time.

Time in Josephine passed even more quickly than it had in the P.T.S. The weeks flashed by, partly because we were so busy in the ward, and partly because every other week I heard from the Professor. His letters were as pleasant and impersonal as they had been in the P.T.S. Now I knew he was single, that impersonality really puzzled me. He never suggested meeting me, barely mentioned himself or signed his name with anything but the initials of his Christian names. If he had not enough interest in me to make one date why bother to keep on writing? Yet he did. And because I loved getting his letters—I would have been grateful even for a typed postcard from him—I wrote back regularly on the alternate weeks.

My set asked about him occasionally. "What's happened to your P.T.S. Professor, Frances? Ever met him?"

I answered no, quite truthfully; they assumed he had faded from my life and stopped asking questions. If Estelle noticed his handwriting on a letter addressed to me in the 'D' pigeon-hole she never mentioned it. She was obviously having her own problems, and because I disliked being questioned about the Professor, I did not question her about Bart. He continued to behave in the most absurd fashion; haunting both Josephine and Estelle, and doing nothing but look haunted. One of these fine days I knew I would have to do something about those two, the difficulty was going to be finding the time. Josephine was hectic; we had started regular thrice-weekly lectures; I always had at least two back lectures to write up—and every other week I used a good two evenings on my letter to the Professor.

I decided to have a splendidly casual chat with my mother about him. I went home for a day off. I had chosen the wrong day. They had started de-beaking the day before; both my parents were in the turkey-houses all day. They refused my offer to help. "You're having a day off, darling. Why not go and look up some one in the village? Take the car."

At lunch I talked about Luke Anderson, hoping to get the conversation round to the Professor.

"Luke's on holiday. We've got a locum." Father handed me a plate. "Seen anything of that man he brought round?"

"We haven't met. He writes, occasionally."

He nodded absently. "He must like writing letters. Wish I did. Meg, how many have we done so far?"

"Three hundred and eighty." My mother passed him the vegetable dish. "We should make the eight hundred by to-night," she added, and we went back to talking turkeys.

Josephine was a different ward next day. Lily Ellis had had a heart attack in the night. Her bed was back in the ward and hidden behind curtains. The women were strangely subdued. "Shame poor Lily Ellis is so poorly, dear. How is she? Better? Give her my love when you go in to her, Nurse."

I was far too junior to be allowed near her that day. I felt lost without her and very anxious. She had become more than just a cheerful patient to me; she was one of my great friends. The balcony was vast and empty without her, and old Mrs Astor embroidered diligently as if she dared not keep herself unoccupied.

It was several days before Lily showed any sign of improvement, but at last her curtains were drawn back. I was delighted to be allowed to help nurse her again, not only because I wanted to be with her, but because the fact I was there showed how much better she must be. The sense of strain faded from the ward. The other women waved and smiled at her. "Better, dear?

That's lovely. Your old lady on the balcony will be pleased to have you back."

Mrs Astor often talked to me about Lily. "She's a good girl, dear. I've never known her grumble. I do miss her."

I plaited her long white hair. "She'll soon be back with you. She's looking almost herself to-day."

She gave me a long, queer look. "Yes, dear. That's good." She was silent until her hair was finished. "That nice young Mr More has been such a comfort to me. He sat out here for over an hour yesterday, keeping me company. Isn't he a friend of yours, dear?"

"Yes. His cousin is in my set." I put away her brush and comb, thinking how pathetically easy it was to give gentle old ladies the wrong impression.

Mrs Astor promptly taught me how easy it was to get the wrong impression about gentle old ladies. "I've seen him smile at you, dear. Is he Nurse Dexter's young man? I've noticed how he's always looking for her—and at her. Have they had a little tiff? Is that why Nurse Dexter pretends not to see him? She's such a sweet girl to us—so kind. But she never smiles at him. I haven't been able to avoid noticing the difference."

I said, "Mrs Astor, is there anything you haven't noticed?"

"I don't mean to spy, dear, but I get so interested watching all you busy young people. I like to watch and think about you all. I love young people. Youth has so much courage and gaiety; it does me good to have you around me." She took one of my hands. "I hope you don't mind my mentioning this to you, dear, but I know Nurse Dexter is your great friend. She seems to me to look very sad in repose. Has she had a hard life, or is she troubled by this little tiff? Such things seem so important when one is young—and youth should not be sad. Wouldn't that nice boy be only too willing to make it up? I think he would. As you are their friend—couldn't you help them?"

"I wish I could, Mrs Astor. It's not quite as simple as it sounds."

Sister appeared on the balcony before we could say any more. "Come and help me with Mrs Ellis now, Nurse."

Lily looked unbearably frail and ill, despite the report I had given Mrs Astor. Her pulse was fibrillating badly; her respirations agony to watch; her spirits were higher than ever. "See them lovely roses my Bert fetched me up this morning, Sister?" she gasped. "From me own garden."

Sister admired them. "Beautiful, Mrs Ellis."

"You ought to see me garden, Sister. Two yards by four—and six inches of solid soot."

Sister talked a great deal about roses, I guessed to save Mrs Ellis having to talk. Later that morning she came into the kitchen as I was collecting Mrs Ellis's lunch tray. "Mind you

70

sit down and let her take as long as she wishes over her meal, Nurse."

"Yes, Sister." I wondered why she had come to tell me this. I would not have dared not sit down when feeding a patient in Josephine, since that was one of her strictest rules.

She frowned at the wafers of sliced chicken and small bowl of strawberries. "Where is the cream, Nurse?"

I hesitated. "Mrs Ellis doesn't care for cream, Sister. Had I better try and persuade her to take some?"

"No." Her expression suddenly reminded me of Mrs Astor's when I had said Lily would soon be with her on the balcony. "She may have what she fancies and as much as she fancies. If she does not want to eat, you may just sit and talk to her for a while. I have observed that she enjoys a little gossip with you. A chat cannot harm her now. Take that in."

I settled down by Lily, and we had a glorious chat about life, roses, turkeys, Bert Ellis's promotion to charge-hand in his bottle factory, and Mrs. Ellis Senior's passion for shopping in super-markets.

She talked eagerly, and ate hardly anything. I did not attempt to coax her after what Sister had said, even though I could not follow why she had said it when she was normally so insistent that we persuaded our patients to eat well.

"No more, ta, duck," said Lily wearily.

I put down the spoon. "A little drink? Lemon? Would you like iced milk? No? All right, love."

"I wish," she whispered, "every one could take the hint same as you, duck. That poor Nurse Dexter tried so hard with me dinner yesterday. I was real sorry not to be able to take it for her. Weren't no use. It wouldn't go down." Her eyes followed Estelle, who was clearing plates on the other side of the ward. "What's come over her, duck? Why she looking so down in the mouth? She had words with that young Mr More what's courting her?"

"Lily. How do you do it? Second sight?"

She chuckled. "I got eyes in me head. I can spot a bloke what's courting when I sees one. It don't take much savvy to see Mr More thinks the world of your pal. Mind, he acts proper, what with his writing notes and taking histories. Cor! Does he write them notes. He must have a ruddy book by now, duck! And always trying to catch her eye, he is, but she won't have nothing to do with him! Have they had bad words?"

"My dear, they hardly know each other."

"Then what you waiting for, duck? You wants to give them a shove, like. Or have you got your own troubles with your own young man?"

I smiled. "I haven't one. No time. And besides, my feet hurt too much."

71

She laughed out loud. "Your feet! Nurse Dorland! You are a one!"

Sister's head jerked up. She looked at once at Lily and I expected a quick frown in reprimand. She merely smiled. "You sound merry, my dear," she called. "I am pleased."

Estelle and I discussed Sister's attitude to Lily when we went off that night. "I can't understand her," I said reflectively. "I wish we knew more medicine. Maybe then it would make sense."

"Player was talking about it when we did the sluice to-night. She was just telling me Lily's heart had gone into failure ages ago, when Sister called her to tidy beds. I'll look it up when we get over."

"Hang on." I recognized the inevitable figure on a windowsill twenty yards off. I looked round quickly. The corridor was empty. I beckoned to Bart. "He ought to be able to explain."

Her expression froze as he came towards us, uncertainly. I ignored both their attitudes. "We want to know some medicine. What exactly is meant by a heart going into failure?"

He glanced at Estelle. She gave him one of her best 'Miss Dexter' nods. Not surprisingly, he stiffened, then smiled affectedly. "I'm flattered, ladies, but, alas, a mere student man."

I could willingly have shaken him. "Bart, be serious. We want help, not a good laugh. We're worried."

"Oh." His manner altered instantly. "What's up? Not Lily Ellis again?"

Estelle looked at him sharply as if taken aback by this reaction, but said nothing.

I said, "Yes and no. She hasn't had another attack—Thank God—but we want to know. What's gone wrong? Why?"

He looked at his feet. "Just about everything."

Estelle said, "What's her prognosis? She has got a prognosis?"

I think they were the first words she had ever addressed to him of her own accord. He raised his eyes to her face. "I'm sorry, Nurse Dexter. She hasn't. She's booked."

I said, "I'm sorry, but you're both above my head. What's a prognosis? And what's booked?"

"The forecast of the course of a disease," he said quietly. "Booked is—well, our word for—the finish." He flattened one hand in the air and tilted it slightly. "She's been"—he tilted it again from side to side—"like that for months. According to Curtis, all that's keeping her alive is guts. She doesn't want to die, poor kid."

I simply did not believe him. I might have done so had we been talking about Mrs Astor, or any of the older women in the ward. Lily was our youngest patient. I could not associate her with death; she was too full of life, too young, too much fun. Death was for the old and tired, not for people like Lily.

Then I had to believe him. When we arrived on duty three

mornings after that conversation with him, we found the small ward was in use. The small ward was the single room off the main ward that was only used for very ill patients who were not expected to recover. It had never been used during our stay in Josephine.

The door was open, the interior hidden by a red screen. Red in hospital, as elsewhere, is a sign of danger.

The senior night nurse looked grey with fatigue when we reported to her. "Dexter, will you do all the early routine. Player will help you. Dorland, Sister wants you to take over from my relief. She's with Mrs Ellis in the small ward."

It was a warm August morning and I felt very cold. "I'm to special her, Nurse?"

She nodded. "Yes. She's been asking for you. Sister says you are to stay with her. Don't leave her at all. If you want anything ring. Sister's gone to early breakfast. She'll be back in a few minutes, and will come in to see her."

It was very quiet in the small ward. Lily was sleeping heavily, and when the night relief nurse handed over, I sat with one hand on her left wrist, feeling as if I had stepped into a nightmare. The fact that I was sitting doing nothing at that, perhaps the busiest hour of the hospital day, only added to the nightmare. I was frightened of my inexperience, frightened of the hours ahead, and above all frightened I might show my fear.

She woke briefly after Sister's third visit. "I'm glad you're here, duck."

I sat and held her hand for most of that day. Sister, Nurse Garret, Dr Curtis, the Senior Medical Officer, his registrar and houseman were in and out constantly. We were seldom alone for more than a few minutes. No one said anything; did anything. They looked only at her and then went away, avoiding each other's eyes. I gave her little sips of glucose and lemonade, at first through a straw, then with a teaspoon. "Ta, duck," she sighed heavily, "ta. No more now."

Sister took my place when I went to lunch, and during the afternoon sent me off-duty for one hour. "Sister will make up this off-duty to you another day, Dorland," explained Garret in an unusually pleasant tone. "She wants you to stay with Mrs Ellis to-day. You've been her great friend. All we can now do for her is let her have a friend hold her hand."

I was supposed to have tea in that hour. I could not face the dining-room. I walked round and round the hospital until I could go back.

She seemed to have rallied a little when I returned and my wavering hopes soared. Her husband and mother-in-law smiled at me, pathetically pleased by this change. "Lil's looking more herself. She'll be pleased you're back again, Nurse. We've heard so much about Lil's Nurse Dorland."

73

A long, long time later, Sister told me to close the door and remove the red screen. "Then go straight off, Nurse. Home Sister knows you have been kept on duty late. You need not report in. Just go to your room and your friends. Good night, Nurse, and thank you."

I walked very slowly down the main corridor. It was empty and silent, and somewhere a clock was striking a quarter to ten. My eyes felt as if they had been rubbed in sandpaper, but I had not wept one tear. I was too sad for weeping.

I walked on without realizing where I was going. Only when I passed Casualty did I notice I had missed the exit we always used on our way to the Home. I hesitated, wondering if to take a short-cut through Casualty; it would be quite safe as Sister Cas. would not be on at this hour, but I might meet some one. I did not want to meet any one. There must be another side exit into the grounds. The corridor was full of doors. I walked on again.

I had gone another fifteen yards or so when I saw a small alcove I had not noticed previously. At the end of the alcove was a door obviously leading to the outside. I tried it; it was unlocked. I closed it behind me and found I was at the top of a narrow flight of steps leading down to the car park. It was quite dark; I had not been in that part of the grounds before; so I stopped at the top to get my bearings. I did not even see the man in the light mackintosh coming up the steps until he stopped a couple of steps from me.

"What are you doing here, Nurse? You shouldn't be using this door. It doesn't matter this once, but don't do it again."

I recognized his voice instantly, but was beyond surprise. Nothing could have touched me at that moment. I just looked at him. "It's you, Mr Slane. I'm going off. I saw this door and came through it."

He stayed poised on that second step for perhaps twenty seconds. Then he was beside me. He bent slightly to look at my face. "Frances Dorland. What's up? Is something wrong?"

I said, "Yes."

6

THE PROFESSOR TAKES OVER

I FOUND myself sitting on the front seat of a car, with no clear idea of how I had arrived there.

"Wait here," said the Professor. "I'll be back, directly."

I waited, without thought or feeling.

A new wing of wards was being built at the far end of the car park. Its darkened outline was splinted with scaffolding. There were no lights yet in the new wing. The scaffolding was strung at intervals with red workmen's lamps serving as warnings, not illuminations.

I was grateful for the darkness; grateful the car had its back to the well-lit hospital roughly fifty yards off; grateful the sky was low and moonless.

He was back before I started wondering where he had gone. Vaguely I recollected his original explanation about calling on one of our residents. He had mentioned a name. I could not remember which name now, nor had I recognized it at the time. We had dozens of residents, but I knew only the names of the three who worked in Josephine.

He got into the driving seat. "Your Home Sister says you may stay out until eleven-fifteen."

"Home Sister?" I looked at him dully. He had not switched on any light inside the car, his face was in shadow. "You did say Home Sister?"

"Yes." He started the engine, backed in a half-circle, and drove us into the road. "I've just been across to see her. The Casualty porter told me which was the Nurses Home. I introduced myself, explained I was acquainted with you and your parents and the circumstances of our meeting to-night. I asked her permission to do what I believe your father would under these circumstances. I'm going to take you for a drive right away from the hospital."

Surprise, even interest, were still beyond me. "Thank you." I rested my head against the back of the seat, closed my eyes, and relaxed. I could not remain relaxed; every pin in my cap was sticking into my head. I sat forward.

He glanced sideways. "Why not take it off? You can put it on when we get back."

We drove in silence. After a while I opened my eyes and saw

we had crossed the river. The long line of light that marked the hospital on the far bank was disappearing behind us.

"Where are we going?"

"Chiswick. We haven't much time and there are odd places down there that could be a hundred miles from Oxford Street. Do you know London?"

"No."

"We're on the Chelsea Embankment."

"Thank you," I said, and he was quiet again.

He seemed to know London like a taxi-driver. We left the main traffic, meandered through side streets, old crumbling Georgian squares, along what looked like cul-de-sacs but were not, until we reached a quiet terrace of Queen Anne and Regency houses overlooking the river. The trees outside the houses were heavy with late summer leaves; there was a cluster of trailing willows by the water; an empty rowing-boat swung placidly on the end of a rope.

He stopped the car by the willows, switched off the engine, sat sideways to look at me. "Did you have any supper to-night?"

"Sister Josephine sent me to early supper."

"That," he said quietly, "doesn't answer my question. Did you eat anything? Or just spin out time?"

"How could you know that?"

He did not answer. He turned on the interior light and reached for the mackintosh he had at some time thrown on the rear seat. I watched him, dazed not merely by the light. I could not even remember his taking off that mackintosh.

He produced a flat packet from one of the pockets, a large bar of chocolate from the dashboard shelf. "I know you aren't hungry, but you'll feel better if you eat something. Have these" —he opened the packet, laid it on my lap, and snapped the chocolate—"and this."

The packet contained sandwiches. "Thank you—I'd rather not."

"I realize that. All the same, have some." He took out a cigarette-case. "Will smoke put you off?"

"No, no. Please smoke." I looked at the food in my lap. I felt it would choke me, but did not want to refuse again in face of his kindness. I ate one ham sandwich, and the chocolate. Both tasted as if made of sawdust and were as difficult to swallow as sawdust.

He did not ask questions or talk at all. He sat smoking, watching the river occasionally, mainly watching me. There was nothing to disturb me in his scrutiny, no strain in our silence. It was only inexpressibly comforting to have him there.

"Have one more sandwich," he said at last; "then I'm going to give you a drink." He took a leather-covered flask from the same shelf as the chocolate. "It's neat, which is why I didn't

76

give it to you first. I doubt it would have gone to your head, but it might have made you feel sick."

"Is it brandy? I'm awfully sorry I really can't tolerate——"

"Whisky." He put the cup in my hand. "If you don't like the taste, eat some chocolate to take it away. But you drink it."

A few minutes later he removed the empty cup, remaining sandwiches, and chocolate paper from my lap, brushing aside the crumbs as if I was a small child.

I apologized for the crumbs. "I'm afraid they'll mess your car."

"It doesn't signify if they do." He opened his cigarette-case again. "You don't smoke, I believe?"

"No, thanks." I realized he was chain-smoking. "Have you given up your pipe?"

"I prefer cigarettes on occasions." He shifted his position, and looked at the river. "Would you like to talk? I'll understand if you wouldn't. But it might help."

I said bitterly, "I'm not the person who needs help. She needed it. But no one could help her."

He nodded slowly. "Tell me about her."

I had given him only the briefest explanation when we recognized each other at the top of those narrow stairs. I would not have believed then, that I could share with any one the thoughts I had had in the small ward all that long, agonizing day, while I watched the dragging hands of the clock, the defeat in the eyes of every member of the staff who came into the room, and the shadow of Death falling over Lily's bed.

Suddenly I was talking. I talked and talked, my words tumbling out on top of each other.

"Sister said, 'Turn off that oxygen, Nurse,' but I couldn't. Lily was still hanging on to my hand. Her fingers were so tight that Sister had to help me to get my own free."

The muscles in his face tightened as he stared at the river, smoking constantly. He did not interrupt, or murmur soothing words. No words could have soothed me just then.

"Bert—her husband—was there all the time. He didn't speak from tea-time onwards. At the end he just patted her arm, then walked out of the room without saying a word. He's twenty-three. He looked like an old man." I shuddered. "He really loved her. If I feel like this—what must it be for him?"

He said, "To-night the poor boy's in hell."

I turned on him. "Mr Slane, why? I know one shouldn't ask that if one works in a hospital, but I can't help it. Why did she have to die? Why does Bert have to be in hell? There are so many unhappy married couples. They were so happy. So—why?"

He threw away a half-smoked cigarette, and folded one arm on the other. "I can't agree that one should not ask why." He twisted back to face me. "I think one should."

77

"What's the point of asking questions that can't be answered?" I demanded wildly.

"I distrust generalizations, but I'm going to make one. All questions can be answered, if one is prepared to take the trouble to find out what they are. You ask if there's any point, because you think you already know the answer. And that thought inevitably disturbs you. Doubt does take one by the throat. It's as suffocating as ignorance, and indeed, often synonymous with ignorance. You've asked me why she had to die? I don't know. I intend to find out."

"You're going to ask some one at Martha's?"

He nodded. "You. Now. Tell me, how did she come to have a bad heart?"

I shrugged. "It's been weak for years."

"Why?"

"I—I think, because she had bad rheumatic fever as a child."

"Why?"

"I don't know."

"Think," he said gently. "How do you get rheumatic fever? Do you catch it like measles?"

"No. It's—oh—from damp. Conditions. Clothes. Houses. Things like that."

"Who allowed a child to live in a damp house? Wear damp clothes?"

"Her parents, I suppose. Or whoever brought her up."

"So what finished this evening began years ago when, through ignorance or carelessness, some supposedly responsible human being neglected Lily Ellis as a child? Right?"

Slowly, I realized what he was doing. "Yes."

"Which makes her death not the cruel and inexplicable act of Providence as you've been fearing, but the logical if none the less tragic follow-on from a human error. Understand?"

"Yes."

He lit yet another cigarette, and watched me over the flame of a match. "I'm sorry, Frances." His voice was very gentle. "Truth may resolve doubt, but it never has been an analgesic."

I said, "I'm never going to let myself get so fond of a patient again. It hurts too much."

"You had her friendship—obviously affection. Wasn't that worth having?"

"Of course, but . . ."

"Everything that's worth having in life hurts like the devil. There's no way round that."

"Yet it seems such a waste."

"No." He studied the lighted end of his cigarette as if it was the first he had ever seen. "Sympathy, love, the rest of that ilk, are only wasted when one gives them to oneself."

78

Without any warning I began to cry. I did not stop until I had soaked both my handkerchiefs and one of his. "I'm so sorry." I mopped my face, eventually. "I really am. I didn't mean to do that."

He did not say a good cry was just what I needed to make me feel better, offer me a shoulder, or any sympathy beyond his handkerchief, and silent presence. I was grateful. I had not wanted to weep in front of him, and I did not feel any better. I felt physically ill and exhausted.

He handed me another drink and more chocolate. "I don't think you need apologize. I wish I had some water to add to this. Take it"—he removed his ruined handkerchief from my hand and gave me another—"and this."

A little later he put away the flask and glanced at the dashboard clock. "I believe we should be moving if I'm to get you back on time."

"Did Home Sister mind my going out with you? Didn't she think it very odd?"

He fiddled with the ignition key. "She didn't appear to do so. Remember, something like this happened to her once."

"I never thought of that." Another thought occurred to me. "What about your friend? I forget his name. Will he have been waiting all this time? I've ruined your evening. I'm terribly sorry."

"Don't be. I was only going to play chess with a man called George Aspinall. We had not fixed it specifically. I merely said I'd look in to-night if I was free. He'll take my non-appearance as a sign that I couldn't get over."

"I see. Aspinall? Physician or surgeon?"

"Physician. You don't know him?"

"I don't really know any one on our medical staff." We had stopped at some traffic lights. "Or anything about Martha's outside of Josephine. I had no idea I should not have used that door. Who's is it?"

He frowned briefly at the lorry directly in front of us. "If he backs another inch he'll sit on my bonnet. What was that——? That door? It's the Dean's private door."

"Oh, no." The second drink had made me feel strong enough to smile. "No wonder it's out of bounds. Do you often come to Martha's? Is that how you know that?"

He nodded at the lorry as it began to move off. "Aspinall's brother was once a colleague of mine. We've been playing chess together for some years. How often I get to Martha's depends on how much work I have to do. I haven't had much time for chess lately."

When we were on the Embankment he reminded me to put on my cap. "Can you reach over? It's on the back seat. I dropped it out of range when I gave you the sandwiches."

79

"I never noticed. Thanks."

He said no more until he stopped the car at the foot of the steps to our Home. "Will you forgive me if I don't get out. I daren't park here. I've just seen three policemen."

"Please do keep the engine going." I jumped out, then paused momentarily, with one hand on the open window. "I don't know how to thank you."

"I'd much rather you didn't attempt it." He reached across and reclosed the door properly. "Would you go in? I'd like to see you in the house before I leave. I can be having engine trouble for the next thirty seconds."

"I will. Good night."

He raised a hand. "Good night."

I heard his car move away as I closed the front door behind me. Home Sister came out of her office. "I saw you drive up, Nurse. I'm glad you met a friend to-night." Her expression was curious as well as sympathetic. "Go up quietly as the lights are out."

I dreaded breakfast and the inevitable questions from my set next morning. To my surprise and infinite relief, no one mentioned Lily Ellis, or my late return to the Home.

Later Hannah told me Estelle was responsible for this. "She went round all our rooms that night and bullied us all—Fay included—into silence. She really went to town, Frances! I expect you were pretty relieved not to talk about it. What time did you eventually get over? After eleven?"

"Something like that." I had not yet told her of the Professor's phone call, and had no intention of telling her how I had met him. She was a pleasant girl, but quite incapable of keeping anything to herself. She had made him public property in the P.T.S. and would have no hesitation in doing so again. She would willingly promise not to breathe a word to a soul; past experience had taught me that from Hannah that meant not telling more than five people in strict confidence. I had not minded at all in the P.T.S. I would now. "I've seen her in her chip-off-the-old-Dexter-block moods in Josephine. She can produce the most fantastic drive when she wants to. Often I wouldn't get done at all if she didn't rustle round and help. She's quick as Player already."

Hannah looked thoughtful. "Dear Naylor'll be shaken if she collects a gold medal when we finish. We won't." She sighed. "Ah me. They say you can't have everything. I look at Estelle and think—no? Looks, brains, cash. She's got the lot."

"Not quite."

"Frances, duckie, please—no corn! Don't tell me she lacks the love of a good man. If she wanted a man—any man—she'd have him. Estelle gets what she wants. Besides, is the man yet born who wouldn't break his neck in the rush if Estelle Dexter showed willing? Even if she looked like the back of a bus? Which she doesn't."

I did not argue with her since I knew I would never persuade her to my view, and have never seen that you gained anything but a headache from ramming your head against a brick wall. Now we had left the isolated and idealistic atmosphere of the P.T.S., Hannah's character was either altering or returning to normal. I was not yet clear which. She seemed to like Estelle as much as ever, but where in the P.T.S. she had never seemed in awe of her money, now, possibly because she was assimilating the comments of the nurses-in-training as a whole and not merely those of our one set, she seemed obsessed by it.

I thought over Hannah's new attitude during the next few days and, at the same time, Lily's and Mrs Astor's advice. I wondered if Bart saw things as Hannah did. I watched him and Estelle covertly but constantly. This was not hard, as he was part of the furniture in Josephine. He always treated me as his oldest and closest of friends—until Estelle appeared in the clinical-room to do the flowers, or the bathroom to scrub mackintoshes. The temperature would then freeze, despite the late summer weather that was breaking records for sunshine, if Estelle looked at him at all, she used the expression most people reserve for a tedious child, while he was content to look and behave as if made of solid wood.

There were occasions, particularly as the real temperature rose, when I could gladly have banged their heads together. They seemed to be making themselves intentionally miserable and after Lily's death I was in no mood for tolerance. I missed her dreadfully; came near to resenting the other women for being alive when she was dead; had to nerve myself to go on the balcony or into the small ward; and still winced at the sight of one special red screen.

The Professor rang me about a week after Lily's death. It was quite late. I was about to have a bath when Estelle bellowed through the door. "Outside phone for you, Frances!"

He said he knew it was late and would not keep me long, but wanted to know how I was. "The world the right way up again?"

I hesitated. "Not really. You see, being still in Josephine, it's not very easy to forget her."

"I can understand that. All the same"—he hesitated too—"although grief is agony, it's the agony of a moment. The indulgence of grief can be the blunder of a lifetime."

"You—you think I ought to snap out of it?"

"I wasn't going to put it quite like that—but—yes."

"I see." I sighed. "Oh, dear. I've been wallowing."

"It's hard not to. Tell me—are you by chance free next Saturday evening?"

I stiffened hopefully. "Yes. I'm off from five-thirty."

"Do you care for ballet? I find I've two tickets which I can't use myself. Would you care to use them for me?"

I tried not to sound too hollow as I thanked him.

"Good. I'll put them in the post to-morrow. Good night."

Estelle looked out of her room as I walked by to the bathroom. "Family?"

"Friend of," I stretched the truth without qualm as Hannah was sitting on her bed, "with two tickets for the ballet on Saturday evening. I suppose you can't get off as I am. How about you, Hannah?"

Hannah said she would get off if she had to bribe Sister Arthur herself. "It'll be something to look forward to. Arthur's a furnace these days. You girls don't know how lucky you are to be in Josephine. Facing the river it must have some air."

"Air?" queried Estelle. "Now what would that be? Any idea, Frances?"

"Not me. I work in Josephine."

Josephine grew more airless with every passing day, despite the wide open windows and balcony doors. The medical staff shed their jackets and waist-coats; their white coats were limp and more grey than white. The students rolled up their shirt-sleeves, and slung their jackets from their hands, donning them only for ward rounds, removing them before they passed the row of fire buckets at the end of Josephine corridor.

In the grounds the yellowing plane-trees were motionless as if too hot to risk exhaustion by moving a single leaf. The women in our ward lay as still as those leaves, covered only by their top sheets, too warm even to wear their wireless headphones. They propped these on their pillows a few inches from their ears; and the faint chattering and music that filtered constantly through the ward seemed to add to the pressure of the atmosphere.

Sister Josephine's invariably quiet manner grew even quieter, until she seemed as ominously silent as the air before thunder. Garret's speed was unaltered, but her temper became razor-edged. Nurse Player's amiable nature seemed impervious to the heat; not so her cap and apron. The starch wilted in her uniform as rapidly as in Estelle's and mine, since being the three most junior members of the nursing staff our work was seldom sedentary. We took two clean aprons on duty with us instead of the normal one and always needed to change before the ward opened at nine. Estelle's hair clung damply to her head like an extra yellow cap; while the heat had the reverse effect on my hair. "For God's sake, Dorland," stormed Garret at least three times a day, "do something about your hair. You look as if you've been pulled through a bush backwards with all those curls on end. Cut it, if all else fails."

At lunch on Saturday Hannah swept into the dining-room in

a fury. "I could kill Sister Arthur," she announced, helping herself to a glass of water, "here and now! I can't make to-night. I've been changed to off this afternoon! I told her I was going out, and all she said was 'what a pity!' Pity! Bah!"

"Hannah, how miserable. I am sorry." I looked round the table. "Any of you girls off this evening?"

No one was, but Alice Linton said Sylvia Franks had a day off, was not going home, and would almost certainly be in her room when I got over later. "She'll love to go with you, Frances."

"That'll be fine—if I survive an afternoon of extra cleaning in this temperature. Who do you suppose was the jolly soul who ordained that all the major extra cleaning should be done by juniors on Saturday afternoon, when the rest of the world is setting forth to play?"

Hannah looked a little more cheerful at the realization of what else her changed off-duty was causing her to miss. "Rub up your lamp, duckie. It's flickering."

"Huh. By the time I've scrubbed forty bed macks it'll have been out for hours. We change the lot on Saturdays."

Bart was sitting on one of the wooden benches under a plane-tree when I eventually limped off-duty. He got slowly to his feet. He was very sun-burnt, the tan suited him, making him look quite outrageously good-looking. "You walk like I feel, angel."

I looked round automatically. Home Sister was being unusually nice to me these days, but I did not want to run risks. There was no visible sign of authority, so I stopped. "How do you expect me to walk after running up and down Josephine all day?"

He apologized and asked obviously, "Off?"

I nodded. It was less exhausting than speech.

"Booked? Or can I take up that rain-check on our last date?"

"Did you take a rain-check on it?"

"Of course. And since we're still on speaking terms I gathered you understood that. Well? Care to spend a quiet evening with uncle?"

I was too hot and weary to be civilized. I had not forgotten the ballet, but I was still very curious about him. "Why?"

He raised his eyebrows. "Why not? I'd like to have you join me."

"So I gather. But why?"

"See here," he said impatiently, "if you've another date, say so. Maybe you want to go out with the girls? Is—what's her name—Estelle—off?"

"She was off this morning," I retorted with equal impatience, "as you must have noticed since you've been in Josephine most of to-day."

He shrugged. "Can't say I did."

"Oh, yes, you did!" I had reached flash-point. "You always

83

do notice her. So why bother to date me? Why not ask her? Not just this evening—other times?"

"And why would I want to do that? God! You are the most impossible girl! Why can't you accept an invitation without a man having to make a Federal case out of it?"

"Hunch."

"Oh, no! Not that! Spare me the womanly intuition!"

"Gladly. If you and Estelle'll spare me having to watch you act like a couple of refugees from Freud. Seriously," I added more calmly, "I'd like to help."

"Just a Girl Scout?" he jeered.

"That's me."

He grinned briefly. "So long as I know. Well, now," he had calmed too, "can we go back to square one? Find a park bench? Look at some ducks? Soothing birds, ducks. Nothing like a soothing background for a full meeting of the Lonely Hearts Club."

I had a better idea and said so.

He shook his head. "It's good of you, angel, but, frankly, no."

"Don't you like ballet?"

"Very much. But the More finances don't rise to it," he explained with a refreshing lack of pretence.

"This is for free." I told him how I had come by the tickets, using the official version I had first used on Estelle and Hannah. "Sylvia may be out. In any case, I haven't yet asked her. If I couldn't find her I was going to have to waste one and go alone. You may as well come. It doesn't start until seven-thirty, so we can sit on a bench first."

He winced extravagantly. "Ouch. These coals of fire are burning."

I took that as an acceptance. "Give me half an hour to change."

He was waiting in the front hall of our Home when I left the lift thirty-five minutes later. We strolled to the nearest public park, chose a bench by the lake, watched the ducks, drank coffee from thick china mugs, ate even thicker hamburgers, and talked Estelle.

"Just date her, you say! It's so simple! Angel, the More finances just stretch to coffee and hamburgers on a park bench. I can't offer you a proper dinner. As for her—I don't even own a ruddy dress suit."

"If she wanted the bright lights and expensive meals she could have them any time. Why can't you forget her cash and treat her as a human being?"

"That is so easy," he replied drily. "Do I also overlook the minor detail that she can't tolerate me?"

"Would it make any difference if she liked you?"

"It would be a pleasant thought—it wouldn't help otherwise.

How could it? I've nothing to offer her. I don't even earn a living."

"You will."

"And since when has a medical qualification been a short cut to wealth? It'll be years before I'm able to support some one like you as a wife. It would never work with her. Her only hope is to marry some well-heeled character."

"Do you have to talk marriage from the start?"

"Surprisingly enough"—he sounded surprised—"I do—with her. I happen to love her. I never intended, or wanted, to love any one yet. I saw her—and it was all over. I thought; that's her. I didn't twig who she was, which was why I came up to call on you girls in the P.T.S. Once I heard the score I realized all I could do was get back on Luigi and beat it like a bat out of hell. I meant to steer clear of her." He looked at me. "Like hell I've been able to do that now I know I've only to walk into a ward to see her. I've not been the only man to do that. I doubt there's a character in the Medical School who hasn't taken a look and opted out. There's only one man in Martha's in the position to do otherwise."

"There is?" I asked absently, wishing I did not see his point of view so well.

"Old Marcus. But he retired to his ivory tower years ago."

"Him? He's far too old."

"Oh, I dunno." He stretched his legs and leant his head against the back of the seat. "He's not such a bad chap. What if he does keep himself to himself? It's his life. Now I've run up against Estelle, I feel mighty sorry for the man. He's stiff with brains as well as lolly. A man with his brains wouldn't be able to delude himself that any woman would be able to see him for his lolly. He probably took to his microscope in self-defence. It's the same with her." His voice softened. "That must be why she hands out the frozen mitt to one and all?"

I nodded. "Once I thought her reserve was just shyness. It isn't. She's never shy with the patients."

"Think I haven't noticed that while writing those reams in Josephine?" His smile was self-derisive. "Have I made notes! I've also noticed how you're the one person to whom she lets down the barrier. Which was why I tried to date you last time—and to-night. Now call me a heel and have done!"

"I knew you weren't asking me for me."

"How so?"

I smiled smugly. "Womanly intuition, dear."

He grinned. "I deserved that."

"Want me to pull a string?"

"I did. Even this evening. Not now."

"What's made you change?"

He said that while he had been waiting for me to change he

had walked round the car park. "I made myself take a good look at that car of hers. It would take my first year's salary as house-man to keep that machine in petrol—if she went slow on using it. So there's no dice. Like me to opt out of the ballet?"

"Of course not! We ought to move soon."

"Before we do—mind if we make a deal? I've opened my big mouth far too wide this evening. You won't let it go any farther?"

I hesitated. The Professor had been in my mind throughout our conversation. I was not sure that he could advise me on this, but I very much wanted to discuss it with him, if only to help me get it in proportion.

He misunderstood my hesitation. "Frances," he caught both my hands, "don't you dare wonder how you can put in the right word to her. Or ask Hannah or any one else to do likewise. You're not to breathe a word about how I feel about her. Get me?"

"I won't tell any one you're in love with Estelle," I promised obediently, adding the mental reservation; so long as I keep Estelle's name out of it, I can ask the Professor.

He kissed my cheek lightly. "Good girl. Hey"—he held me against his shoulder—"don't look round as it'll be too obvious —but there goes old Marcus on his way back to the old firm."

I waited a few moments before releasing myself from his hands. "Which way?"

"He's gone behind the island." He stood up, held out a hand, and pulled me to my feet. "Let's move or we'll be late. And for a break, let's talk about you. How's your love-life?"

"Haven't got one."

He smiled. "Too bad. Hey—how about that aged bird-watching character? Hannah told me something about him. All those avuncular letters sound mighty fishy to me."

"Maybe." I had to smile as he was watching me. "Not if you knew the Professor. There was nothing like that about him."

"With due respects, angel," said Bart, "there's something like that about every man. Let's run. We want that bus."

The ballet was good, but not as superb as I made out in my next letter to the Professor. Once it was posted, I had the in-evitable doubts and wished I had not been so enthusiastic. He would probably think I was begging for more tickets; be nauseated by such pure saccharine; never write to me again.

"Has your mother changed her letter-writing day?" Estelle asked as we hurried to a medical lecture the following Thursday morning, and despite our rush, I insisted on going via Matron's Office. "I thought she wrote on Mondays?"

"She does. I was just hoping one of my sisters has remem-bered my existence. They're all home on holiday. I love getting letters. Don't you?"

"Depends whom they're from, dear." She reached the pigeon-holes first, sorted through the 'D's,' handed me an envelope. "Frances, you can't stop to read it now! We're late. Think of Sister Tutor's blood-pressure."

"Sure." I grinned idiotically as if I found the thought of Sister Tutor's blood-pressure exquisitely funny. "Mustn't give the old girl a stroke."

If I had been alone I would not have given the time or Sister Tutor one thought until I read the Professor's letter. As I had to leave it unopened, it occupied nine-tenths of my thought during Dr Higgs' lecture on Graves' Disease. I fixed my eyes on the round little physician who kept dropping his chalk; fingered the envelope in my pocket while his words flowed over my head and my colleagues wrote pages of notes on exophthalmic goitre, hyperthyroidism, toxic adenoma, and thyrotoxicosis.

Dr Higgs did not approve of too many notes being taken. He stopped by my desk on his way out. "Interested in medicine, Nurse? Eh? Thought you must be. Wise girl. Fascinatin' subject. And you'll learn it better if you carry on keeping your eyes and ears open and hands still. Good morning."

Sister Tutor beckoned me as he left the room. "One moment, Nurse Dorland. What did Dr Higgs have to say to you?"

When I gave her a shortened version of this she clicked her tongue against her teeth impatiently.

"Dr Higgs is far too conscientious a man for it to occur to him that you were gazing at him to cover your lack of attention. I hope you feel ashamed of yourself! If I see you going to sleep with your eyes open in a lecture again, I shall send you to Matron. I strongly advise you to do something to conquer that childish habit before you begin work in Out-Patients. Sister Out-Patients will not tolerate absent-mindedness in her nurses."

I apologized meekly, and automatically, then realized what she had said. "Out-Patients, Sister?"

She smoothed her cuffs primly. "That is what I said, Nurse. You should be aware of the fact. I pinned the change list to the board outside Matron's Office earlier this morning. You have eyes, Nurse. May I suggest you use them for the purpose for which they were intended."

I was as surprised to think Estelle had missed that notice as I was by her news. Estelle was the most observant person I had ever met. I had spent some time in the lecture wondering if she had recognized the Professor's handwriting, decided she must have done, but had had the good sense—and good manners—not to mention it as I had not done so.

Sister Tutor gave me another little homily on the disasters that must inevitably attend any nurse who lacked observation, then dismissed me. Estelle was waiting anxiously in the corridor. "What was all that about? Rocket?"

I nodded. "That's not all. We're changing." I told her about the list. "Did you see it?"

"No. Let's go and look now."

We walked as quickly as we dared back to the Office, because we were already bound to be late when we returned to Josephine. We discovered our whole set was changing wards as the new P.T.S. set was due to start in the hospital in a couple of days. Estelle was going to the General Theatre; Hannah to Josephine.

"I'm sorry we're splitting," she said as we walked on. "Of course, it was bound to happen." Her expression suddenly froze. "I expect," she drawled, "I'll find it quite amusing to spend the next three months hiding behind a yashmak."

"Maybe you will," I replied absently, looking round. I was sure Bart was somewhere near, although I had not yet seen him. When Estelle switched into that dreadful Top Deb. voice he was always close at hand.

He was there all right. He was leaning against the bust of Lord Lister about ten yards from us, talking to three other students. He waved casually in our direction as we went by. The look he gave Estelle was not at all casual. She ignored him and drawled on about the theatre until we had left him well behind. "Do you think you'll like O.P.?" she asked in her normal voice. "I've heard Sister O.P. is an absolute old devil."

Garret was waiting for us in Josephine. She looked very annoyed. "Nurse Dorland, did you scrub the linen-room shelves last evening?"

"Yes, Nurse."

"Come with me." She nodded curtly to Estelle. "You get on with the routine. Now, Nurse Dorland"—she swept towards the linen-room and threw open the door dramatically. "Look at the chaos you have left behind you! Three of those pillow-cases—two hand towels—are facing the wrong way! And you have put thirteen sheets on a pile, not twelve! I've never seen such a shambles! Get this straight before you do anything else!"

I said, "Yes, Nurse, I'm sorry, Nurse," and tried not to look as delighted as I felt. I had thought the Professor's letter would have to wait until I went to lunch, but she had given me the perfect refuge in which I could read in private.

I tidied the pillow-cases and towels quickly, then heaved forward the steps, climbed to the sheet shelf, sat on the top step by the shelf, and read my letter.

He wrote his now usual page and a half. He was happy I had enjoyed the ballet; pleased I had been able to take one of my friends. . . .

"Nurse Dorland!" Garret stood at the foot of the steps looking about to explode. "What do you think you are doing up there?"

I said, "Reading a letter, Nurse."

"Do you suppose I have no eyes in my head? Put it away at once! What do you suppose would happen to the patients if we all retired to linen-rooms and sat on the top of ladders when we wanted to read our post? Have you no conscience at all? If you think you will be permitted to get away with this behaviour in Out-Patients you had better think again! Sister Out-Patients will know how to deal with you!"

Estelle overheard Garret's strictures as she set the patients' lunch-trolley in the kitchen. She was really upset. "Frances, do be careful. Two in a day is two too many," she warned me at lunch.

I promised to be careful, and promptly dropped the plate of Irish stew I was carrying.

Sister Dining-room was quite as angry as Garret had been. Hannah, who had overheard about my morning, shook her head unhappily. "This can't go on, Frances! For God's sake, girl, take a grip. Sister O.P.'ll go round the bend if she hears about things like this."

I felt a miserable failure, a disgrace to my set, inevitably bound to bring sorrow to my aged parents, until I remembered my parents were not yet aged—and the Professor's letter.

I had to talk to some one, so I wrote to him that evening:

The shadow of the gallows looms large, as Home Sister forecast. And after the appalling build-up every one's given Sister O.P. I am not sure it would not be a happy release. Of course, there's always the river, but I can swim quite well. I believe it's hard to drown if you can swim? Still, it seems I have got to be sensible, so I have decided to turn over a new leaf.

Estelle looked round the door as I signed my name. "So there you are! You were so quiet I thought you must be in Hannah's room with the others."

"I'm feeling very virtuous, attending to my correspondence. Notice my halo? Well over the ears?"

She smiled. "It had better stay there, Nurse Dorland. Remember Sister O.P."

I groaned. "Must I?"

"I'm going to miss not having patients." She wandered aimlessly round my room. "It'll make a change."

"Need a change?" I asked carefully.

"It's always a good thing to get around. More experience."

Shock tactics had worked with Bart. I decided to try them on her. "No medical clerks in the theatre, either."

"Just what," she drawled, "do you mean by that?"

"You won't have to keep ignoring Bart More."

"Bart More?" she asked icily. "Why would I do that? He's a friend of yours—not mine."

"Bart More." I ignored her final remark. "Don't ask me why you avoid him. That's something I wouldn't know. Just as I wouldn't know why he watches you when you aren't watching him and vice versa."

"Frances, you do talk the most ghastly rubbish at times."

"Could be. But I'm not at this moment—as you know. So, why? I won't spread it about, but I'd like to know. I think you like him one hell of a lot."

She sat on my bed. "I'm really not interested."

I sat by her. "Come off it, Estelle. I haven't your brains, but I've three sisters. I know when a girl's interested and when she's not. You are. So why?"

Her manner thawed visibly. "You must see why. It's impossible from every angle."

"Because of your cash?"

She hesitated. "More than that. Grandpapa."

"He surely didn't say you were to take the veil because you've taken up nursing?"

"No," she agreed slowly. "But when he gave me permission to come here he said he only gave it because he could trust me to be sensible."

"He's dead right. You are. Surely he wouldn't object to your just getting to be friends with a student?"

"He would. He doesn't hold with platonic friendships—as I've told you. Particularly when the female half is me."

"I suppose I can see his point. You're his one and only ewe lamb, due to inherit no small fortune, and very good-looking. You aren't as other women and it's no use pretending you are."

She said reflectively, "I've never met any one like you. You've no inhibitions about saying the sort of things most people leave unsaid. But where their silence embarrasses, your talk doesn't."

"Couldn't you shed a few inhibitions with Grandpapa?"

"Uh-huh. You don't know Grandpapa! If he suspected a Martha's student was giving me the green light—and that I thought he looked pretty nice—hell, yes, I do—well, he'd have me out of Martha's and back home before I had time to pack. I'm under age, remember."

I was very pleased to have this admission from her, even though it was not apparently going to do any one any good.

"Estelle. He couldn't object to Bart. Bart's no fortune-hunter."

She smiled without humour. "According to Grandpapa, every man who's ever looked my way has been one—and I'm afraid he's right. Heavens, Frances—you don't know what it's like— I know it sounds a piece of cake to be me—it isn't. Grandpapa says he trusts few women and no men where I'm concerned. We had a long chat the night before our P.T.S. term began. He made me promise I would not so much as accept a date with any man who was not personally known to him, or who had not first asked his permission. I know that sounds Victorian. . . ." She broke off apologetically.

"How old's Grandpapa?"

"Seventy-nine."

"Then he was raised under Victoria. Can't blame him for running true to form."

She smiled properly. "You two ought to meet. He'd like you, and you wouldn't be frightened of him. But, Frances—can you see any of these boys asking Grandpapa if they can take me to the movies?"

"N-no." I sighed. "There must be an answer, though. The Professor," I added unthinkingly, "says there's an answer to everything."

She looked at me keenly. "When did he say that? Seen him lately?"

This was Truth Night in the Nurses Home, so I had to be honest. "Once. He's telephoned a couple of times."

"And sent you those ballet tickets?"

"How on earth did you guess that?"

She laughed. "I've no sisters, dear, but a few brains. Found out any more about him?"

I nodded and told all I knew.

"He visited your family?"

"All bird-watchers together, as I forecast."

She seemed about to say more when Hannah swept in and asked why we were looking so gloomy. "The tea's stewing, girls. Do come along, or it'll be too bitter to drink."

7

AFTERNOON IN THE SUN

THE senior nurse-in-training in the Out-Patient Department was called Simpson. She was tall, dark-haired, with very blue eyes. She wore a fourth-year belt and spoke to the tip of my cap. "O.P. Four'll show you what to do, Dorland."

It was my first morning in the department. I had no idea who, or even what, O.P. Four was. I looked hopefully at the four other girls in the changing-room. Three wore the same fourth-year belt as Simpson; the fourth was a second-year nurse. No one took any notice of me or bothered to explain what was obviously an elementary fact of O.P. life.

The department was a new world to me. The conversation in that changing-room taught me that in this world a new language was spoken. "The S.O.P.O. was so right," insisted Simpson. "That B.I.D. belonged in Cas. We can't admit stiffs with all our follow-ups. The S.M.O. was furious about it. He went along to Cas. to speak to the S.C.O., himself."

"Why should a B.I.D. come in at all?" asked another girl. "We're a hospital. Not a flipping morgue."

A third girl said she could understand about B.I.D.'s because of our P.M. room, but what really got her was Sister Mary's creating to her because an infant was B.B.A. "You would have thought I induced the poor little creature when I had to escort him to Mary. The S.G.H.P. said both should have gone to Christian. I ask you!"

She was not asking me, for which I was grateful, being utterly dazed by all these letters. She did not so much as glance my way, nor after that first remark did Nurse Simpson or any of the others. They wandered off, leaving me waiting for the second-year to finish rearranging her hair.

At last she was satisfied with her appearance. She spun round in a burst of efficiency, smoothed her apron, and produced two tin boxes from beneath one of the shelves. She thrust one at me. "O.P. Five's cleaning things. Will you start on the children's room?"

She was a plump, moderately pretty girl with light brown hair and a faintly disgruntled air. She did not explain further or offer to show me to the children's room. Fortunately, on my way in I had noticed a large spotted rocking-horse in one of the many rooms off the long corridor dividing the department, so when she shot off in one direction I hurried in the other in search of the rocking-horse.

It had a friendly face and looked lonely and out of place in its aseptic surroundings. I patted it as I set it in motion while dusting. "You and me, pal, both," I murmured aloud.

The second-year nurse looked in about five minutes later. "You ought to have finished, Dorland. We've all the other rooms to do—five medical, fifteen assorted surgical, plus this. The room cleaning is all done by O.P. Four and Five. I'm Four. You're Five."

"Yes, Nurse." I tried to sound briskly efficient. "Is there a Six?"

"Obviously not, as you're Five! Every new nurse in O.P. starts as Five, regardless of her actual hospital seniority, as the work here is so specialized. Simpson's Head Nurse, Carver O.P. One. Simpson's due to move in about a month. When she goes we'll all shift up one. You'll be Four then," she added a little unnecessarily, but with patent doubts on the subject. "It's a bit unusual, our having any one as new as you here. I suppose Matron must know what she's doing."

I made no comment. I could scarcely say no and feared that if I said yes she would look even more disapproving.

"Oh, well. I suppose I'll have to take you round. Come on. Incidentally," she added over her shoulder, "I'm Vickers. Monica Player's in my set."

The piece of information cheered me. Hospital sets in some strange manner tend to have a form of family resemblance within their numbers. Monica Player had been a pleasant and very helpful senior. I beamed at Vickers' back. She glanced round, noticed my expression, but did not return my beam. I switched it off quickly.

"Twenty-one rooms in all," she announced half-way through our tour. "Those over there"—she gesticulated vaguely, "belong to the S.M.O., S.S.O., S.O.P.O., and S.G.H.P., so they don't concern us as they are only offices. No patients are allowed in the offices. We do only the patients' rooms The rest get cleaned by the lay staff."

I had to stop her. "I'm sorry, Nurse. I can't work out those letters."

She tapped her foot impatiently. "I simply can't waste time explaining. You'll have to have one of Sister's printed lists. I'll just tell you now—the S.O.P.O. is the Senior Out-Patient's Officer and our permanent resident. The S.G.H.P. is more or less permanent too—when he's not in Cas.—he's the Senior Gynaecological House Physician. There are dozens more. Wait here. I'll get a list."

The list momentarily added to my confusion. There were

approximately sixty men on the resident medical staff; the majority appeared to work in Out-Patients during some period of the day; each man being known by the initial letters of his specific appointment.

Vickers ran rapidly through our routine as we scampered on. "After cleaning, we stock and test. We report to Sister at a quarter to nine every morning. Although O.P. never shuts, we open officially at nine each morning and all the rooms remain open until 8 P.M. Only the acute rooms are open at night, unless there's a major crisis. Then they can open the lot. Sister," she went on as we reached the last room, "is very particular about none of the patients' rooms being left unattended by the staff in the day."

I looked again at the list and counted the O.P. nursing staff. "How do we manage that, Nurse? Twenty-one rooms—eight on the staff counting Sister and her Staff Nurse."

"If I were you, Dorland," she retorted sharply, "I wouldn't try to be funny! You may think you're quite important, having important friends and so on, but we simply aren't interested in your private life here. The dressers and clerks help, naturally! They're perfectly capable."

Her reaction astounded me. She looked genuinely annoyed. I could not conceive why she should have taken such umbrage over Estelle—and she could only have been referring to Estelle, since, with the exception of Bart, I had no friends, important or otherwise, in the hospital. She was clearly waiting for me to make some answer, so I fell back on some advice Player gave us in Josephine. 'When in doubt, agree, apologize, and keep quiet.'

If I had any real doubts, she dispelled them when, with the four seniors, we waited outside the door of Sister's office at sixteen minutes to nine. She gazed pensively round the steadily filling department. "I believe I can guess why Matron sent you to us so soon, Dorland. It'll prevent your having delusions of grandeur—do you good to be reminded how the other half live. The half who don't drive around in expensive Continental cars," she added triumphantly, as if she had brought off a magnificent witticism.

Estelle's car was French. I longed to retort that I had only been in that car twice since we left the P.T.S. I very nearly did. Again Monica Player saved me. "Never hit back at a senior, even if she is in the wrong. It doesn't pay. Act dumb and pretend the crack's gone over your head. That'll annoy her more than anything you can say."

I assumed the Idiot Pro expression I had not used since I left the P.T.S. and Staff Nurse Naylor. "Yes, Nurse."

She looked at me sharply. The seniors looked amused. I widened my eyes a little farther. They felt about to drop out.

The Staff Nurse opened the door. "Come in, Nurses."

The immediate prospect of Sister O.P. prevented my brooding on the long-term prospect of working with a tiresome colleague. I had never seen Sister before. Her appearance in every way lived up to her reputation.

She was a square, solid, elderly lady with iron-grey hair and light grey eyes. She did not talk; she barked. "So you're Nurse Dorland, hey?"

"Yes, Sister."

"Don't slouch, child! God gave you a back-bone. Use it!"

"Yes, Sister."

"You've worked in Josephine Ward?"

"Yes, Sister."

"You've done no departmental work?"

"No, Sister."

"You'll have a great deal to learn, won't you, Nurse?"

"Yes, Sister."

She looked as dubious as Vickers had done earlier. "Sister Tutor tells me you are apt to be absent-minded. A sad fault, Nurse. Conquer it."

I swallowed. "Yes, Sister." And since she had not dismissed me, I waited as Sister Josephine always insisted we waited in front of her desk with our hands behind our backs until she said the actual words, 'That will be all, Nurses.'

Sister O.P. peered over the top of her desk, and glared at my feet. "Glue under your shoes, Nurse? Short of breath?"

I stepped back as if the floor was red-hot. "No, Sister."

"You have relieved my mind, Nurse. And why do you still wait? Can you not see that my Staff Nurse is waiting to show you your morning's work? Do you consider my Staff Nurse is free to await you in your own good time?"

I crossed to the Staff Nurse who was standing by the door, feeling as if I had walked into my father's bulldozer.

The Staff Nurse gave me a charming smile. "We'll begin in Room One, Nurse Dorland."

Nurse Vickers had made me wary, and I reserved judgment as to whether our exceptionally attractive Staff Nurse was as charming as her smile. It did not take me long to shed that wariness. Staff Nurse Neal was a genuinely friendly person; she treated me as an equal, chatted as if we had known each other years. She was unlike any other staff nurse I had yet met in Martha's; she behaved like a normal human being who knew more than I did because of her years of hospital experience, but took no credit for those years. She was obviously very popular with the patients. Every few minutes during that morning some man or woman advanced on us, seized her hand, said it was real good to see her again it was, and how was the Doctor keeping?

I had noticed her wedding ring directly we left Sister's office.

As I listened to and watched her I wondered if marriage had given her her human touch and, if so, whether something could be done to marry off Naylor in the P.T.S. and Garret in Josephine. I wondered about her husband too. If Vickers had been less hostile I would have gone straight to her for information, but that was clearly out of the question. Then Neal gave it to me unasked. "My husband was S.O.P.O. here last year—before he decided to specialize in pathology," she remarked after one of her many reunions with old patients. "They've got wonderful memories. They never forget a thing."

"I wish I could say the same, Nurse."

"Don't worry about that," she said cheerfully. "No one remembers anything about the workings of O.P.'s during their first week here. It'll suddenly all fall into place." She looked at the corridor clock. "That skin clinic's running over-time as usual. We can't help out in there as it's time we went back to Sister. I'm not sure which lunch she wants you to go to, or when you'll be off. Wait outside her office. I won't be long."

The office door had been half-open all morning. Neal did not close it when she left me in the doorway. I waited, watched the coming and going of patients, long white coats, short white coats, nurses and students, and wondered, not for the first time in Martha's, how any of the medical staff ever had time to do any real work, because they were always hurrying from one point to another, staring at the floor, and clutching huge sheafs of notes. And surely rubber-wheeled roller-skates would be ideal for nurses? They would be so much quicker and far more graceful than the swaying jog-trot used by all my fellow O.P. girls.

A quiet discussion on off-duty had been going on in the room behind me. I paid no attention until something Neal said made me listen instinctively. "Is that the child you were telling me about, Sister? The Dorland Sister Tutor mentioned?" I could not catch Sister's answer, but Neal's next words told me more than I wanted to know about Sister Tutor's comments.

"Then do you suppose we'll keep her long, Sister? I don't."

I had no wish to hear Sister's confirmation of this view. I moved a few feet from the doorway, stared at the waiting patients and thought bleakly about my future.

"Nurse—here." An elderly lady, in a red hat sitting three chairs away beckoned me urgently. "Is that young doctor over there trying to get your attention? That dark-haired young doctor—over by the wheel-chairs, dear."

I looked round vaguely. Every other physician and surgeon in O.P. appeared to have dark hair. "I don't think he can be, thanks"—and then I saw Bart.

He caught my eye at once, spread his hands dramatically, and came towards me.

I scowled to keep him off. He ignored my scowl and climbed on over the wheel-chairs. The lady in the red hat smiled archly. "I thought he must be your young man, dear. I watched him trying to get your attention for ever so long."

I thanked her again as Bart reached me. "Go away," I said between my teeth, "far, far away. Sister and Neal are both in the office."

"In a minute. Where is she? And what are you doing here? Why aren't you in Josephine? I've combed Martha's."

"We've all changed. She's in the General Theatre. For Heaven's sake—go away!"

He obeyed this time and just in time. Neal came out of the office as he walked by at the double, correctly gazing at the floor. "You are to go to one-thirty lunch, and be off this afternoon, Nurse Dorland." She smiled. "I expect you'll be glad to have an extra afternoon off?"

I could not see any genuine reason for preferring to be free from two to five, instead of from five-thirty onwards, but since she had been so pleasant and seemed to expect me to be delighted, I beamed and said I was most happy to have an extra free afternoon.

Vickers came into the changing-room a little later when I was tidying my cap before going to lunch. "Is Bart More another of your friends?"

I cursed all itinerant students mentally. "His cousin's in my set, Nurse."

She smiled unpleasantly. "Quite a famous set, what with this and that. All the same, I think I ought to warn you—that cuts no ice here. No one—just no one—impresses Sister Out-Patients."

"That I can well believe, Nurse," I said drily, and went to lunch.

No member of my set was at that meal. When I returned to the Home afterwards our floor was empty. The heat-wave had finally broken, but the afternoon was far too fine to waste indoors, even though my conscience insisted I should stay in and write up Dr Higgs' lecture on Graves' Disease. I squashed my conscience by reminding it that Sister P.T.S. was the fount of all Martha's nursing wisdom, and she had always told us that every nurse needed a brisk walk in the open air every day. "It is your duty to care for your health, Nurses. A healthy nurse is a happy nurse; a happy nurse makes happy patients."

I had no real patients in O.P. but it was obviously my duty to spread happiness among our drifting follow-ups. I changed out of uniform, and strolled back to the hospital to care for my health on the stone-flagged terrace that ran the length of the building on the river side. My feet refused to be brisk after their morning in O.P., and the terrace was the ideal spot for getting the maximum of air with the minimum of energy. It was away from the noise and smell of traffic, quiet, and after two in the afternoon generally empty. The students had all gone in to rounds or lectures when I reached it, apart from a man in a boiler suit at the far end, I had the terrace to myself.

I leant against the embankment wall contentedly, too soothed by lunch and the sunshine to think of anything in particular as I watched the river and the traffic on the opposite bank. I had been there perhaps five minutes when I first had that odd sensation you get when some one is watching you. I turned slowly, looked up and down. Even the man in the boiler suit had disappeared. I was quite alone.

I looked towards the ward blocks which lay on my right. I had intentionally not stopped in front of any of the wards in case some Sister might see me, disapprove, and remember my face if I ever worked in her ward. The Admin. block was directly behind me; Matron's office was in that block, but faced on to the small courtyard between the blocks; the Dean's offices, the Hospital Secretary's, and, I believed, a board-room lay under the top-floor Lab. I looked up at each floor, then for some time at the great plate-glass window. It stared down at me, as unwinking as a glass eye. There was no one at any window, nor was it likely that any of the occupants of those floors would be taking time off to watch me, but the sensation persisted so strongly that I moved away.

There was a door in the embankment wall just beyond the Admin. block. It was labelled 'Members of St Martha's Hospital only.' I had not used it previously, but as I was a member of Martha's I could not see how even the Dean could object to my using it now. I crossed the bridge, and in a few minutes reached the public park we all regarded as an extension of the hospital, remembering the last occasion when I had used a side-door for the first time. I wished I could have told Lily about that; she would have been so pleased for me. And then I wished I had not been born with a photographic memory, and winced mentally.

The Professor would say I was indulging in grief, I thought suddenly and dragged my thoughts away from that small ward. I did not attempt or want to drag them from him. I strolled on aimlessly, wondering if I was really in love with him, in love with the thought of being in love, or merely fascinated by a man who was so unlike any man I had had as a friend or acquaintance previously.

There was a wooden bridge over the lake in the park. I leant on one rail for some time, watching the water, and many small children playing on the grass in dresses and suits that had been faded by the abnormally long summer. An endless stream of couples ambled by. I watched them too, and was a little surprised to find that they did not make me feel lonely. Like most young women alone—and possibly young men—couples generally had that effect on me, yet, although I would have loved to amble with my Professor, that afternoon I did not feel alone. Perhaps there was something to be said for a photographic memory, I decided, leaving the bridge. He did not have to be with me for me to see his face, and being alone I was free to carry on a splendid mental conversation with him; a conversation which was wordless, and yet allowed me to be brilliant and clever.

My feet reminded me I was on duty at five. Perhaps I ought to go back and do that lecture. Perhaps.

It was too late. I had noticed an empty bench close to the lake. I forgot all about the thyroid gland. I even forgot that I had shared that particular bench with Bart, until the ducks rolled out of the water and up to my feet. They waited expectantly as they had done that evening before the ballet. "Sorry, ducks," I said aloud. "No hamburger crumbs, to-day."

"Do you think," asked a voice directly over my head, "they'd care for an egg sandwich, Frances?"

His presence had been so vivid in my imagination, that for one moment, I thought I could only be imagining his voice. I looked round very slowly. He was there. He smiled, and I felt as if the sun had risen twice in the same day.

"Don't look so startled," he said. "I'm no ghost."

"I'm so sorry. I was miles away."

"I saw that from the other side of the lake. I tried to get your attention. You looked straight through me." He moved round the bench, but did not sit down. "Do you often come here in the afternoon? I've not seen you before."

"Not often." I folded my hands primly. I had to be prim until I recovered my mental breath. It would shake him rigid if I gave him the welcome I wanted to give. "Do you?"

"Fairly frequently. My office is quite near"—he jerked his head at the long grey line of Government buildings on our left —"just a couple of minutes from here to be accurate."

I made a mental note to haunt that part of the park on every free two-to-five I was given in future. "Isn't it a wonderful afternoon?"

He agreed the afternoon was perfect and looked at the still waiting ducks. "Do you want to feed them?"

I looked up at him, and stayed looking because he was apparently fascinated by the birds. I had not seen him in such a strong light previously. The sun exposed the lines under his eyes, making him seem older and thinner than I remembered, and yet more attractive than any man I had ever seen.

"Have you really got some food on you?"

"Yes. Here." He pulled a paper packet from one of his jacket pockets. "They'll be a shade stale. They won't mind."

I unwrapped the packet. "Do you always carry sandwiches around with you?"

He turned to me, grinned, and shed about ten years. "One can scarcely blame you for having that impression." He glanced at the bench. "Expecting any one? Or on your own?"

"On my own."

"Mind if I join you?" he asked politely.

Equally politely I said I would like him to join me. I sounded exactly like Estelle in her Miss Dexter mood, I thought savagely. I had to let off steam somehow, so I chucked over half the sandwiches to the ducks.

He sat by me in silence. I had to say something. I talked about sandwiches. They made a change from the weather. "Do you eat a lot of them?"

"I usually have them for lunch."

"Is this your lunch?" I asked quickly.

He smiled. "Not to-day. I had ham to-day."

"You have them every day? Truly?"

"They're convenient."

We seemed to be having two conversations. The important one was unspoken. "If you eat them."

"I meant to," he said apologetically, "and forgot. My secretary's very good about having them sent up and worries if I leave them lying about. To save a great deal of unnecessary fuss I push the packets out of sight as soon as they arrive. I use a drawer in my desk—a pocket—or the car. The man at the place where I leave my car at night is used to unloading spare food from the dashboard. I believe he keeps chickens or something. Don't know where. He leaves the whisky."

I was no longer surprised he looked thin, and too concerned for him to pay attention any longer to the laws of civilized behaviour which had had me by the throat since I turned and found him standing behind me. "Just what do you have for lunch?"

"Coffee. Tobacco."

"How long have you been living on that?"

"God knows. Years. Hasn't done me any harm."

"Nonsense," I said firmly; "it must have. That kind of food's no good for a man. No food value in it. My mum would have a stroke if my father started skipping meals."

He considered me thoughtfully. "Your father must have a certain amount of physical work. My job's sedentary."

"That's got nothing to do with it at all. Honestly, I do know what I'm talking about. I know I'm new to hospital, but any one in Martha's would say the same. You don't know the risks you're running with your health. Why can't you go out to lunch?"

"It's such a waste of time. That's why I gave it up."

"You really ought to start it again. Or, if you can arrange it, have a proper meal sent up."

He smiled faintly. "You seem to have very strong views."

"I have. Because, as I've said, I do know what can happen. You wouldn't think of running a machine without fuel—so why try to run a human body without proper food? It's asking for trouble. If you keep on, you'll crack. Hasn't your secretary or some one told you this?"

"No." He took out his pipe, pouch, and matches. "Which makes me most grateful for your kind—if somewhat stern—warning."

"Have I been rude? I'm very sorry. I didn't mean to be."

"You haven't been at all rude." He slapped his pockets absently. "I don't believe you could be."

The sun rose a third time at that. "Are you looking for your matches? They're under your pouch."

"They are? Oh. Yes. Thanks." He filled his pipe. "I've no business to be sitting here. I should be working."

"I should be writing notes on the thyroid gland." We smiled at each other. "It would be wicked to waste this sun."

"Criminal. Do you get any in your room?"

"Actually, yes. It faces south. Does your office?"

He shook his head, still smiling. "It's a typical small back room."

"Are you what used to be called a boffin?" I asked curiously.

"Used to be? Now, that"—he said—"dates me. I thought boffins were still called boffins?"

"I thought it went out with the War. The Second World War."

"Believe it or not, that's the war I call the War. The Crimean campaign was a little before my time. Not much. Just a little."

I laughed. "You weren't even at Mafeking?"

"Alas, no. Tell me," he went on more seriously, "do you remember my war?"

"Only vaguely. I was five when it ended."

He nodded to himself as if he had expected that answer.

"Were you in it?"

"Inevitably. Every one of my generation was involved."

"I mean—did you fight? Were you a soldier?"

His eyes were amused. "I spent six years in the Army. I wouldn't care to claim that made me a soldier."

I tried to visualize him in uniform. I could not do it. "Six years. That's a terrific slice out of your life."

"It seemed more like six hundred at the time." He looked at me meditatively, and I had the impression he was not seeing me at all. "I was twenty-two when I went in. I feel now as if it only lasted a couple of weeks."

I wished he had not said that. Knowing his age made no

difference to me, but his talking so openly showed that he was quite content to underline the fact that we belonged to different generations. He obviously thought of me as a pleasant, perhaps amusing child. And nothing more. Two of the suns went down fast.

"Daddy was in the Navy. He didn't enjoy it much. He used to get seasick, poor darling."

"What happened to the turkeys?"

"We didn't have any then."

He shifted his position slightly. "This reminiscing must be very boring for you. Let's have your news. How's the new job? Gallows still looming large?"

"Larger than ever, even though I've only been in O.P. one morning." I threw the last crumbs on to the yellow, patchy grass and folded the sandwich paper. "My lamp's so dim, it's good as out."

"What happened this morning?" He crossed his legs and settled into a more comfortable position at the far end of the bench. "Sister live up to her reputation?"

"She did. It wasn't merely that." I told him of Sister Tutor's report, and the one-sided conversation I had overheard. "There's just one bright spot about that. If I get chucked out of O.P. I won't have to work with Vickers."

"Vickers? Hold on—I'm lost. Nurse? Student? Doctor?"

"Nurse. She's O.P. Four. I'm Five. We get called by our numbers like the cards in Alice's garden." I smiled briefly. "It's all rather absurd. She's only in her second year, but oh, so senior. And the others, so help me, are all fourth-years."

"And oh, so senior?"

"Heavens, yes. They don't speak to me or even see me. When the head girl has to talk to me she talks to the tip of my cap. Shook me a little at first, but I'll get used to being invisible. I don't mind that sort of thing from genuine seniors, which, to be fair to them, is what they are. Fourth-years in the wards have a lot of responsibility. They act-Staff Nurse and so on. It must affect their attitude."

"Possibly." His eyes smiled. "Some people grow with responsibility; others just swell."

"Vickers swells while you watch. She's in the same set as Monica Player in Josephine, but totally different. Player never made a single crack."

"From which I gather Nurse Vickers does?"

"She does." I explained her fixation about Estelle. "Do you remember my telling you I ran into something like this in the P.T.S.?"

"Very well. What's this girl's name? Estelle——?"

"Dexter. That's right," I added, as he obviously placed her instantly. "Hamilton Dexter's only grandchild. Honestly, that

102

moron Vickers behaves as if Estelle's cash is a personal insult to her. Have you ever heard such rubbish as that bit about my having important friends? Friends, me foot! Apart from my set I only know one person in Martha's, and he's an impoverished student. He had to turn up this morning, too."

He glanced at me. "Surely, you were quite pleased to see a friendly face?"

"There's a time and place for everything, Mr Slane. O.P. in mid-morning is no place for any one's love-life. But he was just a minor detail. What's really eating her is Estelle. Imagine my having to be reminded how the other half live. Me. A working-farmer's daughter. Daddy isn't broke, but he doesn't make all that much out of his turkeys yet. People only eat turkeys at Christmas, unfortunately. If they had the sense to eat 'em all the year round, maybe we'd have enough to run two elderly cars instead of one. We certainly can't at the present, and, frankly," I went on warmly, "I'm not sure that isn't a good thing. The little I've seen of people really in the lolly has made me quite content that I haven't a wealthy papa."

He refilled his pipe leisurely. "Money isn't everything, eh?"

I smiled. "I wasn't going to be quite so corny. But much wealth and many snags do seem to me to go together."

He watched me over the flame of his match. "You seem to have given this a lot of thought."

"Only since I arrived at Martha's. There must be something about our hospital; we go in for millionaires. Not only Estelle—one of our men. But you must have heard about him? Our head pathologist?"

He lit another match. "Should I have heard about him?"

"Maybe not, if you don't have anything to do with agriculture. His name's Everly. Farm machinery."

He nodded over a third match. "I know his name. So he's at Martha's, too?"

"Very much so. He's one of the brains. And do you know what the poor man has to do?"

"Tell me."

"He hides behind microscopes on our top floor with a variety of deadly bugs rather than come down and meet his fellow men —and women—in case some one wants to up and marry him for his money. From what Estelle's told me of her angle, I no longer blame him."

"You consider it inevitable that he could only be married for his money?" he asked mildly.

"Having seen him, I'm afraid I do. He may be pleasant underneath, but he's not particularly attractive."

"Indeed? How did you see him for the microscopes?"

I smiled. "Quite legitimately. I was sent up with a specimen for him when I was in Josephine. He's reputed to scare the living daylights out of every one from Matron downward, but he was perfectly civil if a shade whoffly." I paused momentarily, recollecting that encounter. "Maybe he was not so unattractive as a young man. Of course, with his cash, brains, and a title thrown in, he must have been one of the most eligible men in England. I wonder why some enterprising deb. didn't snap him up."

"Why necessarily a deb.? Why not a nurse?"

I thought this over too. "From the little I've seen of hospital life—because nurses don't have enough time for a successful social life—and their feet hurt too much. Laugh if you like, but it's true! If you run round a ward or department all day some one else must do any running that has to be done when a nurse is off-duty."

"Nevertheless wouldn't you consider that in this case an extra output of energy might have paid dividends?"

"Obviously the man's a piece of cake in some ways—if you want that kind of cake."

"It doesn't tempt you?" he asked quizzically.

"Me? Having seen him? Oh, dear me, no!"

"Leaving personalities out of it, talking academically, wouldn't you be tempted?"

I said slowly, "I suppose every one has their price. I don't know if that's really true. No one's ever tried to buy me. Naturally it would be very nice never to have to worry about cash, but I think you probably have to be used to having a lot of it, to feel it's the be-all and end-all. If you aren't used to it, it's easier to see the snags. And look what it can do to people. Take Estelle"—I waved her name at him—"she's got one big complex about it. And old Sir Whatsit above stairs—what sort of a life is that for a man who could probably buy Martha's outright? He may have fun raising his little colonies of streps. and staphs., but he'd have far more fun raising grandchildren—which he ought to be doing by now. No. I honestly don't think wealth on that scale does tempt me. I'd like to have enough, but life is quite problematical enough without Estelle's crippling complex, or the state of mind of that poor old man—even if he does have a whale of a time among his bugs."

He was having a bad time with that pipe. He had given up trying to light it, and was knocking it out against the back of the bench. "Why is life quite so problematical? Would the problem be male?" He smiled crookedly. "Please, don't answer unless you want to."

I looked at him and then away. "Actually there's something I've been wanting to ask you about a male problem." I felt quite pleased with myself; with a little care I could switch the subject easily to Bart and Estelle.

He said he could not pretend he was surprised; was not sure if he would be able to assist; but was at my service.

"It's about Bart More."

"I thought it might be," he murmured. "Go on."

I did not go on immediately. I had to choose my words if I was to keep my promise to Bart. "He's in love with a friend of mine."

"Your set?"

"Year," I corrected—I hoped diplomatically. "He's pretty serious. He wants to marry her eventually."

"A reasonable desire for a man in love," he remarked drily. "Is your friend equally fond of this youth?"

"He's not all that young. He's twenty-four."

"I apologize." He continued to maltreat his unfortunate if unsatisfactory pipe. "You haven't answered. Is she?"

I nodded.

"Forgive me—but where's the problem?"

I hesitated again. "I know this'll sound daft—but she doesn't want him to know how she feels."

"Why not?"

"Mainly, because of her family's attitude She doesn't feel they'll approve of him, she is under age, and doesn't want to have an affair behind their back."

He frowned briefly. "Why won't they approve?"

"He isn't qualified yet. He's broke."

"Surely time'll remedy that?"

"In a way—yes."

He asked, "Why only in a way? Because for some years More will inevitably have little money with which to support a wife? Do your friend's parents take the view that she'll be throwing herself away on a struggling young doctor, when, conceivably, she might do very much better for herself materially in another direction?"

This was not what I had been trying to explain, but as it roughly fitted Estelle's position, I agreed.

"One can appreciate her parents' point of view. She's consulted them about More?"

"Not yet. She knows their views on students. She hasn't told any one but me, or let any one else even guess."

"And More?"

"Oh, I guessed about him, even before he told me. He's been so obvious. Even the patients noticed what was up."

"They say there are only two things a man can't hide. When he's drunk; when he's in love."

" 'They' are right. I was certain about Bart long before that evening we went to the ballet. You don't mind? I took him with your tickets, not one of the girls."

"My dear child, why should I mind?" He smiled properly to prove his words. "I was delighted to have them used as you pleased. Glad you had a good evening," he added, and gave his pipe what became its final whang against the seat. The stem cracked in two and the bowl flew towards me.

I caught it in mid-air. "Bad luck! Have you another?"

"Not with me. It's immaterial." He pushed both parts in a pocket. "I'll have to be moving directly. Let's get back to these friends of yours. This business of its being a problem obviously distresses you and for that I'm sorry. But I'm not convinced there is any occasion for distress. I can well understand your friend's impatience and yours. You're all very young. Youth is always impatient, even though, ironically, youth alone has time for patience."

"Time'll sort things out? They'll get over it?"

"Not necessarily. I hope they will merely succeed in getting over the parental opposition. Parents generally come round in the long run."

"I hope you're right." I remembered Estelle's description of her grandfather. "I don't know."

"I do." He stood up. "We are discussing my generation now. I may not be able to follow how the minds of your contemporaries work; I know my own. Give them a little time; use not deception but discretion; they'll see things as you do, if they love their daughter—which I'm sure they do."

It was too late to say we were talking of the generation before his. I smiled weakly. "Oh, yes. They love her."

"Then I assure you you've nothing to worry about. Tell your friend to be honest with More. I'm sure he's only too anxious to be honest with her. And then all they'll have to do is wait a year or two for something some people wait for all their lives in vain, or find too late." He held out his hand. "I must get back to work now, or get the sack. I came out for ten minutes and have been away a good hour. Good-bye, Frances. I'm so glad I met you."

His hand was the normal temperature, but his words were so final that I felt as if I was touching ice.

I thanked him for his advice. He said I had been very good to listen to him so patiently. "I hope the sun goes on shining for you. I'll remember your advice on proper meals. Thanks again for it. Good-bye."

He walked away and did not look back. I watched his fair head vanish in the crowd beyond the far gates, then stood up slowly. I looked round and felt quite unbearably lonely. I left the park at once, went back to my room, and spent the rest of my off-duty working on Graves' Disease. That soothed my conscience, if nothing else.

8

TOP SECRETS AND SCARLET

FOUR clinics were still in progress when I returned to Out-Patients at five. The broad corridor running the length of the department was as crowded with waiting patients as when I went off duty at one.

Nurse Neal considered the crowd anxiously. "Poor dears, they're getting mutinous. They should all have been seen by now. It's no one's fault—but there they are."

Once again I was her official shadow. "Don't we have an appointments system, Nurse?"

"Oh yes. A very high-powered one. Only snag is, it doesn't work."

I asked why not?

"Mainly, because—like all general hospitals—we're running a twenty-four-hour service with what is actually a twelve-hour medical staff. As the men have to keep going and work the kind of hours that would send any trade unionist screaming to his union for a strike, the staff tend to slow down, if only to eat. They also have to drop everything when a crisis crops up, and that's happening all the time. With every interruption the clinic gets held up; the queue piles up; the fixed appointments have to be scrapped, and we have to go round soothing irate taxpayers who think all we need is a little efficiency." She surveyed the muttering patients. "Those post-op. gastrics'll develop new ulcers if we don't do something. Come along."

It took her ten minutes to reassure the gastrics. The fracture follow-ups, rheumatics, and cardiacs needed only half that time. We went back to the office doorway.

"There's nothing like a peptic ulcer for producing an acute attack of haemademia," she murmured.

"What's haemademia, please, Nurse?"

She smiled enchantingly at the middle-aged bus driver who had been particularly irate. "The literal translation, I believe, is a bloody mind. You'll see it written on notes."

"I will? Oh. I see." I smiled. "Thanks, Nurse."

"Don't think I blame them. I'd be haemademic with an ulcer. They are maddening, but that's part of our job here. If you ever get annoyed—don't show it. Remember, in places like O.P. and Casualty, the patients will judge the hospital by the staff they meet—so you represent Martha's. The technique always is to smile." She glanced at me. "I'm not advising that because I want you girls to be little rays of sunshine, but because it'll make life so much easier for you or any nurse. There are few women and—in my experience—no men who don't feel soothed when a pretty girl in a nurse's uniform smiles at them."

I told the girls about Neal when we discussed our new jobs over tea in Hannah's room that night. "She's so normal, she's unnerving."

Hannah groaned. "I wish some one would marry Garret. Does she always pull out the lockers and run her finger along the rim at the back?"

"Always," said Estelle and I together.

"That woman's got a mania for cleaning," Estelle went on. "She must have enjoyed herself in the theatre. You can't conceive how we clean in the General, Frances. We scrub everything every day; cleaning the clean as well as the dirty. I don't think I've put down my little scrubbing-brush once to-day, except to go to meals."

Hannah helped herself to more tea. "I thought you had a long abdominal list this afternoon? You couldn't have scrubbed during the acute abdos?"

"Hannah, dear, you ought to know better." Estelle smiled at me. "Get this. I was Extra Dirty Nurse, which meant dogsbody. We had eleven cases on the list, used an average of six large and four small macks per case. Who do you think was Mack queen?"

"Oh, dear! You always detested the macks in Josephine."

"Eleven abdos?" Hannah whistled. "Bart told me he had been dressing for the S.S.O.'s marathon. I thought he was exaggerating the way he always does."

"Is Bart on the surgical side now?" I asked evenly.

Hannah answered for Estelle. "As from this afternoon, he told me when I met him on my way over to-night. He was surprised to hear we've changed. Of course he could scarcely recognize you behind a yashmak in the theatre, Estelle." She peered into the teapot. "This wants more water."

I did not waste any time when Hannah vanished. "Bart came into the O.P. in a panic this morning. Don't ask me why —he did. I told him you were in the General."

She coloured slightly. "Frances, you ought to sit on your imagination. The man can't pull strings like that. And anyway, he didn't recognize me according to Hannah."

"Didn't he?" I wished more than ever, that I had not made that rash promise to Bart. "And what makes you think that acting dumb is your prerogative?"

"Frances, I wish you'd stop suggesting . . ."

"I wasn't suggesting one thing. I was just asking a question. I know it's none of my business and Grandpapa wouldn't approve and so on, but if I were you, I'd have a little chat with Bart More."

"What good would that do?"

"It might," I said, "stop you both from being somewhat haemadementic."

"I'm not—am I?"

I shrugged.

She said soberly. "I'd hate to hurt him."

I decided that enforced promises could be treated with ever increasing reservations. "I've a hunch he might feel the same about you. For two people who don't want to hurt each other," I added quickly as we heard Hannah's returning footsteps, "you're both doing a pretty bad job."

Hannah apologized for being so long. "Some one swiped my kettle for her hottie."

"A hottie? To-night? It's far too warm," I protested.

She said I only thought that because I had been racing round O.P. "The temperature's been falling all evening. The summer's gone on much too long. It probably ended this afternoon."

Hannah was right. The summer did end that day. And so, apparently, did my friendship with the Professor. He did not write or telephone, or appear in the park, car park, or hospital grounds, on any of the innumerable occasions when I haunted all three places. I even risked using the Dean's private exit. That got me nothing but a ricked ankle, and torn nylons, when I slipped on the steps in my anxiety to get away before any hospital authority discovered what I was doing. The days turned to weeks, the weeks to one month—then another. I used every kind of excuse for him. He was very busy, on holiday, had been transferred to some other city, ill, had an accident, abroad on business. I tried to persuade myself that my instincts were wrong. He had not been saying good-bye properly that day in the park. He only meant he was glad we had met that afternoon. One of these fine days he would get bored with crossword puzzles, remember me, and I would get another letter—perhaps more tickets—or bird photographs.

I received nothing at all from him, and as the second month of silence ended, I forced myself to face the truth. I had always expected that one day he would be bored by our relationship. That day had arrived, and there was nothing I could do about it.

Those first two months in O.P. were the most unhappy months of my life, in or out of hospital. I found departmental nursing quite interesting, but totally lacking in the human side of nursing that you get in the wards. Our patients were all strangers to me; the endless clinics reminded me more of a factory than a hospital; and because I was the only member of my set in O.P., I was very much on my own on duty, and almost as much off-duty, since my free time seldom coincided with the ward nurses. Estelle in the theatre was in much the same state where off-duty was concerned, but she had taken to the theatre, and seemed happier than I had ever known her, when we met occasionally at meals or for tea at night. Bart wandered through O.P. roughly once a week, waved at me as amicably as ever, but apart from that vanished from my life almost as completely as the Professor had done. In a hospital as large as Martha's it was far easier not to see than to see a given person, if you worked in separate departments. Each ward and department was its own private world. Out-Patients was notoriously a difficult world.

Oddly enough I got on far better with Sister than I would ever have dared to hope. She was very exacting, but she was also fair. She never expected me to know anything during my first month; never left me in any doubt about what she wanted me to do; and so long as I obeyed her in every detail, not only made no complaint, but sometimes even smiled at me. "You're learning, child. You're putting your mind to your work. That's what I like to see."

There was one great disadvantage about her approval, it accentuated Vickers' original disapproval of my presence in O.P. I had hoped she would grow out of this, but the reverse was what actually happened. "I simply cannot understand why Sister bothers over you, Dorland," she protested one morning after Sister had checked my setting of the S.M.O.'s clinic-room. "It's such a waste of every one's time."

I had never attempted to query her comments until then, as I had been afraid if I did I might lose my temper. I was feeling quite bucked about that clinic that particular morning and genuinely puzzled by her remarks, so I dropped my rule. "Presumably, Sister feels she has to train me, Nurse?"

She looked me over. "You do think you're so clever with your meek little pro act, don't you? Personally, I like people to be honest!"

I stared after her as she swept out. "What the devil did she mean by that?" I demanded of the heart-trolley.

Neal appeared in the doorway. "Did you say something, Dorland?"

"Just thinking aloud, Nurse."

She smiled. "Careful. Can be dangerous," and walked on.

I smiled after her. She was the one person who made O.P.'s tolerable. She treated us all in the same pleasant manner, and often chatted as if we were the same set when we were alone. But, being a staff nurse, she was inevitably far too senior for me to chat to her or run to when I wanted a good laugh, wild

110

grumble, or the odd furious tear, all of which I had shared with Estelle in Josephine. The four senior girls had never relaxed their original frigid attitude towards me, but this never upset me as their behaviour was only to be expected from fourth-years. Probably, not even Vickers would have upset me if I had heard from the Professor, but his silence and what lay behind that silence nagged me like a toothache.

I could not get him out of my mind no matter how hard I tried. And I did try. The early mornings and late evenings in O.P.'s were the blackest periods. From 9 A.M. until 7 P.M. we were occupied with clinics; in my off-duty there was always a lecture to attend or write-up; on my days off at home, the turkey season was working up for Christmas and no one sits around day-dreaming on a busy turkey farm when plucking-time is drawing near; at night I was too tired to stay awake. But during those cleaning hours in the department when my hands were occupied, but my mind free, I came close to wishing I had never gone up that hill. If this was love I did not want it. It hurt too much.

One Saturday evening around eight-thirty I was checking and dusting the cylinders in the oxygen cupboard when I heard Vickers calling for me.

"What do you want Dorland for?" asked Nurse Simpson from the stock-room next door. Simpson had not be transferred as we all expected, and was acting Staff Nurse for the week-end.

"To help me finish the linen-room, Nurse."

"Finish it yourself," said Simpson sharply. "It's Four's job, not Five's. Let the poor girl get on with her own work, and you get on with yours. And while you're here, Vickers, I may as well say what I've been meaning to say for ages. You're being much too tough with Dorland, and very dense. She's not a bad kid and never steps out of line. We thought she might at first, but she's shown us her private life is her affair, which it is. You ought to have enough sense to realize you're playing with fire, narking at her as you do. If Sister heard you, she'd be furious. None of us are supposed to know anything—and we wouldn't know anything if Tom Neal hadn't told his wife. I promised Neal it wouldn't go any farther."

"It hasn't gone any farther, Nurse," muttered Vickers sullenly.

"I should ruddy well think not! It's the top secret of Martha's. Don't you forget it. And don't forget that if Dorland felt bitchy—and I wouldn't blame her after your cracks—she could pull a string that would land you in Matron's office just like that! Now go and get on with your linen, and leave that kid alone."

I leant against the nearest cylinder, and dropped my duster.

111

I did not attempt to pick it up for at least two minutes. And when I did recover my mental and physical breath it took all the self-control I possessed to make me go on with my checking and dusting, and not burst into the stock-room to ask Simpson what on earth she was talking about. What strings could I pull? Why? And what was all this about Tom Neal? I knew Neal's husband was called Tom—but had never seen him.

When nine o'clock came I was a living question mark. I had to find some one who could explain this to me, and the obvious person was Bart. If he could not answer me at once, he could find out, being free to roam the hospital, and from what I gathered on chatting terms with the entire staff.

I went straight to Estelle's room when I reached the Home, intending to ask if he was on theatre call for the week-end or at his digs. If he was on-call I could ring him; if not, the porters would know his address. I would write and ask him to ring me.

Estelle's room was empty. She must have gone out in a great hurry because her cap and apron were lying on the floor. She was far too tidy a person to leave anything lying about without good reason. I picked them up gently, dropped them in her laundry basket, and wondered if she had a date with Bart. It must have been suddenly arranged because she was at second supper, and had not said anything about going out. Perhaps she was treating her promise to Grandpapa with reservations too. If so, though I could see her grandfather's point, I was all for it.

I went along to Hannah's room and was surprised to find her in bed. "Hallo? Did you get off early?"

"No." She smiled, but did not sit up. "I thought I'd give my poor feet a rest."

I sat on the end of her bed and looked at her anxiously. "Are you all right? You never want to rest."

She said she had a cold coming. "I've had a wretched head all evening. My throat's sore-ish. I'll be fine after a good sleep."

"You look a bit pink. Think you've a temp.?"

"Doubt it. I never have a temp. Stop flapping, girl." She moved her wrist out of range as I reached for her pulse. "I was hoping you'd come in. I've got some terrific news. Where do you think our Estelle is?"

"I was just going to ask you. Date?"

She grinned. "She has. With Matron. Poor old girl, she was in such a dither. I've never known her like it, before. I think that's what made her open up. She said I could tell you, but no one else."

"Tell what? And why Matron? At this hour? What's she done?"

"Honest to God, girl! Will you give me a chance? She hasn't done anything. It's about the new block. Guess what?"

"What?"

"Matron wants to see her about the opening date. Her grandpapa has donated it—can you imagine that! Apparently he's always wanted it to be anonymous, then something's made him change his mind. She had a letter this morning from him saying he's going to allow us to call it the Dexter Wing, and is coming along here for the opening, and the reception."

My brain gave an almost audible click. "That's what Simpson was getting at! Tom Neal must have heard it somehow——" and I explained.

"Neal? He works in the Central Lab. He would know. That Lab.'s shifting to the new block." She beamed at me. "The Dexter Block. Can't you just see us all basking in its reflected glory! And poor old Estelle looked utterly crushed—you'd think Grandpapa had done something shameful. She made me swear blind I'd only tell you. She's scared stiff of it getting round before the last possible moment."

"It's round O.P. already."

"Then don't tell her. You know what she's like about her cash."

I nodded. "Grandpapa can't be too grim if he goes round donating new blocks to hospitals."

"People can have generous sides as well as tough sides. Take Marcus Everly. You know what a so-and-so he's supposed to be? Well, did you know he gave not only the P.T.S. house, but the whole hill to the hospital?"

"Did he now? How did you hear that?"

She laughed. "Dear Fay heard Sister Robert saying something about it to Sister Arthur."

"What would we do without our Fay to tell us what's going on! I should have gone to her at once when I overheard Simpson! But, Hannah, aren't they crazy? As if I'd run to Estelle, or she'd run to Grandpapa, because Vickers is being foul to me! Bats. All of them." I stretched lazily. "So old Marcus gave us the hospital? Maybe that's why Hamilton Dexter bunged in the new block? Must be fun to be like that. Take this mountain, chum—and how about a new hospital? Two million? Why not?"

She laughed again, then sat forward, and rubbed her neck. "Ouch. That hurt. My glands are getting worse."

I considered her seriously. "I'm not sure I like the look of you, duckie. Relax. Nursie is going to get a thermometer."

I met Sylvia Franks in the corridor. She was looking worried. "Frances, have you got a thermometer?"

I stopped. "I was just going to find one for Hannah. Some one else feeling ill?"

"Alice has a wicked throat. It's her day off, and she's been lying down most of the day. I think she ought to report it. What's up with Hannah?"

I explained. "There must be some mighty queer bugs around this corridor. Wonder who'll be the third?"

Estelle stepped out of the lift. "Hallo, girls." Her smile was weary as she came slowly towards us. "Any tea going? I'm dehydrated plus. I don't know what the temperature was in the theatre to-night, I do know I've never known it so hot. She fingered her forehead. "It's given me a splitting head."

Sylvia and I exchanged glances. I asked. "Got a sore throat? Any aches and pains?"

"How did you guess? My throat isn't too bad—my back's ready to break in two."

We told her about the others. I touched her arm experimentally. "You're even warmer than Hannah. You get to bed fast. I was on my way to borrow your thermometer. Can I get it and take your temp. too?"

She was obviously too ill to argue. "If you say so."

Sylvia borrowed the thermometer for Alice Linton while I helped Estelle into bed. "I wonder what bug you girls have picked up."

"'Flu or something. Did Hannah get a chance to tell you about Matron?"

"Yes. Estelle. I really am thrilled! I'd adore to have a Dorland Block. Was Matron nice?"

"Very," she replied flatly.

I hung her cloak in her cupboard then turned to look at her properly. She was clearly sickening for something, but she sounded very much more ill than she looked. "Is this honestly being hell for you?"

She closed her eyes. "Grandpapa's timing always was perfect."

"His timing? What's that got to do with——" I broke off, suddenly understanding. "Bart? Have you told Grandpapa about Bart?"

"No." She opened her eyes. "I've just told Bart about Grandpapa. Right now—when I came out of Matron's office."

I sat on her bed. "So you're on speaking terms at last?"

"Have been for some time." A smile flickered through her eyes. "Since your pep-talk. It's been quite fun in the theatre. Sister Theatre says she's never known such a keen dresser."

"Sister Josephine could say the same. You must be doing that lad a power of good, Estelle."

The little smile vanished. "If you could have seen him ten minutes ago, you wouldn't have said that. For the record, the Dexter Block is the last straw."

"But why?"

114

"If you can think of a better way of reminding him who I am, I can't. He said so himself."

"My dear, he'll get over it."

She patted my hand. "You're a nice soul, dear, but you still believe in fairies. I don't."

Her touch reminded me belatedly of her temperature. "We can't go into this properly now; we'll work something out later. Don't get too gloomy, it'll send up your temp. I'll go and see where Sylvia's got to with that thermometer."

Sylvia came out of Hannah's room as I walked into the corridor. "Hannah's just over a hundred. Alice is a hundred and two." She returned with me to Estelle. "You do look muzzy, Estelle. You must be higher than Alice."

Estelle said she felt muzzy, but her temperature was not as high as Alice's. Sylvia shook down the thermometer. "You go for Home Sister, Frances. She likes you. I'll stay."

Home Sister was perturbed. "All three, Nurse? I'll come up now." She was even more perturbed when Dr Spence, the S.M.O., diagnosed scarlet fever. "Dear, dear," we heard her cluck as she and the S.M.O. walked slowly towards the lift at the end of our corridor, "how unfortunate! I hope these are not the first batch of a scarlet fever epidemic."

Sylvia and I exchanged another of the many glances we had been exchanging for the past half-hour as the S.M.O. said he hoped not, too. "Most sincerely. But I doubt we'll escape one. Where do those three nurses work?"

"Nurse Dexter in the General Theatre; Nurse Linton in Arthur Ward; Nurse More in Josephine Ward."

"Two wards and one department, plus all the nurses on this floor, and the dining-room staff are already close contacts." He sounded resigned. "The infection's over half the hospital already. I wish I knew where they picked it up."

"You've had no patients develop it?"

"No." Through the crack in my slightly open door we watched him smooth his prematurely thinning hair thoughtfully. "I only hope they picked it up outside, and we haven't a carrier in our midst. Are they particular friends? Do they go out together? It's hard to see the connexion between the general theatre, a male orthopaedic, and female medical."

Sister said Nurse Dorland was Nurse Dexter's great friend, and she was sure I could answer his question.

"Nurse Dorland? Could I see her, Sister?"

Sylvia murmured, "This I must watch. I'll have to copy your technique, Frances . . ." then stepped back behind the door as Home Sister knocked. "Are you there, Nurse? Come along."

The S.M.O. asked me immediately if I had had scarlet.

"Yes, Doctor."

"That's something." He smiled briefly. "How about your three

115

friends. Have you any ideas where they could have met the same contact?"

Home Sister gave me an encouraging nod, as if I was a small child about to repeat a lesson. "Think hard, Nurse."

At which my mind inevitably went blank. "I can't remember . . ." I broke off. "Oh, yes. They went to a film together on Wednesday morning. The Press showing of that new children's film. They said, apart from the critics, they were the only adults in the audience."

Dr Spence looked relieved. "The ideal place to pick up any of the infectious diseases. Wednesday would be right for scarlet. Good." He nodded at Sister. "Let's hope that's the answer, Sister. I'll ring up the M.O.H.'s office later and find if any school cases have been notified. I'm pretty certain the answer'll be yes. There's always the isolated case about. Well—thank you, Nurse. Good night, Sister. I'll fix up about the ambulance. Expect it in forty minutes."

Sister waited until the lift carried him downward, then returned to me. "Nurse Franks may help you pack for your three friends, Nurse. I shall be going with the nurses in the ambulance. When we have gone I want you both to have baths, wash your hair, leave all the clothes you are wearing now soaking in disinfectant in the first bathroom, and then label the bathroom 'out of bounds.' You'll see to that, Nurse? Good girl."

Sylvia bounced out of my room when Sister vanished. "The old girl eats out of your hand, Frances! Why?"

"Search me. Maybe she wants a turkey for Christmas."

An Office Sister arrived on our floor a few minutes later. When the porters arrived for the three girls, she helped Sylvia and I to strip their beds." The bedding will have to be stoved. Put it in the first bathroom for now. I'll lock these doors for to-night. The fumigating can wait until morning. Good night, Nurses. Thank you for your help."

Sylvia said I could have the bath first as she wanted to wash her hair in the hand-basin. "I can't bear shampoo dripping down my back."

I turned on the bath and shed my uniform. "What do we do with our halos? Soak 'em in carbolic, too?"

"No. They'd tarnish." She grinned. "Do tell me—since when have you had this magic touch with blue dresses? I don't remember Sister P.T.S. oozing charm at every pore when you were around, but now you're obviously the Sister's pin-up. Do you suppose they all want turkeys for Christmas?"

"Expect so." I tested the water, absently thinking of the three girls. "I hope they aren't going to be ill."

"No one's ill with scarlet these days." She plunged her head into the basin. "All the same, Estelle looked pretty ill, even though her temp. was only a hundred and one."

116

"She did." I relaxed, and let the warm water soak up the back of my head; that is, I relaxed physically, not mentally. I was too genuinely worried about Estelle to do that. I had not had much nursing experience, but I had had enough in Josephine to recognize how people look when they are, or are about to be, very ill. Estelle had worn that look when she was wheeled to the lift. The little she had been able to tell me about her conversation with Bart might have accounted for some of the wretchedness in her appearance, but surely not for all? "I wish I knew some medicine."

"Don't panic, Frances. Leave that to the S.M.O." She reached for a towel, and scattered shampoo suds all over the floor. "They haven't got the plague—though no one would guess they hadn't after all the fun and games we've had up here to-night."

Some one banged violently on the door. "Frances, are you in there?" demanded Agatha Carter's voice.

"In the bath and washing my hair. Why?"

"Bart More's on the internal phone. He wants you."

"Oh, no! Tell him he can't have me—no . . ." I suddenly realized I wanted to talk to Bart very much. I would have preferred knocking his well-shaped head against the nearest stone wall, but since he was larger than I was, I realized I should have little hope of doing that. "Agatha, explain I'm all wet. Ask him to hang on. Say I want to talk to him, too."

"I will."

Sylvia wound the towel round her dripping hair. "I suppose he's heard about Hannah?"

"Probably," I agreed untruthfully to save argument. "Chuck me that other towel, please."

"Frances!" Agatha was at the door again. "Are you out?"

"Yes?"

"You can get back in. He can't wait. He's got to get a train that leaves in fifteen minutes. He said he just called to let you know he was making tracks. He'll let you know when he gets back."

"Blast the man!" I opened the door furiously. "He might either have let me bath in peace or at least waited to hear about Hannah and the others."

"What about Hannah?" Fay Kinsley appeared behind Agatha. They were both in mufti. "And what are you two doing in there? Turning the place into a Turkish bath?"

Sylvia looked at me and began to laugh. I was very cross with Bart and worried about Estelle, but I had to laugh with her. For the first time in our hospital career, Fay had to come to us for news. "Keep back," we spluttered, "we're unclean—we've been in contact with the plague."

Fay looked gloriously prim. "What is all this nonsense?"

We told her. "You should have been in, Fay," added Sylvia. "It was some party. Dr Spence, Home Sister, an Office Sister, porters, ambulance men—the lot. It's too bad you missed it."

Fay said she considered us utterly cold-blooded and adolescent. "I thought Estelle and Hannah were your friends, Frances. You might at least pretend to be upset instead of just standing there draped like a French movie star laughing your head off."

"I might," I agreed, "if I wasn't so cold-blooded. I'm not just cold, I'm iced. Come in if you must, but forgive me. I'm getting back into the bath."

One of them slammed the door at that. Sylvia leant against it, laughing weakly. "There's only one thing for you to do. Don't wait until Christmas. Send her a turkey right now."

9

TEXT-BOOKS CAN BE WRONG

DR SPENCE was right. By the end of the next week Martha's was hit by what every one hoped would be a minor epidemic. Half-way through the following week a major staff crisis developed. As the incubation period for scarlet fever was short, a steady trickle of nurses, students, and housemen vanished in ambulances to the fever hospital on the other side of London, and in their absence a general post went on among the remaining hospital staff.

We remained unaffected in Out-Patients until the middle of that second week. Simpson, our head nurse, was sent on night-duty in Alberta; Wade, O.P. Two, was removed to the ortho-paedic theatre. Sister O.P. rearranged all the work among the four of us left to her, and that evening Vickers went down with scarlet.

Next morning Nurse Carver, head nurse and O.P. One, actually smiled at me. "As you alone have had it, Dorland, you'll probably find yourself coping with the lot in O.P."

Nurse Stevens, O.P. Two and Three, who had never addressed an unnecessary word to me before, asked, "Think you'll enjoy being kin to the Ancient Mariner, Dorland?"

I had barely time to recover from this double shock when I had a third, and far more shattering one. Sister O.P. appeared in the changing-room. It was half-past seven in the morning; she was not due on duty for another hour; I had never seen her with her cuffs off.

She came in rolling her sleeves high. "Let me have Nurse Vickers' cleaning tin, Nurse. Now then—I'll clean the fracture and skin room. You get on with your routine. Nurse Neal has just started stocking and testing."

Carver noticed my expression, and lowered one eyelid. A little later she stopped in the children's room doorway. "Sister's always like this in a crisis. She can be murder when all's going well . . ."

"And when she finds her nurses gossiping at this hour of the morning!" Sister's awesome figure suddenly loomed behind Carver. "Get on with your work at once, Nurse Carver!"

Carver apologized and vanished. Sister came a couple of steps into the room, and watched me scrubbing a glass trolley. "That's cloudy, child!"

"I'm sorry, Sister." I put down my brush, and took up the soft cloth I used for polishing glass. The cloth was damp with much use; the glass remained cloudy.

Sister watched me impassively. "How many more trolleys have you to do?"

"Seven, Sister." I rubbed violently, and waited for the inevitable lecture on the inefficiency of junior nurses.

"I presume Sister P.T.S. taught you to scrub and polish glass trolleys as you are doing, Nurse?"

"Yes, Sister." I was still waiting.

"You must always do as you were taught in the P.T.S., Nurse. You carry on with your work. I will do these two for you. Will you kindly find me some clean newspaper and methylated spirit?"

I gaped at her momentarily, then rushed to collect her requests.

She received the newspaper and spirit with a brisk nod. "Carry on with your work, Nurse." She poured the spirit on the first glass shelf, crumpled the newspaper, rubbed the shelf briskly, then held it to the light. It was spotless. "An aseptic and quick, if unorthodox method, Nurse," she barked. She dealt with the second shelf, then the second trolley. "Finish the others, quickly, Nurse." She glanced at the bottle of spirit, nodded to me and swept out.

I did not hesitate. I put down my soft rag, and never scrubbed another glass trolley in O.P.

Vickers' absence, and the scarlet epidemic transformed life in Out-Patients. Instead of being a strained department, it became positively hilarious. Sister's temper improved hourly, her bark was almost jovial. Neal was pleasant as ever. Carver and Stevens treated me as if I was one of their set. I found myself looking forward to going on duty instead of dreading it, as previously, and genuinely regretting going off at the end of each day. Our corridor seemed so empty without Estelle and Hannah, and the seven others of my set who had scarlet; the nights were far too long and too quiet.

Possibly because we really were over-working in O.P. for the first time in my life I was suffering from insomnia. And so I had time to think and think about the Professor. And think I did as I stared at the black ceiling, and my thoughts were far blacker than the darkness around me.

It was fairly easy to be sensible about him by day; there was no time to be anything else. Every morning I faced the fact that I was never going to hear from him again; every night that fact made me twist and turn until my pillow felt as heavy as lead and my well-sprung mattress stuffed with sawdust.

I dreaded the nights so much that I began looking forward

to Bart's return from wherever it was he had gone. It was too cold for sitting on park benches now, but he could have stood me a cup of coffee in some dockside cafe. Once I even went along to the Casualty porters to ask if they had his address.

Sam the head porter scratched his head. "Mr More's gone on his holidays, Nurse. He didn't leave no address with us, but the Dean'll have one if you wants to reach him."

I thought this over for twenty-four hours then decided I did want to reach him. I wrote a short letter telling him about the girls.

According to Home Sister, they're doing nicely. I miss them a lot, and want to see you. Ring me when you can, but make it after eight P.M. I'm seldom off before then any day, these days.

I added a P.S.

Sam says you're on holiday. What on earth are you doing having a holiday so close to Finals? If Galahad's big-game hunting in darkest Africa to forget, wouldn't he be more sensible to come back and qualify?

I called in at Home Sister's office on my way out to the post that night. Nurse Charles, the assistant Home Sister was at the desk. "Sister is over at the fever hospital, Nurse Dorland"—she seemed very grave—"so I'm afraid I can give you no report on the nurses until she gets back."

I could not understand why she should look so serious; we had all heard our girls and the various men were doing reasonably well. But she was a sober person who took life grimly so I thought no more of it, thanked her and crossed the road to post my letter.

Sister O.P. looked grim when she joined us for cleaning next morning. I caught her looking at me a couple of times, and wondered what I had done wrong. She was a very much more human person these days, but she was still Sister O.P. and Sister O.P. never lets anything pass.

At ten-past-nine a strange second-year came into the fracture-room. "Are you Dorland? Will you go to Sister? I'm from Cas. I'm to take over from you with this clinic."

"Right, Nurse. I say—do you know why?"

She shrugged. "No one tells me anything."

Sister was in her office. "Come in, Nurse." She looked me over. "You are very white, child. Do you feel well?"

"Yes, thank you, Sister."

"I don't believe you, Nurse. You are much too pale. Go off for two hours and have some fresh air. Walk by the river.

121

Come back at eleven with some colour in your cheeks. Off you go!"

I did not feel at all like going off or taking a walk by the river. It was a dull grey morning, raining fitfully and a sharp east wind was blowing up from the docks. But no one disobeyed Sister O.P., even if the hospital was in the middle of a scarlet epidemic. I went back to the home to leave my cap and fetch a mackintosh.

As I opened our front door Mrs Higgs leant out of her lodge. "There you are, Nurse Dorland! Good. I've just been ringing your floor. Call for you. Go into Three and I'll put the gentleman through."

My immediate thought was that Bart had got my letter. I picked up the receiver in Three and realized he could not have had time, unless he was back in the hospital. "Bart, you're back. I'm so glad. Did you get my letter?" I asked without waiting for him to announce himself. I had no doubts about my caller's identity. Bart was the only man who had telephoned me in months.

"I'm sorry, Frances," said the Professor's voice as calmly as if we had met five minutes and not two months ago; "it's me—Slane."

I thought myself too shaken for speech; I had not realized how deep my training had already gone. I heard my voice say equally calmly, "It's my fault for jumping to conclusions. I was expecting Bart More to ring me—or rather I hoped he'd ring me. How are you?"

He said he was very well and had been out of town for a while. "And you?"

"Oh, fine, thanks."

"And the hospital?"

I said the hospital was not so good and explained why.

"Scarlet fever? Sounds most unpleasant."

I leant against the glass wall and blinked to see if I was awake. Nurse Charles scuttled across the hall carrying a vase of flowers. I was awake. I should never dream about poor old Nurse Charles. "Luckily, it's not very serious these days with the sulfa drugs and what not," I said, quoting all I had heard from my fellow nurses during the past two weeks. "Estelle and Hannah should be coming out soon. They were in the first batch."

"Indeed? I saw Hamilton Dexter having breakfast at my club this morning. I suppose," he asked casually, "he's in town because of his granddaughter's illness?"

"I shouldn't think she's ill enough for that. Perhaps he's up on business."

"Possibly." He was silent momentarily; then he added in a rather odd tone, "Is one quite out of danger from complication by the end of the second week? I had it when I was sixteen—I

122

seem to remember there being some fuss about the second and third week."

"Really?" It seemed so natural to be chatting to him again, and he was chatting so naturally, that the long empty weeks that had filled the endless two months since our last meeting faded like last night's dream. "I honestly don't even know my fevers. We haven't had our lectures on them yet."

"Couldn't More give you the details?"

"He should be able to—if I knew where he was. He's taken a holiday of all crazy things. Just vanished. He doesn't even know anyone's got scarlet for all I know."

There was another small silence. "Vanished? How's that?"

I told him the truth, if not all the truth.

"So after hearing what you describe as an overwhelming bit of news, he took himself off? I follow his reasoning."

I looked across at Mrs Higgs and wondered why I had never realized she had such a pleasant face before. "I can't. He ought to realize he's hurting her badly."

"But does he?"

I had to be fair. "I rather doubt it. That's why I want to see him."

"So you wrote care of the Dean? That was intelligent."

"Not really. Sam, our head porter, gave me that tip. Our porters," I added cheerfully, as happiness broke through properly and I realized I was actually talking to him again, "are incurably sentimental. They see themselves as so many bluejacketed cupids."

He said he was sure they must be exceedingly helpful under certain circumstances. "And now I must tell you why I've bothered you with this call."

I stiffened. He was obviously married; going abroad for years; emigrating. "I'm afraid I've been talking too much, as usual."

"No. No. In point of fact I thought I'd give you a ring to ask how you were getting on. It's a long while since I heard from you, and, being back again, I thought it might be an idea to find out if all was well with you. Is it?"

I hesitated. I could not conceivably tell him the truth or remind him that he had been the person to write, since the last letter in our correspondence had been written by me. "I—I think so, thank you."

"You don't sound very sure."

"Life," I said tritely, "is always full of problems."

"I know. You think everything's splendid, turn a corner, and there's life waiting for you with a sandbag." He paused, then asked with strange abruptness, "Have you got a good memory?"

"It's sort of photographic. I remember things as pictures."

He did not tell me, as any one else would have done, that I

was repeating myself unnecessarily. He merely said, "That's convenient. Then can you recollect one letter I wrote you in your P.T.S.? In the days when we were dealing with curdled custards? In case you've forgotten—which is only too probable, since you must have many other things to remember—it was a letter in which I said I'd be happy to help out with any problems. You've obviously been too busy to take me up on that recently, but if you should"—he paused again—"need help, let me know."

I had often read about people's hearts bounding against their ribs in moments of emotional stress. I never believed it actually happened. It happened, all right. "It's very kind of you. I haven't liked to keep on bothering you."

"Frances," he said slowly, "I'm going to tell you something. When a man gets to my age he seldom says and never writes anything he doesn't mean. So don't forget what I've said. I'm glad you are well. I hope young More returns soon. I'm pretty sure he will. Good-bye—but remember, if you want to get in touch with me you know where to find me." And before I could even thank him for phoning he had rung off.

Sister O.P. gave me an approving nod when I returned at eleven. "The fresh air has done you good, Nurse. You look a different child. Go along and help Nurse Neal with the skins."

I had only spent an hour in the skin-clinic when Sister summoned me once more. "You are making up your lost off-duty to-day, Nurse. Matron wishes you to go on night-duty in William MacPherson to-night. And for the next hour you are to go to Casualty. Go along there now."

Sister Casualty looked doubtfully at my first-year belt. "You've not worked here before, Nurse? Oh, well. We're lucky to have you. Go and help with the dressings in Room 15. The senior dressers are in there. They'll be very useful to you."

The masked dressers, with sleeves rolled high and ties buttoned in their shirts, greeted me like old friends. It took me a few minutes to realize they were old friends. They had been clerks in Josephine. "Have you heard John Jones has been smitten with the plague?" one asked.

"The Jones in Josephine? Our houseman?"

"That's our John! What with old Curtis having been called over, the entire cardiac firm seems to be moving across to fevers."

"Dr Curtis called over? Who for?"

None of them knew. They shook their heads, I shook mine. We agreed that whoever needed Dr Curtis had had his—or her —chips. There was no slur on Dr Curtis in that reflection. He was considered one of the best cardiologists in England by out-

124

siders; at Martha's we considered him far away the best; but the fact that another hospital had sent for him automatically meant that the medical staff of that hospital were very worried. Hospitals seldom call in consultants from other hospitals, except, it was generally accepted, as a last hope.

I looked round the dressing-room. It was filled to capacity with men with minor injuries. "Who's the houseman?"

At that moment Dr Perry the Senior Out-Patients Officer walked in. "Sorry I'm late, gentlemen." He nodded my way, then recognized me. "You an exile too, Nurse? Let's get on. Forgive the delay"—he washed his hands—"but I've had to do a round in place of Dr Jones. I suppose you've heard he has it?"

"Yes. I'm so sorry." I handed him a towel.

"Thanks." He dried his fingers carefully. "It's tough all round. The S.M.O. looks fit to drop this morning. You've heard about Dr Curtis? Rough, that. Well—who's first?" He glanced through the pile of admission cards on the standing desk. "Who's Mr J. A. Holloway?"

A man in a wheel-chair by the far sink held up one hand. "Here, Doctor."

Dr Perry walked over to him. "What've you been doing to this foot, man? Dropping bricks on it?"

Mr Holloway grinned. "That's right, sir."

"Were you wearing this?" Dr Perry picked up a discarded boot and examined it. "Stout. Good. Let's hope it's saved you a fracture." He wrote rapidly on a card. "Nurse. X-Ray in a chair, please. Wet plates back here. Next?"

It seemed only five minutes later that Sister Casualty was beckoning me from the door. "Thank you for your help, Nurse. You must go to lunch. I'll take over in here."

I went back to Out-Patients for my cloak, walked out of the department into the main corridor, and Bart.

I jumped back. "The very man I want to see. When did you get back? I suppose you've had no chance of getting my letter?"

He looked at me in a peculiar fashion. He seemed dazed. "Letter? I haven't had any letter from you."

"I've just said—you haven't had time. I only posted it last night. It was to tell you about Estelle."

He said dully, "So you know?"

"Of course, I know she's got scarlet. She was in the original batch. But, Bart—why did you have to vanish?"

He looked up and down the corridor. "I've got to talk to you, Frances. When are you off?"

"I'm on my way to lunch now. I want to talk to you too. It'll have to keep until afterwards."

"What I have to say can't keep. Come to the canteen."

125

"I can't——"

"You've got to," he said simply. "Come."

I looked at him momentarily, then did as he said. I did not know what was wrong; I only knew from his expression that, whatever it was, it was very wrong. I went with him to the canteen. We chose a table against the far wall. We did not bother to eat or drink anything.

He sat down stiffly as if he was very old. "I don't believe you can know about Estelle."

I sat very still. "What about her?"

He avoided my eyes. "Curtis has been called in. He saw her last night—again this morning."

"Curtis? For scarlet?" My voice cracked. "Why?"

"According to Nigel Curtis"—his voice was without emotion —"she's got suppurative pericarditis. Understand?"

"From scarlet?" He nodded. "No. At least, I know roughly what it means, but not how she could get it."

He turned on me savagely, "God, woman! Don't you know anything? It isn't common—according to the books it occurs, quote, in a small percentage of cases. And she's had to get it. Curtis was hauled in—he hauled in Marcus Everly—they both spent most of last night there. Hamilton Dexter went over with Curtis last night. They sent for him during the evening. You know what that means?"

I said very carefully. "She's on the D.I.L.?"

"And what the devil else would she be on?" he snapped, with the petulance of extreme anxiety.

I had been so happy since the Professor's phone. Now I was in a nightmare. I had to wake up out of it. I had to discover we were not talking about Estelle. But I was awake—and we were.

"Bart. What's the prognosis?"

He shook his head.

"Bart. There has to be one."

"All right," he said bitterly, "all right. Maybe there is a good one. Maybe I missed it this morning. Maybe I looked in all the wrong books. God, Frances! I looked in the lot. I've been reading up on it since I got back to town just after eight. There's not a ruddy word on it in our library I haven't read. I'm a bloody mine of information on suppurative pericarditis as a rare complication of scarlet fever. And I can't give you a damned answer because I daren't."

And I dare not think we were talking about Estelle. Women are not supposed to make good friends to each other. I did not know if that was true or not. I only knew I was as saddened as I would have been had she been one of my sisters.

"How did you hear?"

He explained he had been on a walking tour with Nigel Curtis.

126

"He's in my year. We were in Salisbury last night. Nigel rang his mother just to say hallo. Mrs Curtis gave him the news of the old firm, and said his old man had been called over to see one of the nurses. Since the nurse was Hamilton Dexter's granddaughter, she obviously made news. Nigel passed it on to me." He lit a cigarette. "I came up by the first train. Not that there's anything I can do. I just had to be up."

I was too distressed for coherent thought yet. "Why has Curtis called in Marcus Everly?"

"Frances, do you have to be so bloody dumb? It's suppurative. That means pus. Pus means bugs. Who's the bug king here?"

I was quite glad to have him storm at me. It acted as a safety valve for him and did not touch me at all.

"What can he do about the bugs?"

"Am I a bleeding pathologist?" He stubbed out his cigarette. "Frances, I'm sorry. I really am. I shouldn't give you hell like this."

"That's all right. You're in it—why shouldn't I share it. I like her, too."

He touched my hand. "I know."

We sat in silence. At last I said, "You had better write to her."

"Sure." His lips twisted. "And maybe send her a lock of my hair?"

"Bart. I'm serious."

"And what do you think I am?" He pushed his hand through his hair. "You're a good kid. You mean to be kind. You don't know what she's up against. She's on the D.I., and the mortality rate, for your information, is——"

"I don't want to know it." I slapped the table with the flat of my hand. "I refuse to believe Estelle's booked. And I refuse to listen to any more of the nonsense I've listened to before from you about her." I met his eyes. "You must write to her. You won't be allowed to see her—but you can write."

"It's too damn late. She'd be too ill to read. You don't understand."

"Maybe I don't understand much medicine. Or men. But I know a packet about women, particularly young women. And I have nursed very ill women. The most irrational things can make a power of difference to a very ill woman; I've seen it happen. I'm just talking about what I've seen—get that—and not what I've read up in the books! I haven't read any books. But I've seen things—things like an indigestible cake cooked by some miserable husband who has never done so much as the washing-up before, a bunch of withered dandelions, or a get-well card in smudged capitals with finger-marks all over it. I've seen these things sway the balance with the women in Josephine. I remember three women"—I had to stop for breath—"three

D.I. women, who were too weak to hold an envelope or read, but not too weak to read the writing on that envelope, smiling when they should have been dead. We used to read them their letters, then prop their envelopes on their bed-tables so that they could lie and look at them. Don't tell me what the books say! I don't give a damn! I'm telling you what actually happens in real life!"

"But—but—it wouldn't make any difference to her."

I turned on him quite as furiously as he had on me. "Do you have to be so bloody dumb? Can't you tell when a girl's in love with you?"

He just looked at me, then slowly tapped his chest.

I nodded.

He stood up carefully, as if he had been ill and was not sure his legs would support him. A group of students at the next table watched us openly. We ignored them. We might have been the only two people in the world.

I got on my feet. "I must go to lunch. I'm on nights to-night."

"Where?" His voice did not seem to belong to him.

"William MacPherson."

We walked out of the canteen. In the corridor he stood still. "I'll be taking a letter over to her this afternoon. If I've any news of her I'll bring it up to Willie Mac, to-night."

I was breathing as if I had been running hard. "Good. But what about Night Sister?"

"To hell with her. I'll get up somehow."

I was very late for lunch. Sister Dining-room was very annoyed. "It is most inconsiderate of you to be so unpunctual, Nurse Dorland."

I apologized mechanically, helped myself to a plate of food, and carried it over to the half-empty first-year table.

Sylvia pulled out the chair beside her. "I'm so glad you've made this meal."

"Thanks." I sat down.

She looked at me. "Frances, what's up? You look queer."

I said that was how I felt and told her why.

The whole of our table was listening before I had finished; my news spread quickly to the other tables; a strange, strained silence settled over the normally lively dining-room. The silence was in the Home all that afternoon and evening when I lay in bed unable to sleep, watched the sun go down, and thought of Estelle dying.

The hospital smelt different by night. The air was heavy with a mixture of cooking, coal, ether, and iodoform. I wondered how any one could sleep or work in that atmosphere and if it really was as intolerable as it seemed to me or if acute anxiety had put an edge on my senses. The main corridor was probably

128

no more deserted than was usual for that hour of the night, but as I walked to the dining-room it seemed to be a desolate place. I had asked Nurse Charles for news of Estelle before leaving our Home. She had told me Matron and Home Sister had gone over to the fever hospital; "I'm afraid," she added, with the typical hospital understatement that so infuriates the outside world, "Nurse Dexter is not very well." I had not been infuriated; I had been frozen with fear. "Not very well" when translated meant desperately ill.

She need not have said any more after telling me about Matron. Matrons do not leave large general hospitals at eight at night to visit sick members of their staff in other hospitals without good reason. I glanced at her office as I went by. An Office Sister was pinning a notice to the board over the letter pigeon-holes. The lights were on in the outer office, but Matron's private room beyond was in darkness. I could see this because her door was half open—all the office doors in Martha's were left open when their occupants were elsewhere. That darkened room made me wince mentally. I was as scared of Matron as we all were, but because she was out of the hospital I felt as I used to when I was a child, and my mother was out.

At Martha's the night staff took supper in the evening, dinner in the middle of the night, breakfast in the morning. Tea and coffee were provided at all meals. The girl sitting next to me at the junior table told me that some hospitals served breakfast at night and supper in the morning. "We much prefer it our way round. I expect you will too." She looked at my belt. "First-year. First nights?"

"Yes."

"Poor thing." She smiled pleasantly. "I'm Ames. In Henry. Where are you going?"

"William MacPherson."

She looked at me keenly. "Are you Dorland?"

"Yes." I braced myself.

"Isn't Estelle Dexter in your set?"

"Yes."

"Is it true she's on the D.I.L.?"

"Yes."

A girl on my other side turned to us. "Matron's been over there all evening."

"Oh, God!" said Ames. "Are you sure, Polly?"

The girl called Polly nodded. "Poor girl must be on her way out."

I said nothing. I caught Ames looking at me and then frowning at Polly. "Dexter's in Dorland's set," she said simply, and for the rest of that meal no one at our table spoke at all. I thought they were quiet because they were night nurses. It was not until nights later that I discovered that night nurses' meals

129

were hilarious affairs, and permitted to be far more noisy than any in the day-time.

The night senior in William MacPherson was named Nixon. She was a tall, very slim young woman with a cool voice and prim manner. William MacPherson was a male general surgical ward. When the day report was over Nurse Nixon took me into the kitchen. "Your first night duty, Dorland?"

"Yes, Nurse."

She handed me a work-list. "I wrote this out this morning. You had better read it through while the milk's heating for the men's drinks. I'll take you round and give you a quick diagnosis class directly I've got my evening drugs out."

Her work-list covered both sides of four large sheets of writing-paper. I read it through twice and wondered how any one night would be long enough for me to do all the work listed. I knew I had no hope of remembering it yet, so, as the kitchen was apparently my domain at night, I clipped the pages to a spare bed-ticket and propped it on the dresser. I consulted that list roughly every ten minutes throughout the night. When I did this a little after midnight I found an extra sheet had been added. "Sorry, no change. B.M.," was scribbled in pencil across that sheet. I looked at the words for a few seconds, then removed the page and pushed it into my apron bib. I had no feelings at all at that moment. I was not a person; I was a machine in a starched uniform. And because I was a machine I was able to keep up with that work-list.

Once, like the echo of a forgotten song, I remembered how happy I had been after the Professor's phone call that morning. And then, just as he had said, life had waited for me round the corner with a sandbag. One day, I thought, I'll tell him how prophetic his words have proved. One day. But I did not really believe that day would come. The night was too dark; the ward too dim; and even the patients were shadows.

Nixon came into the kitchen after Night Sister's 2 A.M. round. "I didn't realize Dexter was a friend of yours and in your set, Dorland."

I was cutting bread. I put down the knife. "Was, Nurse?"

"Sorry—I mean—is."

I took up the knife carefully as if it was hot. "Did Night Sister mention how she is, Nurse?"

She hesitated. "No change yet, I'm afraid. Night Sister met Sir Marcus downstairs just before she came up here. He's on his way over to Dexter now."

My ignorance brought me close to tears. "Is that good or bad, Nurse?"

She had been standing in the doorway. She stepped out into the corridor momentarily, looked down towards the quiet ward, came back again. "I'm no physician, Dorland. I can't honestly

130

answer that. But I am an S.R.N., and I do know that if I was Dexter now there are no two men in the world I'd rather have had by my bedside than John Curtis and Marcus Everly. If she can be hauled back from the gates those two men'll haul her."

Her expression was so sympathetic, her voice so gentle, I wondered I had ever thought her prim and cool.

"Some one told me this morning—there's no prognosis."

She came up to the table, and began buttering the bread I had cut. "Some one might be right, theoretically. In actual fact that's never true. I've spent four years here. I've seen people who were booked walk out of here cured. Not once—dozens of times. I've seen the dying become the living—pass me that empty plate—for no good reason at all on paper. And I've seen other people die, for as little reason. Dexter's in a bad way, but she's young, strong, and must have a tremendous will or she would never have come to work here. Nursing's no sinecure—no gentle art—no soft hands on fevered brows"—she buttered efficiently, stacking as she went—"it's just plain damned hard and badly paid work, with long hours and no glamour. You have to be tough to take it—and tough people don't die easily. You'll be surprised how much it takes to kill a strong human being. Dexter may be facing the last enemy right now as the small hours are on us, but she's strong all right. I don't need to know her, to know that."

I said, "She's tough, Nurse."

"So are John Curtis and Marcus Everly. They won't give up easily, either. They wouldn't for any patient, but they'll hang on just that much longer because she's what she is."

"Hamilton Dexter's granddaughter?"

"Not that. One of our pros." She laid a clean, dampened tea-towel over the first filled plate of bread and butter, put it on top of the fridge, and began filling a second plate. "That's what's hit the hospital. She's one of our girls, and there's not a member of Martha's to-night who isn't thinking, There but for the grace of God go I." She glanced at me. "We get used to seeing the patients ill; even used to them dying. When they do we get upset if we know them. We can't get upset for those we don't know. We have to forget them. We'd all have nervous breakdowns if we didn't." She took another look at the ward, then came back. "We haven't any D.I.'s up here, but there'll be some in Martha's to-night. There are names on the list every night. They may cast a shadow over their respective wards, but that's as far as it'll go. Yet because one of our first-year pro's may be on the way out, to-night there's a shadow over all Martha's."

"I thought it would just be over my set." I reached into the bread-bin for another loaf. "And her friends and family."

"She's one of our girls," Nixon said again. "So we're all part of the family. That's why Matron, Home Sister, John Curtis, and Marcus Everly are all up and over there with her. And there's not one pundit on our staff who wouldn't be out of his bed to-night at the drop of a hat, if he was called in. Good hospitals look after their own. This is a very good hospital." She had finished buttering. She covered the last plate and washed her hands. "When you've cleared up in here, come into the ward. There's something I have to show you."

"About Dexter, Nurse?" I asked urgently.

"Take a grip, Dorland," she said not unkindly. "I know you aren't with us at all just now—all the same, take a grip. We've got work to do. Even if we feel like weeping we've no time for tears. Get rid of those bread-crumbs and join me in the ward. I've got to show you how to write a night report. Night Sister insists all juniors learn that during their first night on."

I apologized. "Yes, Nurse. Thank you."

10

A MAN WITH A MICROSCOPE

THERE was a weighing machine in one of the ward bathrooms. It was an old-fashioned machine, a cross between a wheelbarrow and an armchair. The bathroom had white tiles on the walls, green tiles on the floor, and was the room in which the night junior in William MacPherson folded, counted, and listed the soiled linen used in the past twenty-four hours at half-past four every morning. The soiled linen was the final routine item on the list Nixon had made for me. At five we officially started work.

I finished with ten minutes to spare. I spent those minutes sitting on the weighing machine, too weary for anxiety or even coherent thought. To keep awake I counted the floor tiles, then the walls, one at a time. "Eighteen—nineteen—Estelle's nineteen and perhaps she's dead, so she was nineteen—I won't think of that now—twenty—twenty-one—the Professor's forty-two—I wish he was here—I'll write . . ."

"Dorland! What are you talking about?" Nixon came in. "And just what do you think you're doing in that machine? Don't you know you never sit down on duty?"

I stood up stiffly. "Sorry, Nurse." I yawned. "I forgot."

"Don't forget again," she said sternly. "I don't mind you sitting down—you can lie down for all I care—but if you or any other night junior sits at this hour you'll inevitably go clean off to sleep. Martha's night nurses do not drop asleep on duty —and that I do care about. If you feel exhausted lean against something—never sit. If you pass out standing you'll wake up when you hit the floor. So keep on your feet in future. Now come on. It's time we did some work."

Home Sister looked as tired as I felt when I knocked at her office after breakfast. "I'm sorry, Nurse Dorland. I'm afraid Nurse Dexter is not very well this morning."

Nurse Charles had used those words last night without infuriating me; this morning I knew exactly how the general public felt. Why couldn't Sister be honest and say the poor girl was booked, I thought savagely, as the lift took me upwards. How could it help to talk as if Estelle had a cold in the head?

I rang Bart on the internal phone at the end of our corridor

133

before going to my room. It was not yet nine, and there was just a chance I might catch him in Casualty before the morning rounds and lectures started.

The porter I spoke to had never heard of Mr More. I asked for Sam. Sam was sympathetic but unable to help.

"Like me to ask him to give you a ring if I see him come in, Nurse?"

"I don't think so, thanks. I've got to go to bed."

He cleared his throat. "I'm—sorry about that Nurse Dexter, Nurse. Pal of yours, ain't she? They say as she's what you might call poorly."

"Yes," I said, "you might. Thanks, Sam."

I stormed back to my room and sat down to write to the Professor. Writing was the next best thing to talking to him, and I had to talk to some one. My head dropped forward before I finished one paragraph. I tried to hold it up; it was too heavy; it went on dropping forward until the back of my neck ached. I left that letter unfinished and lay on my bed, meaning to take a short nap and then go on writing. I fell asleep as if I had been pole-axed. Some time in the afternoon I woke to find I was very cold, had ruined a cap, and left streaks of black shoe-polish on my white bedspread, since I had forgotten to take off my shoes.

It seemed only five minutes later that Sylvia Franks was shaking me. "Frances, your first supper bell's gone. Get up!" She gave me another shake. "Awake? Good. Listen. I've only got a couple of minutes—Sister Margaret sent me over for a clean apron. Estelle's as she was this morning according to Home Sister at tea-time, and I've just been stopped by Bart More. He asked me to say he's sorry he missed your call this morning and hopes you got his message in Willie Mac."

"I did. Thanks. Anything else?"

She shook her head. "Should there be?"

"I hoped so. Maybe he'll ring later."

"I don't suppose he will or he wouldn't have stopped me," she pointed out reasonably. "I'd adore to ask leading questions, but I simply haven't time. Just tell me quickly—how did you get on in Willie Mac.? Senior decent?"

"Not too bad. Thanks for coming in."

Home Sister was in our hall when I raced downstairs a few minutes later. The lift was in use, and I could not afford to waste time waiting.

Home Sister disapproved of racing, and I expected a stern warning when I leapt round the final turning on the stairs, then slowed—obviously only because she was there. She merely smiled kindly. "Oversleep, Nurse? Poor child. This must be an anxious period for you in every way."

I thanked her mechanically. While I cut the bread in William MacPherson kitchen a couple of hours after, I thought about Home Sister. She was a nice old thing, and I was growing quite fond of her, but I could not understand at all why she should be so indulgent with me.

Nixon's head came round the door. "Leave the bread. Those post-ops. have come round. Come and help me sit them up."

One of the four men who had been operated on that afternoon was having a blood-transfusion. Nixon altered the speed of the drops of blood falling through the glass drip-connexion. "He's got to have one more pint of whole blood after this, then switch to glucose-saline. This"—she illuminated the vacolitre on the stand with her pocket torch—"will take about twenty minutes to run through. Ever changed blood before? Then I'll show you how. Join me in fifteen minutes."

We were changing the vacolitres when Night Sister arrived for her first round. She looked up the ward, saw what we were doing, and drifted to the centre table.

"I'll have to go," muttered Nixon, altering the rate again. "This is running all right. Dump that empty in the sluice for the moment—rinse it later. You must stay in the ward while I'm held up with Night Sister, so you may as well begin my four-hourly temps. The book's on the desk."

A few of our men had not yet gone to sleep. "You going to be our regular night, Nurse?" one asked.

"I believe so." I offered him a thermometer. "Under your tongue, please."

His name was Doughty, and to-night he had a face. I knew his name because Nixon had made me learn all their names by heart last night. "Night Sister'll test you on the names any time after and including your second night."

The other men had faces as well as names, but they were not yet people to me. They were not really patients, either. As I had only nursed women previously, patients were still always female in my mind. I knew how to treat sick women; I had no conception of how to treat sick men; nor had I realized how heavy men were in comparison with women.

I did not talk to any of our men that night, but as I did not wish to seem unpleasant, took Neal's advice on smiling. Much to my surprise, her advice worked excellently.

Nixon beckoned me to the centre table when Night Sister's long, slow round of all the men was over. "You've gone down well with our men, Dorland."

"Me, Nurse? But I don't know them—or they me."

"Don't kid yourself they don't know you. Patients know all there is to know about a new nurse after she's been five minutes in a ward. They watch everything. They think"—she smiled slightly—"you're ever such a nice little nurse. Ever so quiet with a real lovely smile. Now, sit down." She drew out the chair

135

by her. "I've news for you. Night Sister said I could pass it on as she knew you'd want to hear it. It's all right. It's quite good."

The table was shielded by two red screens. The ends of the screens were left open to allow any one at the table a clear view of both ends of the ward. The overhead light directly over the table was pulled down to the full length of its flex. It hung only a few inches over our heads, and, being swathed in a red shade cover, threw a pool of rose-coloured light on the table.

I sat down quickly and folded my hands in my lap. My apron looked pink. "Good? About Dexter?"

She nodded. Her cap was also pink. "She's beginning to respond."

"To what? I thought there was no treatment? I looked it up yesterday——"

"What did you look it up in?"

I named a standard text-book of medicine.

"When was that written?"

"I don't know, Nurse." I wished she would get on and stop this futile cross-examination.

"I do. Before the last war. Practically before the sulfa drugs, certainly before penicillin and the mycins. So just forget all you read and listen to me. See here." She took a clean case-history sheet from Sister William MacPherson's file and drew a rough diagram of the heart. "Here's the pericardium. She's got a purulent effusion here." She shaded an area. "Right? Well, she had a paracentesis this morning."

I had to stop her. "What's that, Nurse?"

"I keep forgetting how little you know. They drew off some fluid."

I looked at the drawing, then at her. "Direct? Isn't it a moving target?"

"Of course. It's fairly simple if you know how. I've seen John Curtis do it—oh, half a dozen times. He sticks in a long, wide needle first—the needle moves with the beats—then fixes on the syringe. Roughly"—more shading—"it goes in here. Between the fourth and fifth left interspaces." She put down her pencil, and tapped my chest with one finger. "About an inch from the sternum."

"Simple," I echoed, feeling torn between concern for Estelle and academic interest. "How much is taken off?"

"Can be a few hundred c.c.'s. I'm not sure how much they took off Dexter. Point is this—shifting the fluid gives the patient a lot of relief and the Path. Lab. something tangible to work on."

"Isolating the bugs?"

"That's right. Until they know what they're dealing with

136

they can't know what weapons to use." She turned her head sharply to the left. "That's either Chalmers coughing in his sleep or Davis about to be sick. Go and see."

I returned a few seconds later. "Chalmers coughing. Davis is asleep, too."

"Good." She looked up and down the ward. "Then we can go on. They're all right for the moment and far quieter than I expected us to be to-night. Of course, we've still one empty bed."

I sat down again. "Think we'll have an admission?"

"We haven't had one for three nights. We're due for one." She frowned at her drawing. "What was I saying?"

I told her. "Just what is she responding to, Nurse?"

"Chemotherapy. Oh, Lord—you don't understand? That's the treatment of disease by chemical means. It's all chemotherapy these days—plus nursing plus plus, where hearts are involved. That's where the path. boys come in. And why John Curtis needed Marcus Everly. With some ailments you can hit back sort of at random. But all these new drugs put a strain on the heart, and you can't risk that to some one who's heart is already in a bad way. They had to be absolutely specific. They are now. She's shown a slight but definite improve—— Oh, damn!" The buzz of the night bell on the duty-room telephone hissed up the ward. "I thought this quiet was too good to last. There goes our empty bed." She shot soundless out of the ward. She was back immediately. "Acute appendix for operation to-night. On the way up now. Go and fill two hotties while I shove in the electric blanket."

The new patient was a youngish man with dark hair and anxious eyes. His name was Huckle.

"Been in hospital before, Mr Huckle?" asked Nixon.

"Not me, Nurse." He glanced nervously at the drawn curtains round his bed. "Never had the knife, neither. Proper turn up for the book, this is."

Nixon said she was sure it was and held up an operation gown. "I'm afraid this may seem a bit odd—it ties at the back."

" 'Streuth." He grinned suddenly. "Proper draughty."

"Not if you're lying down. No—we can manage, thanks—don't try and move or you may bring the pain back. That's it." She shook out the long, thick woollen stockings I had brought with his theatre pack. "These'll keep your feet warm."

The stockings amused him as much as the gown. "Hand-knitted, eh? You nurses knit 'em? Reckon," he added, without waiting for an answer, "you must be quite glad of the job of a night. There can't be much for you to do, seeing as the lads are all asleep."

Nixon caught my eye momentarily. "I always enjoy knitting," she said amicably, and went off to scrub her hands before preparing his skin.

When he was ready she told me to scrub my hands. "You can give his premedication injection. I'll witness."

Huckle looked surprised to see us. "More carry-on?"

"Just a little more. An injection into your arm. It won't hurt." Nixon rolled up his gown sleeve. "It won't put you to sleep, either. It'll just make you feel very-nicely-thank-you."

He smiled up at us. "Bit of all right, eh?"

She watched me critically, then patted his hand. "Didn't feel that, did you?"

"Nah." He raised a finger at me. "Reckon you're used to bunging in needles, eh, Nurse?"

I had given three injections in Josephine. This was my fourth attempt. "Oh, yes, Mr Huckle."

Nixon told him I should be going to the theatre with him. "Now try and sleep a little before the trolley arrives."

My mouth felt dry as I rinsed that syringe. Nixon had followed me into the sluice. "Been through with a case yet, Dorland?"

"No, Nurse."

"Never mind. You have to start some time, and must to-night as I can't leave the ward. Don't look so worried. You won't be expected to know or do anything, apart from holding his hand when he goes under, and have an anaesthetic bowl handy on the return journey, in case he vomits. The theatre staff'll show you where and how to dress up; the theatre porters'll know exactly how to cope if anything goes wrong on the way up or down. Just do what they tell you. Let's see—who's on theatre call to-night?" She thought for a moment. "Blakelock and Paton are the porters on. Blakelock's wonderful; Paton can be moody, but he knows his stuff. Nurse Howard, the senior staff nurse, is on, too. Pity."

My heart sank. "Why, Nurse?"

"She doesn't like ward nurses cluttering up her theatre. Don't feel hurt if she sends you up to the gallery. She's done that before. She's not too bad," she added, smiling faintly at my expression; "she just doesn't like ward nurses. Think you'll feel queer?"

"I don't know, Nurse," I said truthfully.

"If the floor does start coming up at you, keep your head down. Tie your shoelace or pick something off the floor. And don't watch the incision to-night. That's always the worst moment. All right?" She turned to go, then swung round. "I nearly forgot. I saw this sitting on the sand in the fire bucket by the door ten minutes ago. It's for you."

I recognized Bart's handwriting on the envelope she handed me, and pushed it in my apron bib to read later. I forgot all

138

about it until I took off my apron in the theatre changing-room, and it dropped on the floor.

Staff Nurse Howard watched me pick it up. "Don't you bother to read your post, Nurse?"

I put it in one of my pockets. "I forgot to read it, Nurse."

She raised an eyebrow. "Nurses are supposed to have good memories," she announced, in a very fine copy of Sister Out-Patients' favourite tone.

"Yes, Nurse," I agreed, and attempted to tie my turban.

"Nurse," she drawled, "you are about to attend an operation, not take a bath. Give it to me and stand still." She flicked the linen triangle into the correct folds. "The point goes over your head—so—and the ends tie at the back, then tuck in. Like mine." She turned her head for my inspection. "See? You must prevent its riding up—and never fix it with a bow in front." She looked me over. "Take one of those gowns on the left; the top one. It should fit you. Now all you need are over-boots—that cupboard on your left—and a mask. Take one from the jar just inside the anaesthetic room. Put it on and keep it on until your man comes out of the theatre."

Huckle looked as pleased to see me as I was to see him when I rejoined him in the anaesthetic room. "Hallo, Nurse. You do look different. I'm glad you're back. I was feeling on me own, like. Proper strange."

I could hardly explain that I felt the same, so I smiled. "I'm back to stay." I tied on my mask. "In disguise."

"You are an' all!" His hands gripped the sides of his stretcher nervously. "Rare do, this is. Never thought I'd be moved up in the like, I didn't."

I touched his right hand. "Like to hang on to me?"

"Ta, Nurse." His fingers tightened round mine. "I know this'll sound real soft, but I'm—well, I'm—not too happy about all this."

"I don't blame you. You've never been in hospital before. It must be an awful shock for any man. Don't worry about it sounding soft. No one in their senses likes having an operation."

"You don't say?" He brightened visibly. "'Streuth, I'm dry. I could do with a pint, right now."

"That's the injection you had in the ward. It makes you dry."

He sighed drowsily as the effect of his premedication deepened. "Got to know a lot to be a nurse, ain't you? Queer life, though. Seeing blokes sick and being cut up and the like. Don't worry you nothing?"

"Not at all." I was glad I wore a mask. "One gets used to these things."

He said he reckoned one did. He sounded relieved.

The theatre porter was fiddling with the knobs on the

139

anaesthetic trolley. He caught my eye, jerked a thumb upward, then returned to his fiddling.

Huckle sighed again. " 'Streuth. I could sleep for a week an' all."

The anaesthetist had come in. "Sleepy? Splendid." He pulled down his mask. "Remember me? I listened to your chest in Casualty. Just let me have your right arm. That's the form. Get his sleeve up, Nurse—and you make a fist, lad. Right. Now"—he held his syringe poised and swabbed the injection site with spirit—"just a little prick coming."

The telephone bell jangled in the theatre corridor as Huckle went under. "Oh, God," murmured the anaesthetist, continuing his slow injection, "if that's another surgical emergency I'm getting out. What's the matter with them all to-night? Aren't there other hospitals in London? Eh, Nurse?"

I glanced round before answering in case he was speaking to another nurse. Doctors in large hospitals do not as a rule address unnecessary remarks to junior nurses. I was the only nurse in the room, so I said I had heard there were other hospitals.

"Then why can't they take their acute abdos. there?" demanded the anaesthetist, laying aside the syringe and picking up a laryngeal tube. "What"—he readjusted the angled mirror on a head band and slipped it on his head—"is wrong with Thomas's, Guy's, and Bart's? Good hospitals? Of course. So why don't the customers use them and give poor old Martha's a rest?"

The porter who had answered the telephone returned at that moment. "Not an admission, sir. The Night Sister just wants a word with Nurse Howard."

"Thank God for that," said the anaesthetist piously. "Let's have that gag, Blakelock. I want to get this tube in."

We heard Nurse Howard's voice clearly as the corridor phone was only a couple of feet from the open anaesthetic room door. She sounded annoyed. "Actually, we are just about to start, Sister. Mr Fraser's scrubbing now." She paused. Then: "We've only got one, Sister. Sister Theatre likes us to keep a spare. I suppose," she added, with obvious reluctance, "he'll have to have it, if he wants it. Right away? Oh." There was a second long pause. "I see. May I just—that is, would you mind holding on one moment, please, Sister?" She came into the anaesthetic room. "Nearly ready, Dr Elks?"

"Not nearly. I'm ready." The anaesthetist did not look up. "Stand by to shift that trolley, Blakelock."

Nurse Howard turned to the porter. "How heavy is he, Blakelock? Can nurse and my duty nurse lift him?"

The porter shook his head gloomily. "Not unless we want him on the floor, Nurse. He's all of fourteen stone."

"I see." She looked at me. "Dr Elks, do you need the ward nurse? Can I borrow her?"

"Take her. I don't want her." He glanced up suddenly and nodded at me. "You'll appreciate that I'm speaking professionally, Nurse."

Howard ignored his rider, and returned to the phone. "Sister, can I send it up with the ward nurse? She's very junior and will only be in the way. I know he doesn't like——" She stopped speaking as Sister apparently interrupted her. "I don't know. From William MacPherson. Oh? It'll be all right? Thanks, Sister. I'll send her up now."

"I don't know where you're going, Nurse," said the anaesthetist, "but before you go would you tighten the top strings of my mask. I haven't got a hand."

Howard joined us. "Is your name Dorland, Nurse?"

"Yes, Nurse."

The anaesthetist glanced round sharply, nearly causing me to break one of the mask strings I was retieing. His eyes were amused and curious. Howard's eyes over her mask were equally curious.

"When you've done," she said politely, "would you come with me, please, Nurse?"

I followed her into the theatre duty-room. She took a sealed test-tube from the large refrigerator in the far corner. "Take that up to Sir Marcus, please. You'll know how to get to his office, of course."

"Yes, Nurse. Should I change first?"

She hesitated. "Not at this hour of the night. Take off those overboots and go as you are. When you get back, change your gown and come straight into the theatre." She gave me the tube. "Be careful with that. It's precious. If you drop it Night Sister'll have to open the main dispensary."

I wondered what the tube contained. I did not like to ask her. She would probably tell me to read the label on it. I had already done that, and was no wiser. Certainly she seemed to have mellowed in the last few minutes, but experience had made me wary with staff nurses. She might be another Naylor—an angel of sweetness one moment, the reverse the next. Nixon had not warned me about her for nothing.

The main corridor was empty and silent. Night Sister was sitting in the outer office of Matron's office as I went by. She glanced up. "That's right, Nurse Dorland. Take it up quickly."

I was very glad Garret had sent me up to the top floor lab. previously. Night Sister and Howard clearly assumed that every night junior knew the way there, and I should not have enjoyed confessing ignorance to either.

The Dean's office was in darkness. Only one light was on in the alcove, another in the private lift. The top floor was blazing with light and very quiet. I hitched under the top of my gown for my watch. It was five past twelve. I wondered why the pathologists were working late, then instantly decided Estelle was worse. Luckily, before I got in a complete dither, I remembered there were other patients in the world—and if Estelle was keeping them up surely Marcus Everly would be over at the fever hospital as he had been last night, and not sitting here on the other side of London.

There was no one in the lab. with the plate-glass wall. The glass was uncurtained, and, as before, I wished I had time to stop and look at the view. Instead, I looked round for a notice to tell me what to do next. I found one on the door on my left. "Pathologists' offices. Private."

I knocked on that door. Nothing happened. I knocked again. With the same result. I looked at the door and wondered if the old man was deaf. He had certainly heard that incubator bell last time. Perhaps he only heard bells?

I looked about for something to ring, or a label to tell me what to do. I found neither. I could not risk putting the tube in the fridge by the incubator, since Howard had told me to deliver it in person, or waste much time as, from her conversation with Night Sister, I had gathered there was some urgency about its delivery. I knocked very loudly and more than a little apprehensively. I had come up on a perfectly legitimate errand at his request, but the prospect of interrupting a man who was reputed to scare the living daylights out of Matron was not a pleasant one. I stood back slightly, expecting him to bounce out in fury. As nothing happened at all I wondered quite seriously if he had dropped dead.

So I opened the door and found myself in yet another lab. It was smaller than the previous one and equally empty. There were three doors off that lab; a light showed through the fanlight of the door on the extreme right.

Once again I knocked. He was neither deaf nor dead. "Come in, Nurse."

The small office was plainly furnished, and, apart from the flat-topped desk in one corner, another lab. The inevitable waist-high china shelf ran the length of one wall; the remaining walls were lined with two elbow-tapped sinks, several bookcases, and three large glass-fronted cupboards filled with stone jars, bottles, test-tubes, and instruments. In the centre of the room was a rather worn zinc-covered table holding a microscope and angled lamp. A man in a white shirt with his sleeves rolled above the elbows sat with his back to me looking into the microscope. A thin man with fair hair.

He did not look round or pay any attention to me. He wrote something on the open pad by his right hand, and went on looking into his instrument. He had his back to me, but when he wrote that note he altered his position slightly, and gave me a brief but clear view of his right profile.

I stood stock still. I should have recognized, and been happy to recognize, that profile anywhere in the world until that moment. But that office was the last place in the world in which I had expected to recognize it, and the shock made a mockery of happiness.

"Excuse me, Nurse," said the Professor, "I just want to finish what I'm doing." He did not even glance up. "I presume you're from the general theatre. Would you leave that tube in the holder on my desk. Thank you for bringing it up."

I could not have moved if the hospital had been on fire and filled with patients having major arterial haemorrhages. I clutched the tube and stared at him speechlessly.

He looked round briefly. "On my desk, please, Nurse." He returned to his microscope.

My scalp pricked under my turban, my hands turned coldly damp, the mask it had not occurred to me to remove felt heavier than lead. I had never fainted in my life, but I knew quite well what those symptoms meant. I thought, Oh, God, I'm going to pass out.

Somehow I managed to get that wretched tube in the wooden holder on the desk. The floor came up at me as Nixon had warned me in a different context. I did not dare risk bending to retie a shoelace. It was too late. If I bent over I should go over. The room was revolving round me; at least three men were sitting at that table ignoring me. I rested both hands flat on the desk to steady myself, then instinctively pulled down my mask, forgetting everything but my desire to breathe without restriction.

He must have looked round again. I was too muzzy to notice anything beyond that fact that he was on his feet.

"Sit down in that chair behind you, and get your head over your knees. I've got to wash before I can touch anything."

I obeyed and closed my eyes. A few seconds, minutes, or it could have been hours, later I felt a hand pressing on the back of my head. "Right down. That's better. Stay there for a little while."

The hand moved; I heard him walk away. His footsteps sounded a long, long way off. Somewhere nearer a drum was beating loudly.

Something cold touched my right hand. I blinked. A medicine glass came into focus. "Can you hold it?" he asked.

I sat up slowly. "Yes. Thank you."

"Ammon. Aromat." He put the glass in my hand. "Sip it."

His using that name added the final touch of nightmare. My friend the Professor would have called it sal volatile. My hand shook badly, spilling some of the liquid on to my gown. I drank the rest far too quickly, so as not to spill more. It burnt my

143

throat and momentarily choked me. I coughed and spluttered; the drum went mad; and then suddenly the room stopped revolving; I was able to breathe and identify the drum as my temporal pulse.

He brought me a glass of water. "You'll need this."

"Thank you." I knew I ought to look at him. I did so. "I'm sorry to be such a nuisance."

He was watching me closely. His face was expressionless. "I'm sorry you should have had this shock."

It was a relief to discover there was going to be no more pretence. "I thought that other pathologist was you. I didn't think you had anything to do with Martha's—apart from playing chess."

"I know." A muscle twitched high in his left cheek, but his tone was as unemotional as his expression. "You must have seen either Dr Eastwood or Dr Carruthers—my colleagues up here." He took both glasses from me, rinsed and dried them, and replaced them in one of the glass-fronted cupboards. "Slane's one of my Christian names." He returned and leant against his desk. "I didn't realize you were on nights in the theatre."

"I'm not. I'm in William MacPherson."

"Why are you in theatre clothes?"

I looked at him, and wondered if I had passed out in the theatre. This had to be a dream. There was no alternative. You do not have to talk in dreams, so I did not answer.

"Jobbing in the theatre?" he prompted.

I woke up then. 'Jobbing' was hospital slang for a nurse on loan. He had walked our wards once. He would know our slang. Our? It belonged to him. But not to my Professor.

I explained.

"I see." He reached for the telephone on his desk. "I'll let Night Sister know you aren't fit to go back."

I stood up without knowing or caring if my legs would support me. "Please, don't. I'm quite all right now. I must go back. My senior's alone in William MacPherson, and we're busy to-night."

His hand closed over the receiver without lifting it. "I'm afraid I can't agree that you're fit to work. I don't doubt that your ward is busy, but no one will expect you to keep going when you're obviously unwell."

I had loved him very much; I still did. Love is not something you can turn off like a tap at will. Because I loved him he could hurt me more than any other human being; to-night he had done that. He probably had never meant to hurt me. He probably began our friendship for a joke, and kept it on as another joke. Just a good laugh. A riot of fun. The great man had come down from his ivory tower, amused himself being avuncular to

144

a junior pro., but had wisely not trusted her with his real name. That would have been so indiscreet, and he had in every way been the soul of discretion. If I had known who he was I might have had ideas about his money, been tempted to step out of the clearly marked hospital line because a man in his position had bothered about me. Of course it would have gone straight to my head. And he might have lost consequence if any one had known he had been mixed up with me. Every houseman in Martha's ignored the first-year nurses. A senior member of the hospital staff could not even admit to knowing such creatures existed.

My jeering brain no longer had room for shock or pain. This would really hurt later, when my icy anger thawed.

"It's very kind of you to be so considerate, Sir Marcus"—I used his title intentionally—"but I really have quite recovered."

He straightened from the desk. "You have?"

His eyes were infinitely weary. I noticed the fact academically. "Yes, thank you."

"Good." He walked to the door, and held it open. "Thank you for bringing up that culture. Good night."

"Good night."

I heard his door close as I let myself out of the main laboratory. I looked back then. There was something I wanted to see. It was there all right, pinned to the outer door. 'It' was a smallish typed list of all the pathologists in Martha's. There were a good many names on that list; Tom Neal's came halfway down. The first name ran, "M. J. S. S. Everly, M.C., M.D., F.R.C.P., Director, Pathological Department, St Martha's Hospital, London."

I looked at it for several seconds. And then in the absurd way in which you do wonder about inessentials in moments of emotional stress I wondered how he had won his M.C. If it was not for services rendered to MI5, it ought to be. I got into the lift, slammed the gates, and went back to the theatre.

11

A LONG, EMPTY EVENING

I SHOULD, I thought, have guessed if not the incredible truth—at least, some of the truth. I should have realized he was a Martha's man, and not just blindly accepted all he told me about himself. Yet it had never occurred to me to doubt him or want to doubt him.

My thoughts chased each other round in an unhappy circle as I finished cutting the bread-and-butter; laid the breakfast trays and trolley; set the sluice for the morning washings; folded linen in the tiled bathroom.

Just before dawn Nixon told me Night Sister had been talking on the telephone to the Night Sister in the fever hospital. "Dexter's having a good night so far." She looked at me keenly. "You don't look too good. I don't think nights suits you. Go on the balcony for a few minutes' air."

The pre-dawn air was cool, clean, and pale grey. London was a drifting dark grey shadow as mobile as the parchment-coloured river. The world was very quiet, and belonged to me. I did not want it. I went back into the warm, slightly airless ward.

Home Sister looked triumphant when I met her in our lift that morning. "Nurse Dexter has had her best night for over a week. Most satisfactory, dear. Most satisfactory."

I was too braced against bad news to be able to accept the reverse easily. Slowly, in the privacy of my room, the relief I felt about Estelle began to trickle through my defences. Then, quite suddenly, they all collapsed, and I knew that, although everything had changed, nothing had altered as far as I was concerned.

I sat in my armchair, kicked off my shoes, and relaxed physically, while my mind, unasked, occupied itself fitting together a mental jig-saw puzzle. His presence on the hill in that storm; his letters; his being on those steps the night Lily died; Home Sister's willing permission for me to come in late; all these made good sense. The only things that did not yet make sense were why he had bothered to write any letters, or walked into the Home to see Home Sister. My instant reaction last night hit me like a boomerang. For a good laugh? An Everly version of the Kinsey report?

146

I winced inwardly, but could not stop. I had to finish that puzzle. Home Sister was on another piece. Now I knew why she treated me as she did. The knowledge made me feel slightly sick.

I wondered who shared Home Sister's specific bit of knowledge about him and me. There was no point in hoping she would have kept it to herself. He was a Martha's legend in his own lifetime, and anything he did would set the grapevine humming. Was that why Night Sister had given me permission to approach the unapproachable last night? Why Howard had mellowed so strangely? And that anaesthetist nearly snapped a mask string?

I did not bother to answer the obvious. Instead, I thought about Vickers. And at last I saw the point in her cracks.

My God, I thought, he probably owns a foreign car, too. Some one in a hospital always sees everything. Home Sister apart, some one must have seen him drive me out that night. The light inside his car was off, but we had had to drive through the well-lit gateway. It only needed one person. Home Sister's version plus our being seen together was more than enough to hit the hospital with the biggest story for a decade. And my being a junior only added to its gossip value. No wonder Simpson talked about a wretched top secret! And I had blithely filled in the gap with the Dexter Block! I ought to have my head examined!

I could not sit still. I roamed round my room in a bitter fury, and all the thoughts I had had about my Professor twisted and taunted and jeered. I thought him so wonderful—was so sorry for him because he worked so hard—looked so tired—lived on snacks. I had lectured him on his health, told him to eat proper meals and stop living on sandwiches.

And then I thought; but he does work too hard, look tired, and apparently seldom troubles to eat the sandwiches.

That thought sobered me. I pushed my hand through my hair, discovered I was still wearing a cap, removed my cap pins, and put them on the dressing-table as if they were made of gold. A long way back I heard my voice talking to Bart: "If she wanted the bright lights and expensive meals, she could have them any time. Why can't you forget her cash, and just treat her as a human being?"

Perhaps he wanted to be treated as a human being? If I had known who he was I probably should never have been able to treat him as one. Perhaps no one did. He had so much; if he wanted more he could buy it, without two thoughts about the price.

Buy—what? If there was a price tag on love, affection, friends, then none were worth having. Estelle had taught me that was not just a soothing bromide for the poor but a plain

147

truth. I might not know much about men; I knew a great deal about young women. The poor-little-rich-girl line might be suitable with some people; not with her. She never asked for pity, but she was the loneliest girl I had ever known. She wore her loneliness like a cloak of dignity. She had shed that cloak with me. And so had he.

Estelle had often helped me in Josephine, and with my lectures, but never so much as she helped me that morning. Because I knew her, neither danger nor damaged pride could blind me indefinitely. Now I knew the truth, I had to face all the truth; I had to try to look through his eyes, to realize there was scarcely a door in the civilized world he could not open with his money and title. He had a freedom of choice granted to few people, but the only door he had bothered to open he had opened with his brains.

I emptied my dress pockets on to my bed, intending to throw my dress into the laundry basket. Only when I saw it did I recollect Bart's unopened letter. I slit it incuriously. My body might be holding his letter, but my mind was a long way from Bart More at that moment.

After a long paragraph on Estelle's paracentesis and much more hopeful prognosis he discussed his nervous system:

Nervous system is not what it was, angel. It took one hell of a bashing this evening. Hamilton Dexter sent round his chauffeur with a formal but civil note asking yours truly to lunch with him at his club to-morrow. Says he wants to talk to me. I'm not sure what's in his mind; I know what's in mine. I hope she won't mind, but there's nothing I'd like better than to have a straight talk with the old man. I'll let you know what gives.

Remembering what Estelle had told me, I had a fair notion of what lay in her grandfather's mind. He might be old-fashioned, but he was clearly very wise to keep such a strict eye on Estelle while she was so young. She was not an ordinary young woman, and it was foolish to pretend she was.

I smiled slightly, wondering how Hannah was going to react when she heard about Bart and Estelle. Her 'honest to God' would echo round our floor. I took up the letter again, thinking, Dear old Hannah! It would be pleasant to have her back. I doubted if Estelle would ever be able to nurse again; I was going to miss her badly, but so long as she recovered from her illness, that would not matter.

Bart's letter ended with some very generous thanks to me. Something had obviously cropped up when he had signed it. A P.T.O. was heavily underlined. I turned the page over. His writing on that side was an utter scrawl:

Nervous system finally shot to pieces after talking to Joe Carver—brother of Maggie C. in O.P.'s. Frances, you devil! How dare you hold out on me! It's the best story I've heard in years, and, angel, have you rocked Martha's! Never mind. I'll forgive you, and am now basking in the reflected glory, having stood the future Lady E. a hamburger on a park bench. No wonder you've known all the answers. Dead crafty, you country girls—that's what!

I put away the letter. So I knew all the answers, did I? I hadn't even heard the questions. Every one else had heard—not me. Then I realized it was not every one, it was the senior half of the hospital, and the story was only just trickling downwards. It would reach my set soon.

No wonder the poor man had to retire to his lab., if this was what happened when he merely admitted to being acquainted with a nurse and possibly was seen driving her in his car. No one knew he had been writing to me. If they had they would probably have fixed the date by now.

I no longer blamed him for not telling me his full name; I was merely amazed he had risked talking to me. The talk and publicity that must inevitably have followed him all his life must have been agony for some one with his quiet, reticent nature.

I sighed. It had been so much simpler when I was angry. Now I kept seeing his point it was growing more and more complicated. Now I knew what was being said, I should have to do something to stop it. The difficulty was—what?

A vague idea instantly rose to my mind. I should have to get hold of Bart, tell him the truth, get him to help. I could leave him to circulate anything we wanted to circulate. He knew the hospital. Perhaps we could work out something along the lines of Marcus Everly's being an old pal of my father's. He having used much the same line to Home Sister—just why he had taken that risk I still could not fathom, but I should have to think it out later—he had used that line, so we should have to rub it in. We could laugh and laugh and keep on laughing at the idea of any romance. I could invent a mythical young man—even borrow a ring from my mother.

That stopped me again. The Professor had met the parents and told them he was Slane. Why?

It was useless. I did not know any answers, I was growing into a question-mark, and was far too exhausted to think another thought. I felt too tired to sleep until I got into bed. I was not.

Fay Kinsley shook me in Sylvia's stead that night. "Frances, you can't go on sleeping. You've got to be in the dining-room in ten minutes." She removed all the bedclothes over me and

149

hauled on the bottom sheet. "If you don't get out I'll topple you out."

"For God's sake go away! I'm in no mood for dormitory pranks . . ." I got out of what remained of my bed and shivered. "What time did you say it was?"

"Twenty past."

"Eight?" My voice cracked.

"That's what I'm trying to tell you. Sylvia warned me you might oversleep." She threw me my face flannel and turned on the hand-basin taps. "Wash your face in cold water." She sounded exactly like Sister P.T.S. "And brace up. I've got news for you."

"Estelle?"

"Yes. Off the D.L. and on the S.I." She took a clean apron from my drawer. "Where's your dress?"

"I need a clean one. Bottom left." I was not used to this helpfulness from her. "Thanks, Fay. I never knew you cared."

When Fay patted you on the head she had to do it with her knuckles. "A set ought to stick together, Frances. And you're so irresponsible, if we don't see you get on at night, you'd never bother."

I said I did not know what we should do without her. "Thanks for the good news. Seriously ill isn't much, but it's not to be compared with the D.I."

She polished my shoes with an old apron from my laundry basket. "I've got another bit of news. You know the new block. It's going to be called the Dexter Block." She smiled knowingly. "Yes—he's paying for it. The opening's been postponed."

I was hurrying too much to have to do more than look wide-eyed.

"I heard Home Sister discussing it with Nurse Charles when I was reading the notice-board outside her office just now. I couldn't help hearing."

Having done my own eavesdropping on occasions, I had to agree with her. "I suppose they'll wait until Estelle's up?"

She hesitated. "As a matter of fact, they were talking about that too. They—er—don't expect her back, I'm afraid."

"She hasn't a hope in hell of nursing again with her heart."

"You knew?"

"Guessed it." I fixed my cap on quickly.

She said slowly, "Don't you mind?"

I put down my comb. "Very much. On all counts. She loved nursing. I liked her." I reached for the door with one hand and my cloak with the other. "Bless you, Fay. Do the same for you some time."

I left her standing in my room looking as if she had expected me to weep on her shoulder. If I had had time I might have wept, not only for Estelle, but for life in general. As usual, there was no time.

I slipped into the empty place beside Ames as Night Sister arrived in the dining-room to say grace.

"Nice timing," said Ames, as we sat down. "Oversleep again?"

"Yes. I don't know how I'm going to wake up on nights. I never hear the bells."

"Lucky you! I even hear the clock in the hall." She produced two envelopes from her apron bib and opened them in her lap. "Keep an eye on Night Sister while I read. Then I'll do it for you. Or didn't you have time to get your post?"

"No." I poured myself a glass of water I did not want. "Doesn't matter. I'm not expecting any. Go ahead and read. I'll watch Night Sister."

Night Sister always rose for the final grace ten minutes before we were due on duty. Consequently I had plenty of time to walk to the office and look for any post. I did not bother. I had heard from my mother yesterday, and expected no letter from home for a week. I knew I had now had my last letter from the Professor. I had avoided my letter pigeon-hole this morning, and did not want to look at it again just yet. It reminded me too much of the past. I walked slowly towards William Mac-Pherson and for the first time in my nursing career arrived on duty a good five minutes early.

Nixon joined me four minutes later. "You're an eager beaver to-night, Dorland."

Huckle waved to me directly Sister William MacPherson left the ward. "How's my Nurse Dorland to-night? I been looking out for you, Nurse. Had a good rest?"

I said I was fine, and how was he?

"Mustn't grumble, Nurse."

Nixon came into the sluice when I was rinsing the mouth-wash mugs. "I gather you're Huckle's private property?"

"I got that impression too, Nurse."

She considered me with an expression that would have puzzled me twenty-four hours back. Incredulity and respect were equally mixed in that expression. "So we can all breathe again? Dexter's on the S.I. . . ."

"Yes. I'm so pleased."

She nodded, looked as if she wanted to say something else, but was not sure of her ground, then went off quickly.

I finished the mouthwash mugs, rinsed some stained sheets, put them in a covered bucket, and took them along to the wet-linen bin that stood on the balcony.

It was a dark night, and the air was cold on my bare, wet arms. I lingered for a few moments and leant over the stone balustrade, looking down at the darkened grounds.

The Theatre Block ran parallel with William MacPherson. The general theatre on the third floor was fully lighted. I glanced over to those lights, and wondered what would have happened if Huckle had not come in last night, or if Sister Theatre and not Howard had been on call. Would he have gone on letting me believe he was Slane indefinitely?

One of the theatre corridor doors was opened as I watched. The corridor was lined with a row of black oxygen cylinders. The cylinders against the white wall looked like nightmare teeth grinning wickedly. I turned, picked up my empty bucket, and went inside.

Bart was sitting on the steps at the foot of Miss Nightingale's statue when I came out of breakfast next morning. A scarlet and white rugger club scarf was draped round his neck; his hair was standing on end. He practically exploded to his feet when he saw me.

"Angel, I've been waiting hours——"

"Sssh." I held up a cautioning hand and looked round. "Night Sister hasn't come out yet."

"Would I have given you that big hallo if there'd been any blue dresses around. And what the devil do you care about blue dresses now, anyway?"

"We'll go into that in a minute. Heard the early-morning bulletin?"

He beamed. "Best night to date. I got it out of old Sam, who was listening in."

"How did you get on with Grandpapa?"

He shrugged hugely. "He didn't exactly pat me on the head and call me son, but in a positively hellish way he was pretty decent."

"What's he like?"

"Granite, until he got going on her. The sun rises and sets on her head for him. Which made two of us." He coloured. "Tell you something, Frances. You know that letter you wanted me to write? He read it to her."

"Oh, no! Did he mind?"

"He said, quote, under the circumstances he considered I was fully justified in acting as I had. Then he gave me the works."

"Did you mind?" I asked curiously, noticing how he seemed to have changed in the past few days.

"I didn't enjoy it, but in his place I'd have done the same."

"Can I ask—what did you say to him?"

"I love women," he replied dreamily. "Can I, you ask so sweetly, and don't even wait for an answer. If you want to know I told him what I once told you—maybe in rather better English."

"How did he take it?"

"In silence. He was doing his granite act then. When I

finished he just grunted. I thought, This is where you make tracks, chum, and was on my two feet when he said, 'Sit down, boy!' I sat. Then out of the blue he upped and told me his old man was a G.P. Did you know that?"

I shook my head. "Think that's where Estelle gets her passion for medicine?"

"He thinks so. Know something else? His old man was a Martha's man. Which is why he has a soft spot for the old firm."

"She never told me."

"I don't believe she knows. H.D. certainly gave me that impression. He said his old man was a fine character who died when he was a kid. Some uncle educated him, and put him into his own firm. Uncle knew how to do business, nephew knew even better. He went on and up and up."

"And after his life-history?"

"We had lunch. He showed no sign of softening until the brandy arrived. Then—again quote—he gave me his permission to pursue my acquaintance with his granddaughter, providing there is no talk of any official engagement or marriage until (a) she comes of age, and (b) I am in an established position. Fair enough, eh?"

"Very. Bart, I'm so pleased."

"Wait." His voice shook suddenly. "There's a little more. He said she had asked him to say she would like to see me. I can go along just as soon as Curtis gives the word."

"My dear, this really is something."

"You're a good girl." He slapped my arm gently. "Very good. And it seems you're going to get your reward. Now we've finished with my angle, tell me all."

I stopped smiling. "Yes, I must," I said urgently. "I've simply got to tell you——"

"Nurse Dorland." Night Sister was beside us. "No doubt you have a great deal to tell Mr More"—she looked him over coolly—"but may I ask you to choose some other place for these confidences? I cannot have my night nurses standing idly chatting with students in the main corridor."

Bart apologized instantly. "It was my fault, Sister. I stopped Nurse."

"It takes two to make a conversation, Mr More," she informed him primly. "Nurse should not have allowed herself to be stopped." She gave us an old-fashioned nod and walked on.

Bart was contrite. "I was so sure they'd overlook——"

I cut him short. "Never mind that. Look, I must talk to you —obviously not here. Can you meet me somewhere soon as I change?"

He hesitated. "I'd like to—but I'm dressing in the general theatre at nine. Will to-morrow do?"

I thought quickly. Another twenty-four hours would not make any real difference; they might even give me time to work out a more concrete solution. "Yes. In the morning?"

"Nine, outside. Why? Something amiss?"

I nodded. "Keep it to yourself till then."

"I'll be there. You going for your post, I expect? I'll make tracks in the opposite direction."

I had not meant to go along to look for the post, but as Night Sister was still visible at the far end of the corridor from Matron's office, I walked to the office to get out of her sight.

Ames was rooting through her pigeon-hole. She glanced up. "You've got one. I saw it when I collected Joanna Dawson's."

I flipped over the small pile of envelopes in the 'D' compartment, wondering how long it would be before I was able to do that without wincing. One of the envelopes was unstamped. It was addressed to me in the Professor's handwriting.

Ames was talking. I did not hear a word she said. I took up that envelope as if it was brittle as glass, backed unthinkingly to the nearest windowsill, and slit the envelope with my scissors.

It was a longer letter than any he had written previously. He had used Martha's paper, added the time as well as the date. The time was 1.30 A.M. yesterday. I had left his office at about a quarter-past twelve. He might have given it to a porter to deliver, or, more likely, put it in my pigeon-hole on his way out that night. Between 1.30 and 3 A.M., Night Sister and her assistants were always out of the office on rounds. He would know that. He had been a Martha's houseman.

I looked at his signature before reading the letter. It was there in full, for the first time. M. J. S. S. Everly.

"Nurse! Nurse Dorland!" An Office Sister stood in front of me. She looked very peeved. "Nurse, I have already called your name twice. You paid no attention."

"I'm so sorry, Sister." Fortunately, apologizing to a Sister was a reflex action to me. "I'm afraid I didn't hear you. I was reading my post."

"That," she retorted icily, "I could scarcely fail to observe. Will you in future kindly remember that this alcove is not an extension of the junior nurses' sitting-room? And never let me see you lounging in that unseemly fashion against a windowsill in this hospital again! Please put away your letter and come into the office. The Assistant Matron wishes to see you. I was about to ring over to the Home for you, when I noticed you through my open door."

"Yes, Sister. I'm so sorry, Sister," I repeated mechanically, and pushed the letter into my apron bib. Then I realized what she had said. "The Assistant Matron, Sister?"

I did not know her name, or recollect having seen her before.

154

Our Office Sisters were constantly changing. She was tall and slim, with pale red hair and pale, thin lips. "I am gratified to have your attention at last, Nurse. Yes. Sister Black wishes to see you now. Come along."

Sister Black, our Assistant Matron, was the most popular sister in Martha's. She was very plump, surprisingly young, not pretty, but very pleasant-looking. I liked what I had seen and heard of her, but if I had not had that letter in my bib, I should have been very shaken by this summons. The nicest Assistant Matron was still the Assistant Matron.

The pale Sister ushered me in. "Nurse Dorland, Sister."

Sister Black told me to come in and close the door.

That did worry me a little. A closed door in Martha's was always an ominous sign.

"Tell me, Nurse," went on the Assistant Matron chattily, "have you had a heavy night? Are you very tired?"

Half an hour ago I had been exhausted. I said truthfully, "We were quite busy, Sister, but I'm not at all tired."

She said she was very happy to hear that. "You look very fresh. Good. I fear you have a busy day ahead of you. You may have to-night off, naturally, but must report for duty in Catherine Ward to-morrow night."

"Catherine Ward, Sister?" I wondered if I had heard right. I did not know of any Catherine in London.

"Catherine, Nurse. At St Martha's-in-the-country. Sister Illingworth, the Sister-in-charge down there, requires another night junior immediately. We cannot supply a nurse for to-night, but will be able to spare you from to-morrow." She smiled pleasantly. "I am sorry to have to move you at such short notice, and send you ahead of your set, but for various reasons"—she glanced down at an open book on her desk— "Matron considers you would be the most suitable junior to fill the gap. You had scarlet fever as a child?" she added, without looking up.

"Yes, Sister." I squinted at her book and read my own name upside down.

"I see you had diphtheria when you were eight. Did you have it badly?"

"Moderately, I believe, Sister." I tried not to sound too surprised or curious. "I can't remember much about it."

She closed the book. "Diphtheria is always serious, Nurse. Your parents must have been very worried. How fortunate to have it safely behind you! Now go over and see Home Sister. I have already spoken to her about you. Sister will tell you of the arrangements for your luggage and which train you must take. That will be all, Nurse. Good morning."

Home Sister was in a positive dither when I reached the Home. "I am sorry we are losing you so soon, Nurse. Dear, dear,

dear. So unfortunate. Hurry up and get your packing done. Leave your cases outside your door, and take only your night things with you. The rest will go down in the hospital van at twelve. You must take the twelve-thirty train. Come into my office when you are ready and I will give you your ticket. So unfortunate"—she clucked again—"so unfortunate." And she bustled off to find Nurse Charles muttering something to herself about it all being so upsetting for dear Matron, poor Sister Illingworth, and the already over-burdened Dr Sympson.

Nurse Charles arrived in the hall by one door as Sister vanished through another. "Get on, Nurse Dorland. Don't dawdle around waiting for the lift. You have a lot to do."

I had a lot to do, but, instead of doing it, directly I reached my room I stretched out on my bed and took out my letter. Fay Kinsley burst in on me before I was half-way through the second reading.

"Frances, I hear you're leaving us because you're the one pro. in the whole first year who's had dip."

I lowered the letter and gazed at her. "How on earth do you know that? I didn't."

She was very pleased by this. "It's obvious. One of the pros. in the country is a query dip. I heard Sister Mayhew telling Sister Robert when I collected my post this morning. She even mentioned you by name."

I had to take things in easy stages. "Who's Sister Mayhew? I never heard of her."

"The new red-haired Office Sister. She won a gold medal."

"Now how do you know that?"

"Every one knows that! Really, Frances! You ought to keep your ears open. You miss just everything."

I was so enchanted by the realization that there was one thing she had still missed that I very nearly told her what it was. Luckily, she had too much to tell me.

"Nurse Charles was talking to Home Sister about it in the hall just now. I was waiting to make a phone call and couldn't help . . ."

I smiled at her. "I know, dear. What did Charles say?"

"That your having had both dip. and scarlet made you the ideal choice. Matron doesn't want to pass on scarlet, or risk sending down an unimmunized junior. Dip.'s a foul illness, and one junior on the D.I. in the last month is one too many. If this girl has got dip. we'll all be immunized."

"Except me," I corrected smugly.

"That's what I've been trying to tell you."

I got off my bed. "Think this means a second epidemic?" I yawned. "How long's the incubation?"

Inevitably she had overheard this too. "Usually two to three days, Mayhew said."

156

"Very jolly. Take up nursing and get the plague."

Sylvia flung open the door. "What's all this about your leaving us, Frances?"

I left Fay to explain, put my letter in my handbag, and lifted on to my bed one of the empty suitcases Home Sister had sent up. Sylvia opened my wardrobe and handed me the contents absently while she listened to Fay.

"How do you feel about shifting?" she asked finally.

"Punch-drunk." I rolled a skirt. "Life's got clean out of hand lately. Every time I stop to draw breath something happens."

Fay pulled open all my drawers, and said I would have plenty of time for drawing breath in the country. "The wards may be busy, but you'll be very much on your own off-duty. The junior set down there are an up-stage lot. They won't speak to you."

Sylvia said I should have to be up-stage too and keep myself to myself. Neither of us bothered to ask Fay how she had come by this knowledge; nor did we bother to doubt her.

Sylvia thought it tough my having to travel after a night on. Fay said I must take a nap in the train. "Are you going to wear those shoes? If not, let's have 'em. They'll need to go at the bottom."

They organized my packing and me. Sylvia promised to let Bart know I had left London. "I'm writing to Alice to-day. I'll ask her to get one of the nurses to pass it on to Estelle. Hannah'll hear direct from Alice as they're in the same ward."

"Any one else we should contact?" asked Fay. "Your family?"

"I'll ring them this evening." I glanced at my handbag. "No one else, thanks."

Fay was on duty at 1 P.M., Sylvia not until 1.30. She came with me to the station. "Did you give Fay that turkey?"

I smiled faintly. "No. I don't know what's come over her."

Sylvia said she didn't either. "Something's got her all shook-up. You've been dear, sweet, muddle-headed Frances since tea-time yesterday. She even went so far as to admit that she had always been mistaken about you."

"Where was she working yesterday?" I had to raise my voice to beat the hiss of the incoming train.

"Jobbing somewhere—we're all doing that all the time. I think it was Josephine—yes, of course. Your old pal Monica Player's back there pro tem. Fay mentioned her too. Why?"

"I just wondered." I did not explain further as the train was still. I did not need to wonder any longer at Fay's altered attitude towards me. The fact that she had managed to keep her news to herself proved how important she considered it—and I—might be.

I did not attempt to sleep in the train. I had the carriage to myself; privacy was too precious to be wasted in sleep. I read

157

and reread the Professor's letter until I came close to believing it was only from my Professor.

He did not ignore the past. He reminded me of it constantly. "You know my views on explanations. I'm not going to insult your intelligence by launching into one."

Inevitably his letter was more formal than usual. But the apology which he hoped, but did not expect me to be able to accept, was patently sincere. He wrote at length on our friendship, and the words he used seemed to me the most wonderful ever to have been written. He ended:

> I have given you no cause to believe anything I write, so I am not going to ask you to believe the truth in this letter. However, as it is more than probably the last letter I shall write to you, I should like to thank you. You have given me a great deal, Frances. I am very grateful.

I knew that final paragraph by heart long before I arrived at Pine Halt. If only his name had just been Slane. If only. Those two words, I thought wearily, must be the most futile—and the saddest—in the English language.

It was raining lightly at the Halt. A thin wind was blowing down from the hills and the small station looked bare, cold, and very different from the way it had looked last May when I first met Estelle and Hannah.

The station-master was as helpful as before. "Would you be Nurse Dorland, miss? They rang from the hospital to say would I ask you to wait for the students' bus. It'll be along soon."

The rain stopped when the bus arrived. It was empty. The driver asked me to sit in the seat just behind his as he liked a bit of company. "Real chilly this afternoon, Nurse. Had it cold in town?"

"Not as cold as this. You had any snow yet?"

He chatted contentedly about the weather, the number of patients in the hospital, the number of students he would carry on his return journey. "Packed in like sardines, they'll be. Talk of the overloaded ark!"

I made a series of exclamations, I hoped in the right places, but did not really hear him at all. I was watching the country around. It had settled for the winter, the trees were brown and bleak, only the evergreens bore leaves, and the rain dripped from these like slow tears. The bleakness soothed me. It reminded me of the winter at home. The pale afternoon sun held no warmth when it came out, the sky remained grey, the land the colour of deep pewter, with only the brown lace of the empty trees and dark green stabbing fingers of the firs to lighten the grey world. Then, as we reached the foot of the long hospital hill, a scarlet tractor bounced out of a side lane, swung dangerously, and perched half on one bank of the narrow road to let us pass. The tractor-driver was young, and dressed in an old Army greatcoat and leather over-jacket the tractor-drivers wore at home. He even had on the same type of tea-cosy hat with a large blue pompon. I noticed every detail about that unknown young man deliberately. I had to do that to keep my mind off the original owner of the hill and my own future. I even wondered, as again I had at home, what landworkers wore in winter before the last world war provided a generation and their sons with old Army clothes.

Sister Illingworth was too busy to see me when I reported at her office. A Staff Nurse wearing a sister's belt took me to the Night Home, and handed me over to the Home Sister.

The Home was a long, one-storey, brick building, divided into a rabbit-warren of minute rooms. The Home Sister told me all the rooms had french windows and gave me a key. "You may come and go through your window, Nurse, but remember always to lock it and remove the key when you leave your room empty."

My luggage had arrived before me. The suitcases were in my room, my bicycle, according to that Sister, was in the rack. "Unpack quietly. All the nurses in here are sleeping. Go to bed early to-night, after this busy day. Be in bed again by three to-morrow afternoon and report to Night Sister when you go in to supper." She looked at her watch. "If you hurry you should be unpacked by second tea. The dining-room is directly opposite to Sister Illingworth's office."

I felt far stranger than on my first day in the P.T.S. when I went in to tea. A voluntary helper presiding behind the tea-urn poured me a cup of tea, and told me which was the junior table. There were several girls at that table.

I ate in silence while they continued with their apparently fascinating and very technical conversation, in which Klebs-Loeffler, Hoffman's something or other, and something called the *B. xerosis* kept cropping up. They all sounded alarmingly knowledgeable and were obviously as up-stage as Fay had forecast. They reminded me very much of Simpson and her colleagues on my first morning in O.P.'s. I had survived that; I would survive this; survival did not mean enjoyment.

When I left the dining-room I wondered what to do. The silent solitude of my room was not very attractive. I had had all the privacy I needed in the train. I was tired, but far too restless to think of sleep.

It was still light, and would be so for roughly another hour. I decided to use the time taking myself on a tour of the hospital. My months in London had shown me how useful it was to acquire a pro.'s eye view of a hospital.

I quite enjoyed my self-conducted tour. I found the dispensary hidden behind Casualty; the X-Ray department, Path. Lab., and Almoner's offices were a neat trio of Nissen huts disguised by clean white paint and red window-boxes; the surgical stores, repairs and works, chapel, and morgue were straight out of Hans Andersen. Each was housed in a small, weather-boarded hut, and they were clustered together and half hidden by the infringing pines.

The hospital was like a toy in comparison with the parent building in London, and my tour took me less time than it would take me to walk down the main corridor of Martha's proper. I had noticed the names of the wards, but could not go near then as I was out of uniform. I drifted back towards the night nurses' home, but the thought of that silence oppressed me. I turned away and left the hospital by the main gate. Without thinking where I was going, I wandered up the hill to the P.T.S. house.

I paused when I reached it and looked at the building curiously. It was not really long since we had left it, yet it seemed to belong to another lifetime. I thought about my set in general and Estelle in particular. I had to move on. That wretched house reminded me too vividly of her. If ever a girl had a vocation for nursing she had. And because she had gone to a free film show one morning she would never be a nurse again. I wondered if Bart realized how much this was going to upset her. I guessed her grandfather did, and that was one of his reasons for allowing Bart to visit her. I hoped they would let me visit her soon. I would ask for permission just as soon as I had a proper night off. There was so much I wanted to tell her, and one of those things, I realized without forethought, was that as she could not nurse she ought to read medicine. The idea pleased me so much that I nearly went back to write to her at once. The watery sun was disappearing fast. If I wanted to reach the top of the hill I should have to hurry. There was plenty of time. I had a long, empty evening ahead.

It was darker and very slippery under the wet trees. Above tree-level the light returned. I glanced at it only once, then had to pay attention to my hands and feet as the going was exceptionally rough after the rain and I was mostly on all fours.

I reached the plateau, and recovered my breath as the rim of the sun disappeared. I was glad I had made that climb. It was good to be back here, even if I was alone.

And then I heard that footstep behind me.

12

I TAKE THE PROFESSOR'S ADVICE

I LOOKED round at the shelter quickly, hoping I had been mistaken. I did not want to share the next half-hour with any itinerant nurse or student. When I saw who was behind me I remained momentarily transfixed with my head twisted over my left shoulder.

That afternoon in the park I had thought I was imagining his presence. I knew at once I was imagining nothing. He was there all right. His suit proved that. Having only seen him previously in an ordinary grey lounge suit, a mackintosh, or his shirt-sleeves, I had never visualized him wearing the insignia of a senior member of Martha's. His black jacket and pinstriped trousers made him seem an elegant stranger. His expression was strange, too. He looked as if he doubted the evidence of his eyes.

"Frances?" He came towards me. "You? What are you doing here?"

My heart was beating so loudly that I thought he must hear it. "I've been transferred. They're short of a night junior. Some one seems to have diphtheria. I got sent down."

He stopped a foot or so from me. "Come away from that edge—you're much too close." I stepped back, and so did he. "Did you say diphtheria?"

"Yes. One of the nurses has it—I think." I wondered how he did not know this, since the pathologists must have had to deal with the diagnostic swab.

"Oh, that girl. No. She hasn't got it. She's got an acute streptococcal tonsilitis, plus a query Vincent's angina. A nasty throat. Not diphtheric."

"Is that why you're here?"

"Roughly." He spoke with unusual deliberation, as if he was talking in one language and thinking in another. "Why did they pick on you?"

"I'm the only first-year who's had diphtheria."

"You have?" He looked at me, then at the trees below. "When?"

I told him. "I suppose I'm immune?"

He told the trees that nothing was medically impossible, but it was unlikely that I should get it again. "When did they send you down?"

"By the twelve-thirty express." As it was safe to watch him I did so. The other night in his office I had been able to accept that he was not my Professor. Now I had had his letter, even though he was dressed up like a pundit, I could not think of him as any one else.

"You're not going to have to work to-night?" he asked sharply.

"No. To-morrow night. In Catherine."

He looked at me again. "Have you slept at all to-day?"

"Not yet. There hasn't been much time. I only heard this morning." I paused, to nerve myself to say what I wanted to say. "I got your letter this morning. Thank you for writing it."

He inclined his head, but made no comment.

The silence that followed deafened me. I had to break it. "May I ask you something?"

"Of course." His tone did not match the invitation in his words.

"What is—are—Klebs-Loeffler, Hoffman's something, and another thing that sounds like the *B. xerosis*? Are they bugs— I mean, germs?"

He did not answer immediately. He just went on looking at me. Then he smiled. "I call 'em bugs too. Let's go and sit down while I tell you. You've spent far too many of the last twenty-four hours on your feet."

I sat on one end of the long wooden seat against the back wall of the shelter, and held my hands tightly in my lap in an attempt to stop them from shaking too obviously. He leant against the side-wall opposite to me. "The Klebs-Loeffler is a bacillus—also Hoffman's—and the *B. xerosis*. All three are members of a group of the Corynebacterium, with a few others thrown in. You find the Klebs-Loeffler in the false membrane that's characteristic of diphtheria." His smile reappeared. "Want any more?"

"Yes, please," I replied as if he was offering me a plate of bread-and-butter.

"Right. Let's see. Well, the organism is a non-motile, gram-postive, non-sporing aerobe, which produces a soluble exotoxin. Does any of that make sense?"

"The first part—sort of. The last bit—no."

The light was fading, but there was still enough for me to see the expression in his eyes. His smile was not reaching his eyes. "It's a shade complicated. I'll explain if you like, but won't it be more to the point if I just tell you that if you spot the Klebs-Loeffler you know you're dealing with diphtheria. If it's not here you have another look, and rule out dip."

"No Klebs-Loeffler no dip.?" I echoed, as if his words were the most important I had ever heard. "Thank you."

162

He took out his cigarette-case. "How did you come by all this confused learning? Young More?"

"No. The girls at tea to-day."

"You'd better bring the conversation back to diphtheria at tea to-morrow and throw out a few light remarks about non-motile, gram-positive, non-sporing aerobes."

"I'll have to be in bed, then. I'll save them until I get back to my set. That'll shake 'em. Bart too," I added absently, thinking how reality differed from imagination. Although I had tried to be strong-minded in the train, I had inevitably drifted into a glorious day-dream in which he and I met again. I had not got around to working out our conversation. But if I had, never in a hundred years would I have imagined it including a fascinating discussion on the Klebs-Loeffler, Hoffman's bacillus, and the *B. xerosis*. "Like all medical students, he doesn't believe nurses know anything."

"He'll grow out of that." He considered his open case gravely as if it was important that he found the right cigarette. "Your leaving town so suddenly must have been a blow to him. Mind if I smoke?"

"Please do." It was a relief to be able to be honest about Bart if nothing else. "He won't mind my being away. He's got quite enough on his mind without having to bother if I'm around. You remember what I told you about him?"

"Yes. And?"

"Well—it's all working out fairly well." I hesitated. "I think it's going to work very well, in the long run."

"In the long run?" he echoed doubtfully.

"Perhaps I should apologize. I told you the truth, but not quite all the truth about him. It's all right to do that now, as it's quite official."

"I realize I am being exceedingly dense, but what is official?"

I explained in detail. Apparently I did not explain clearly. When I had finished he took me back over each point.

"Your anonymous friend was Estelle Dexter?"

"Yes."

"More was merely in the habit of confiding in you as a mutual friend?"

I smiled briefly. "He didn't honestly make a habit of it. He only really let down his hair in the park one evening. Before we went to the ballet with your tickets."

"I remember." At last he had found the cigarette he wanted. "I saw you in the park that evening."

"You did?" Then I remembered too. "Oh, yes. Bart said you had gone by. I didn't look round. I—er—didn't know you were you."

"No." He glanced at me expectantly, as if he was waiting for me to enlarge on that remark. There was a lot I wanted to ask him, and had wanted since I discovered who he was. Originally I had thought I should never dare question him; now we were together, daring did not come into it. He was a highly intelligent man; he knew very well that I was curious about him. If he had wanted to satisfy my curiosity he would have done so. His silence kept me silent. I loved him. I did not want him to do anything he did not want to do.

He struck a match. The wind had blown inland, the air in the shelter was quite still. The match flame flickered dangerously. "So you were just a disinterested third party?"

I shrugged. "I can't honestly remain disinterested when two people I'm fond of behave like a couple of ostriches. I had to try to pull their heads out of the sand, if only to bang them together. I know there are a good many snags still in the way for them, and Estelle's still on the S.I.——"

"She's not." He cut me short. "She came off at two this afternoon."

"She did? Oh, that's wonderful!"

"It's very good." He sounded as pleased as I was. "I can tell you something more, as it's official. Dr Curtis is bringing her back to Martha's at the end of this week."

"That's splendid!" I sighed pleasurably. "Couldn't be better. Bart'll be on top of the world."

"I'm glad." He sat down on the bench. "One more problem we can tick off. A satisfactory, if, to me, rather surprising solution."

"That Hamilton Dexter should come round?"

"I didn't know Hamilton Dexter was involved until a few moments ago. I had previously thought you were talking about yourself."

"About me? Me and Bart?" My voice cracked slightly. "Heavens, no! Besides, if it had been me, there wouldn't have been any problem."

"No? Oh, yes, I see what you mean."

I looked at him curiously. I should not have said he was being exceedingly dense, but he was taking an extraordinarily long time—for him—to grasp what I was saying. That fact surprised me far more than his presence on the seat beside me in smooth pundit's suiting. It only seemed natural that he should be there. With the exception of that night in his office, I had never been able to remain on edge when with him. I might be as taut as an over-strung fiddle-string when we met. Ten minutes after meeting it was as if I was at home.

Again we were silent. This time the silence was without strain. I was content to listen to it until eternity.

He said nothing until he finished the first and lit a second cigarette. "Frances, have you ever lost a friend?"

I did not know what I had been expecting. I only knew it was not that. "I don't know. Expect so."

164

"I don't. I expect your friends hang on to you like leeches. No one," he added slowly, "in his right mind would let you go out of his life. You're not only a remarkably attractive young woman, you are—in my experience—unique."

"Me?" I couldn't believe my ears.

"Yes. You." He stood up, walked to the entrance, turned to face me. "We both know I owe you a considerable explanation. You've every right to demand one now we've met. You haven't." He paused. "That night in my office, you might have been too shocked, then too angry, to bother. You're neither, now. But all you've asked of me is—Klebs-Loeffler. And I don't believe you intend asking anything more personal. Do you?"

I shook my head.

"Why not?"

I had to answer then. I used his letter as an ally. "I share your views on explanations."

"I'll have to be honest. If our positions were reversed I shouldn't hold those views." He paused again. "I should never have written that letter. I wish I hadn't."

"You do?" I could not follow him now. I loved that letter.

"Yes. It was a mistake. A great mistake. If I had known then what I know now, I should not have written as I did. I expect you can understand why?"

There was no point in polite pretence. "No. I can't."

"I'd like to explain," he said. "Would you mind?"

"No," I said carefully, "no."

"Thank you." He sat down and folded one arm on the other. "It won't take long. Are you cold?"

I said I was not at all cold, thank you.

He took his time. "I've told you I've been under the impression that you were very fond of More. I could well understand his feeling the same about you. I was convinced he did. But for that, you would never have had that shock the other night. And I would certainly," he added, with unusual urgency, "never have written what amounted to a final letter from an old—in every sense of the word—friend."

"You didn't tell me who you were, because of Bart? But," it had to be said, "I hadn't met him when I first met you."

"I know. Now. I didn't previously. I got the impression he was very much in the picture from the first evening I rang you, ostensibly to tell you I had visited your home, in actual fact to ask you to dine with me. You've no reason to believe this, but I dislike deception, and had decided to tell you the truth that night. I told your parents I intended doing that on the first occasion on which I was able to persuade you to come out with me. As I have not been able to do that," he said drily, "I have at least kept my word on that. I'm not counting the night Lily Ellis died. I didn't ask you out that night. I took you for a drive without giving you a chance to refuse."

I could only take this in very, very slowly. And one astounding fact at a time. "You told my parents? They knew? They've always called you——"

"Slane? That was good of them. I asked them if they would until they heard from you."

"Why?"

He said, "May I answer that in a moment? Have you told them what you've found out?"

"No. No one."

"My God," he said softly, "that tells me how much it hurt. I'm sorry. Very sorry."

I ignored that because I had to. It was a long time since I had had any sleep, my armour of detached interest was wearing thin. Gentleness could shatter it far more easily than anything else. "I know Dr Anderson took you to visit my parents, but how did you get hold of my name originally?"

He turned to me. It was too dark to see anything now but the outline of his face. "Why have you taken so long to ask that?"

I told him the truth. "Either I forgot or, when I remembered, didn't think you liked being questioned."

"I see." He was silent for several seconds. "To be strictly accurate, I traced you through the British Museum."

"The—what?" I demanded incredulously.

"The British Museum. It was quite simple. You had given me the name of your village. When I looked it up in the A.A. book I found there were four villages with that name in England, two of them in Kent. That's why I went to the Museum. It was a safe bet that in only one there'd been a Mithraic temple. You mentioned it. I found it."

"I knew there were two in Kent. Ours has a 'cum,' the other an 'in.' But that doesn't explain—me."

"Doesn't it? Frances, you're used to village life. You should know how simple it is to find out any one's name. I merely drove down there the following week, and spent a long while in your post office sending myself a telegram."

"Oh. Of course." I smiled weakly. "Mrs Mercer."

"Is that your postmistress's name? A pleasant woman. She said she was quite used to having strangers in her sub-post-office, and told me all the local sights I must see. When she saw my hospital address she was most interested. She told me Mr Dorland's eldest daughter Frances was at St Martha's—said I must be sure to look out for you, and went so far as to describe you very well. If I had any lingering doubts over your identity she dispelled them by telling me your father kept turkeys."

"How did she know you were at Martha's, if you were sending a telegram to yourself?"

"I explained that I worked there too. Having got that settled, I came down here the following week-end to photograph those hobbys. You know most of the rest. What you don't know you can probably guess."

I did not know anything; my brain was too stunned for guessing. "Dr Anderson?" I asked carefully. "You said you met him by chance?"

"Chance hasn't figured much in our relationship. I just tried to make it appear that way. I looked at the list of local G.P.'s in your post office, noticed Luke Anderson's name, checked in the *Medical Register* to see if he was the man I knew, then made a point of running into him, and getting an invitation out of him. He told me about your father's tape-recordings, and took me round to your home, as I hoped."

I was beyond surprise, even beyond wonder. "Why did you take all that trouble?"

"Wasn't much trouble. It was just a case of following a few leads. I wanted your name, and to meet your parents."

"What would you have done if Dr Anderson hadn't been at Cambridge with you?"

He said that would not have made much difference. "You had to have a G.P. The medical world's a smaller world than most. Once in it you can generally contact any given person. Some one always knows him. If the unlikely had happened, and I had drawn a medical blank, there was another line open to me. Your father uses the machinery made by my firm. I could have got some man to take me round on some pretext."

"I—I forgot about that."

"I'm sorry to have to remind you of it," he said a little grimly. "If you're to know the truth you may as well know all."

"But why—why any of it?"

"Briefly, because I'm old enough to be your father. And happen to share certain views with Hamilton Dexter." He got to his feet, and, as before, walked to the entrance. This time he did not turn round. "I wanted to get to know you, and, circumstances being what they are, felt I ought to talk to your parents as well as to you. We talked at length that day I spent with them. I haven't mentioned this to you until now, because only now have I learnt how mistaken I've been all these months. I've been tempted to do so often. It seemed better to leave it unsaid."

I watched the dark outline of his figure against the early night sky. Below us the pines were a black fringed carpet; there was no moon; the first stars were out.

I said slowly, "If it had been Bart and me, instead of Bart

167

and Estelle, perhaps if I had known who you were, and told Bart, it might have rocked the boat."

He faced me. "You do believe me?"

I could believe without understanding. "Yes. It makes sense."

"Then can you also believe why, in the first place, I gave you only half my name and continued to do that in the letters I wrote, before I knew of More's existence?"

"I'd like to. I can't because you haven't told me why."

"That's true." He put both his hands in his pockets. "Surely you've guessed the answer to both?"

I was about to deny that, untruthfully, when I remembered Estelle. In some incredible and wonderful fashion it seemed he and I were going to be able to go on where we had left off on the morning before Howard sent me up to the top-floor lab. But we could only go on if I was as honest as he was now being with me. I said, "I suppose you have to be careful when you've got a lot of money. And being"—I took a deep breath and plunged on—"a senior member of Martha's, as well as anything else, you possibly felt it might embarrass me if I had known that I was pouring out my life-story and problems to a pundit, and, in another way, it might have embarrassed you to know I knew."

"You aren't offended by that?" he asked oddly.

"Not now. I was—very angry."

"I saw that. And deserved it. What stopped your anger?"

"I thought it over, and it made sense too. I shouldn't have got so cross. No," I added quickly, as he was obviously about to interrupt, "no—it wasn't fair to fly off at a tangent without knowing the whole set-up. It was particularly wrong to do that to some one who's been so consistently kind to me, and helped me as much as you have."

He stood very still. "Frances," he said, "you are a very sweet young woman, and I love you beyond expression. But every man has his limits. If you say I have been so kind and helpful to you again, I am not sure I can answer for the consequences."

I just stared at him. Slowly, very slowly, I realized what he had said. He waited for me to speak, but I was speechless with wonder. Then wonder changed to overwhelming happiness that grew and grew inside me, like a rising fountain of stars.

"I'm sorry if that annoyed you," he said at last. "I didn't want to do that. I shouldn't have told you yet. Possibly never. I keep doing the wrong thing where you are concerned, probably because I'm so anxious to do the reverse."

"Please! Don't say that . . ."

"My dear"—his voice was weary—"you may as well let me finish. I've said too much to go back. So I may as well tell you that I want to marry you, and that, absurd though it may

168

sound to hear a supposedly adult man say that he wanted that after meeting you once, the fact remains that it's true. The situation is not without a certain ironic humour—though I must admit for the present the humour escapes me. Having at last met a young woman whom I love and trust in every respect —the one person I have ever known to be genuinely uninterested in my material angle—I find I have met her twenty years too late. She's kind, gentle, and very generous. But to her I can never be anything else but her old friend the Professor."

His patent unhappiness would have made me jump up, even had he not used that name. "How did you know I called you that?"

"My dear girl, you've called me that unconsciously, on and off, since the night Lily Ellis died. You used it several times that night. I didn't take you up on it then; you were too upset to know what you were saying. Later it came out again and again. You're a very talkative person. You probably don't realize how much you've told me about yourself, your family, your friends. You certainly can't have realized how much I've enjoyed listening to you. For a little while I quite enjoyed being your Professor. Incidentally, how did you come to hit the nail on the head?"

I explained absently, trying to think of some way to break through his defences.

"I reminded you of an uncle? That's reasonable." He lit a cigarette. "Now we've straightened everything out, I think it's time I took you back to the hospital." He threw away a dead match, and out of the blue began to talk about smoking. "I miss tobacco in the lab."

"Can't you smoke there?" I asked to gain time. I had no intention of letting him go yet, but had still to find the right words.

"It's not a good idea if one wants to stay alive." He held out a hand as if I was a child. "Come along. You must be exhausted. I'm going to take you back."

I could not waste any more time in searching for words. "Before we go—there's something I want to say."

"There's nothing more to be said. I've talked far too much and for too long, as it is. Shall we go?"

I stood in front of him. "I was only going to say you have been so kind and helpful to tell me what you have."

He stiffened perceptibly. "You've possibly forgotten that I asked you to dispense with all that."

"No, I haven't forgotten."

He got rid of his cigarette. "I don't think I understand."

"I don't think you do," I said, and explained.

I might as well have made that explanation to the stone walls of the shelter. He refused to believe me. "You hate hurting people, Frances. You don't want to hurt my feelings. You're only a child, a weary child—you're tired—don't know what you're saying. You're fond of me—your attitude this evening has shown me that. I'll not pretend I wouldn't give everything I possess to take you at your word. But I refuse to take advantage of your kind heart." He reached for my hand. "Come. We're going."

"Oh, no, we're not." I pulled my hand out of his. My movements were quite instinctive. I put a hand on each of his shoulders, and looked up at his face. "You may be an adult man—old enough to be my father if you married in the schoolroom—a Director of our Path. Lab.—a fourth or fifth Bart. (I still don't know which)—and own a firm that manufactures half the farm machinery in England, but you don't know one thing about women. I could willingly shake you hard here and now. I love you very much and have loved you for a long time. You're my dear, dearest Professor—and always will be. So will you please stop talking utter rubbish about my being a kind, generous child"—my voice broke, but I kept on in sheer desperation—"and realize that I mean what I'm saying—or I won't be able to answer for the consequences, either . . ."

His arms had tightened round me before I finished speaking. "Oh, my darling Frances," he murmured, and kissed me hard. It was some time later that he raised his head. "Sweetheart, are you sure you don't mind my being so much older?"

"Are you sure you don't mind my having no money?"

He kissed me again, and there was no more talk about age or money.

We went back to the shelter and sat on the bench. He drew my head on his shoulder and played with my hair. "I've always wanted to do this. I've never seen such wonderful curls."

"There's not a Sister in Martha's who would agree with you. I've collected hair rockets all over the old firm."

"You aren't going to be able to collect many more. I hope you don't mind, dearest, but I hope to marry you very soon. I'll write to your parents to-night. Can we go and see them on your next night off? Any idea when?"

"I'll be due for a couple some time in the next week. I'd like to see Estelle, too. Think they'll let me?"

"I'll ask John Curtis. I expect it'll be all right."

I smiled at him. "Does anyone ever refuse you anything?"

"Yes. You did. To-night. Anyway, I'll ask John and let you know what he says. I'll be down here at the week-end."

"That's good." I stroked his hair, then suddenly realized everything. "Oh, God! I'm so junior here that not even the juniors'll talk to me! And you're you!"

"I've just been thinking over that angle. It won't hurt me, but is it going to hurt you? I'd be only too happy to go down

170

and announce everything to-night, but will that mean you have to put up with the kind of things you got from that girl Vickers in Out-Patients? I suppose you've now realized what all that was about?"

"Yes. Don't let it worry you. It doesn't worry me at all now. But there's one thing I'd like to know. Why did you risk going to Home Sister that night?"

His arms closed round me. "You needed help. I wanted to be there to help you. But what about this place? Do we make it public? Or keep quiet until the last minute?"

I looked down the hill. A sickle moon had risen out of the trees, the clouds had all vanished, the stars were all over the sky. Far below the hospital lights shone through the trees, as if a giant had cast down hundreds of surplus stars.

"I don't suppose I'll have to put up with much. I don't particularly mind if I do. And if I run into any serious problems I can always run to my Professor for advice. He's never disappointed me yet. He always tells me what to do."

"Did he tell you to go round threatening to shake respectable pathologists?" he asked softly.

"More or less. He once told me that on certain occasions it's essential to be absolutely honest. Which just shows. He always knows what to do in any given circumstance."

"I believe you're right, sweetheart," said the Professor. "He does indeed." And he kissed me again.

A HOSPITAL SUMMER

BY LUCILLA ANDREWS

SUMMER 1940 – AN ENGLISH MILITARY HOSPITAL –
AND A YOUNG NURSE FACES THE REALITIES OF
DUNKIRK AND THE BATTLE OF BRITAIN.

Few novels have captured the wartime atmosphere of a military
hospital as effectively as A HOSPITAL SUMMER. The twenty-
year old Clare Dillon, almost overnight, learns the harsh realities
of love and war.

'It has bite, shrewdness and even toughness in it, and in spite of
dealing with life and death, as they were encountered by a VAD, it
manages to be continually humorous' – Lawrence Meynell, *Express
and Star*

0 552 08541 3   £1.75

HOSPITAL CIRCLES

BY LUCILLA ANDREWS

Jo Dungarven had all the qualities necessary for a first class nurse.
She was kind, cheerful, sensitive, and nearly always good in an
emergency. She was also, on occasion, downright foolish. She had
a lot of growing up to do.

But third year nurses in a busy London hospital tend to grow up
very quickly. When Jo was sent to nurse a dangerously ill young
man, she forgot the first rule of hospital life – to keep emotions
separate from nursing. It took a great deal of heartache, and
several months of gruelling – sometimes tragic – work, before she
discovered that at last she had achieved maturity.

0 552 09505 2   £1.75

THE MARIGOLD FIELD

BY DIANE PEARSON

THE MARIGOLD FIELD is a story of poor, proud, high-spirited people . . . people whose roots were in the farming country of southern England . . . in the bawdy and exuberant streets of the East End.

Jonathan Whitman, his cousin Myra, Anne-Louise Pritchard and the enormous Pritchard clan to which she belonged, saw the changing era and incredible events of a passing age – an age of great poverty and great wealth, of straw boaters, feather boas, and the Music Hall . . .

And above all THE MARIGOLD FIELD is a story of one woman's consuming love . . . of a jealous obsession that threatened to destroy the very man she adored . . .

'An exceptionally good read. One of those *comfortable* books you can live in for a while with pleasure.' – *McCalls Magazine*

'When Maxie takes Anne-Louise home on Sunday, when his relations assemble loudly at the meal-table . . . there is an instant of the finest, broadest comedy . . .' – *Sunday Times*

If you have enjoyed this book, you can follow the continuing saga of the Whitman family in SARAH WHITMAN, the superb sequel by Diane Pearson.

0 552 10271 7   £2.50

BRIDE OF TANCRED

BY DIANE PEARSON

Miriam Wakeford was full of hope when she arrived to take up her new appointment as needlewoman and companion in the bleak, windswept house of Tancred, high on the South Downs. Her strict Quaker upbringing was no preparation for the experiences which awaited her there . . .

John Tancred, a widower, was a mysterious, moody figure, frequently harsh and sometimes surprisingly kind. His young daughter, Esmee, seemed unbalanced . . . John Tancred's mother was an imperious old lady who ruled the decaying mansion from her wheelchair. Above all, the atmosphere was filled with the evil, violent presence of John's dead father, Richard, who by his excesses had brought ruin, infamy and tragedy to the name of Tancred . . .

0 552 10249 0   £1.75

LAST YEAR'S NIGHTINGALE

BY CLAIRE LORRIMER

Clementine Foster was young, unbelievably innocent and wildly in love with a man who didn't even know of her existence. When, one golden summer night, she stepped in front of his horse, he took her with all the drunken arrogance of a young aristocrat used to having whatever he wanted. The repercussions of that night were to forge bonds of hate, love, and tragedy in both their lives.

For the child that was born to Clementine ultimately appeared to be the only legitimate heir to the Grayshot inheritance. And, according to the law of the times, she had no right to keep her child if Deveril wanted him.

But Clementine was determined to recover her son, no matter what the cost, no matter what she had to do.

0 552 12565 2   £2.95

THE CHATELAINE

BY CLAIRE LORRIMER

Seventeen-year-old Willow, newly married to Rowell, Lord Rochford, believed she held not only the keys to a multitude of rooms, but also to her own happiness . . .

'The book, CHATELAINE, is not actually a sweeping romance. Instead the characters build and build becoming more real on every page. The plot which features hidden babies, a beautiful girl marrying the wrong man and a corrupted doctor, zings along packed not only with action but with information. Miss Lorrimer has done her research and the book is not just a good read; it is a slice of life' – George Thaw, *Daily Mirror*

0 552 11959 8   £2.95

MAVREEN

BY CLAIRE LORRIMER

A giant novel of romantic adventure.
Illegitimate daughter of an English aristocrat and a prim young
governess, Mavreen had fiery beauty, intelligence and a tempestuous spirit no man could subdue. Stubborn in loyalty, passionate in
love, her turbulent romance with a handsome French nobleman
would take her from the high seas to every capital of Europe
before it reached its triumphant consummation.

0 552 10584 8   £1.95

CHANTAL

BY CLAIRE LORRIMER

Torn from the dazzling salons and glittering balls of aristocratic
London, the beautiful, beguiling Chantal is cast adrift on the
stormy sea of destiny. From an evil chateau and a debauched
French nobleman to a deserted tropical island and a bold
Portuguese pirate to an elegant English estate and a dashing
officer, Chantal is swept up in a tempestuous whirlwind of passion
and scandal, anguish and ecstasy. This unforgettable saga of
triumphant love and soaring dreams pulses with the vivid legacy of
Chantal's mother, the incomparable Mavreen, and her bewitching
sister, the untameable Tamarisk.

0 552 11726 9   £1.95

A SELECTED LIST OF FINE NOVELS
AVAILABLE FROM CORGI BOOKS

☐	08541 3	A HOSPITAL SUMMER	Lucilla Andrews	£1.75
☐	08719 X	MY FRIEND THE PROFESSOR	Lucilla Andrews	£1.75
☐	09505 2	HOSPITAL CIRCLES	Lucilla Andrews	£1.75
☐	11660 2	PRINCESS DAISY	Judith Krantz	£2.95
☐	12565 2	LAST YEAR'S NIGHTINGALE	Claire Lorrimer	£2.95
☐	10584 8	MAVREEN	Claire Lorrimer	£2.95
☐	11207 0	TAMARISK	Claire Lorrimer	£2.95
☐	11726 9	CHANTAL	Claire Lorrimer	£2.95
☐	12182 7	THE WILDERLING	Claire Lorrimer	£2.95
☐	11959 8	THE CHATELAINE	Claire Lorrimer	£2.95
☐	12544 X	GAMBLER IN LOVE	Patricia Matthews	£2.50
☐	12406 0	DANCER OF DREAMS	Patricia Matthews	£1.95
☐	12309 9	FLAMES OF GLORY	Patricia Matthews	£1.95
☐	11924 5	MIDNIGHT WHISPERS	Patricia Matthews	£1.75
☐	11868 0	TIDES OF LOVE	Patricia Matthews	£1.75
☐	11813 3	LOVE'S BOLD JOURNEY	Patricia Matthews	£1.95
☐	11401 4	LOVE'S GOLDEN DESTINY	Patricia Matthews	£1.95
☐	11181 3	LOVE'S MAGIC MOMENT	Patricia Matthews	£1.95
☐	11109 0	LOVE'S PAGAN HEART	Patricia Matthews	£1.95
☐	10940 1	LOVE'S DARING DREAM	Patricia Matthews	£1.95
☐	10651 8	LOVE'S WILDEST PROMISE	Patricia Matthews	£1.95
☐	12641 1	THE SUMMER OF THE BARSHINSKEYS	Diane Pearson	£2.95
☐	10375 6	CSARDAS	Diane Pearson	£2.95
☐	09140 5	SARAH WHITMAN	Diane Pearson	£2.50
☐	10271 7	THE MARIGOLD FIELD	Diane Pearson	£2.50
☐	10249 0	BRIDE OF TANCRED	Diane Pearson	£1.75
☐	12607 1	DOCTOR ROSE	Elvi Rhodes	£1.95
☐	12579 2	THE DAFFODILS OF NEWENT	Susan Sallis	£1.75
☐	12375 7	A SCATTERING OF DAISIES	Susan Sallis	£2.50